The Innocence That Kills

BY THE SAME AUTHOR

Stone Boy
The Wisdom of Serpents
The Love That Kills

The Innocence That Kills

RONALD LEVITSKY

Charles Scribner's Sons
New York

Maxwell Macmillan Canada
Toronto

Maxwell Macmillan International
New York Oxford Singapore Sydney

Quotations from the Old Testament are from *Tanakh*: The New JPS translation of the Holy Scriptures.
Translations by Langston Hughes from *The Selected Poems of Gabriela Mistral*. Copyright © 1957 by Langston Hughes. Copyright renewed 1985 by George Houston Bass. Reprinted by permission of Harold Ober Associates and Joan Daves Agency.

Charles Scribner's Sons
Macmillan Publishing Company
866 Third Avenue
New York, NY 10022

Maxwell Macmillan Canada, Inc.
1200 Eglinton Avenue East
Suite 200
Don Mills, Ontario M3C 3N1

Macmillan Publishing Company is part of the Maxwell Communication Group of Companies.

Library of Congress Cataloging-in-Publication Data
Levitsky, Ronald.
The innocence that kills / Ronald Levitsky.
p. cm.
ISBN 0-684-19707-3 : $20.00
1. Rosen, Nate (Fictitious character)—Fiction. 2. Teenage girls—Illinois—Chicago—Crimes against—Fiction. 3. Fathers and daughters—Illinois—Chicago—Fiction. 4. Lawyers—Illinois—Chicago—Fiction. 5. Chicago (Ill.)—Fiction. I. Title.
PS3562.E92218I55 1994 93-42385
813'.54—dc20 CIP

10 9 8 7 6 5 4 3 2 1

Printed in the United States of America

For Jin and Rachel

Acknowledgments

The author wishes to thank the following people: Father Kevin Feeney of Saint Sylvester's Church, Sonia Levitsky for her knowledge of Spanish and the Dominican culture, Officer Bill Lustig and the Northfield Police Department, Rafael Sanchez for the tour of Chicago's neighborhoods, Dick Verbeke and the Lake Forest Police Department, and Holly Weindorf for a glimpse into the human side of podiatry.

I went up the bitter mountain
seeking flowers where they whiten
half asleep and half awake
among the crags.

When I came down with my burden,
in the middle of the meadow I found her,
and frantically covered her
with a shower of white lilies.

But without looking at the whiteness
she said to me, "This time bring back
only flowers that are red.
I cannot go beyond the meadow."

I scaled the rocks with deer
and sought the flowers of madness,
those that grow so red they seemed
to live and die of redness.

When I descended happily trembling,
I gave them as my offering,
and she became as water
That from a wounded deer turns bloody.

—from "The Flowers of the Air"
BY GABRIELA MISTRAL

The Innocence That Kills

Chapter 1

Rosen wanted the two boys locked away in darkness for the rest of their lives. Whatever their psychiatrists might someday learn couldn't change what happened—what they'd done. Rosen wanted to hate them like everyone else in the courtroom, but he couldn't. He was their lawyer.

He sat beside them at the defense table, near the small door that let the prisoners in one by one, like cockroaches shaken from a bottle. The State of Illinois considered his clients "men" because they were nineteen, but they looked like any of a thousand black kids locked up in the Cook County jails, wearing prison khaki shirts with "D.O.C.," Department of Corrections, stenciled down a pants leg. Only what they had done set them apart.

Did the two boys really understand what they'd done? If they'd shown the slightest remorse, perhaps Rosen could've justified his actions in court during the past few days. But they'd sat quietly bored, as if the proceedings were one long Sunday church service that had to be endured.

The assistant state's attorney, a thin, earnest man with longish hair, was giving closing arguments at his podium before the judge. He slowly recounted the brutality against Denae Tyler, each sentence punctuated by outcries from the victim's family and friends. How, one evening six months ago in Evanston, the two boys had lured their neighbor, a fourteen-year-old black girl, into their car. How they'd driven to one of the boy's homes, gone into the basement, raped her and, when she'd cried too loudly, bashed in her skull with a baseball bat. How they'd finished watching a sitcom on

TV, stuffed her into the trunk of the car and driven around for an hour before dumping her body into Lake Michigan, then gone for ribs. How the police stopped them on the way home and searched the car, finding bloodstains and one of the girl's shoes. How one of the boys confessed with a shrug.

" . . . like he'd squashed a bug, instead of the life of an innocent young girl."

"My baby!"

Rosen glanced at the victim's mother, a big woman with stooped shoulders and soft brown eyes, before once again looking down at the table. The prosecutor recounted the evidence and confessions quickly—too quickly, as if the judge might be tricked into confusing justice with the law. But that would never happen.

"Thank you, Your Honor," the prosecutor mumbled and looked at his notes. He was ashamed too, but for a different reason.

After a few minutes of silence, the judge, a florid man with wisps of white hair and steel-rimmed glasses, motioned the defendants to the other podium. Rosen accompanied the two boys, who clasped their hands behind their backs (as all prisoners did). Three policemen stood guard behind them.

The judge seemed about to begin, when he removed his glasses for a moment and, blinking hard, sighed.

"I've sat in judgment in hundreds of cases and heard, I fear, enough acts of senseless cruelty to shake one's faith in the basic decency of man. This is such a crime. To take Denae Tyler, a young innocent girl, who through no fault of her own . . ."

Shaking his head, Rosen felt his stomach tighten. Cruel enough what these two boys had done, but the judge was only making it harder on the dead girl's family by giving them hope.

He droned on. "Certainly there is no doubt that the defendants committed this heinous crime. The testimonies of the arresting officers, the preponderance of evidence, one of the defendant's confession—all lead to the obvious conclusion of guilt."

Rosen gripped the podium. Go ahead, tell them! Tell her family what we've all done!

"However, there are certain rules the police must follow in gathering evidence, as defense counsel so ably pointed out during his cross-examination of the arresting officers."

And the judge catalogued all the errors the police had made. Most importantly, they'd stopped the defendants' car for no reason. "Going to rattle the monkeys in their cage." That's what they'd told the dispatcher—that's what she'd finally admitted under Rosen's grilling. Or the witness he'd found, an old man in an alley, who'd seen one policeman put a gun to the boy's head, after the trunk was open, to force a confession.

Again the judge removed his glasses—was he ashamed to see how the decent people in court would react to what he was about to say?

"The United States Supreme Court has recently given the police more latitude in gathering evidence, even in some cases evidence that has been obtained without probable cause but in good faith. I wish this were such a case, but it is not. As defense counsel correctly pointed out, the police acted with wanton disregard for the defendants' rights under the Fourth Amendment. I have no choice but to dismiss the charges against them and order their release from custody. Court is adjourned."

The only sound was the judge shuffling his papers together before hurrying from the bench. Only when the defendants, neither of whom even blinked at the verdict, were escorted back through the narrow door, did those in court fully realize what the judge had said. They wailed as if the girl's body were laid before them once again. And then they raged—against the boys, the court, and Rosen.

"I'll kill 'em—see them comin' round the neighborhood! Swear to God I'll kill 'em both!"

"Oh, my baby, my little girl!"

"God damn Jew lawyer!"

"I'll kill 'em!"

The police, who had guarded the defendants, now turned to guard Rosen.

"My baby!"

The girl's mother lurched forward and almost collapsed in the aisle. Two men grabbed the woman, while a television camera recorded her misery. Once again Rosen felt sick, stuffing the papers into his briefcase. When someone touched his arm, it flew up to protect his face.

"Nice job, Counselor."

Standing across the table, Elgin Hermes almost smiled. His skin was the color and texture of milk chocolate. In his fifties, he looked ten years younger; only the few gray hairs around the temples and in his mustache hinted at his true age. Hermes' eyes, dark and piercing, were made more intense by his wide cheekbones. A charcoal three-piece suit gloved his lean, muscular body. Putting a hand on Rosen's shoulder, he revealed a diamond-studded cuff link.

"I'm very pleased." His voice, a deep baritone, was made for the stage.

Rosen snapped his briefcase shut. "It's nice somebody is. Maybe you can explain why to Denae Tyler's family."

"I'd like to try. Maybe in time they'll understand that what we did here is important. You understand the significance."

"Sure. It doesn't make it any easier."

A young woman with curly black hair pointed a microphone in his face and turned him toward a camera. "Angelina Mella, WGN News. I'm here, at the Cook County Circuit Court in suburban Skokie, with defense attorney Nathan Rosen. Mr. Rosen, as a member of the Washington-based civil liberties group the Committee to Defend the Constitution, can you tell us the significance of your victory today in court?"

Behind the reporter, the victim's family still shouted its disbelief. Rosen rubbed his eyes. He forced himself to mumble something about the Fourth Amendment and the people's right against illegal searches.

"Thank you," the reporter said. "Standing beside Mr. Rosen is Elgin Hermes, President of Hermes Communications, one of the largest African-American media corporations in the country. I understand that you personally retained the services of Mr. Rosen's organization."

"That's correct, Angelina. First let me say, like any decent human being, I grieve for the poor innocent girl who died and for her family, just as I have nothing but disgust for the defendants. Under normal criminal procedure, they would have been duly convicted and, no doubt, sentenced to death. But just as guilty are the arresting officers who thought that the two men were fair game, because they were black—because they were 'monkeys.'"

"Isn't it true that both your business and home are in Chicago, yet this crime occurred in suburban Evanston?"

"It's about time people realized that police racism is not just happening in Chicago. I'm glad this trial was held in the suburbs, so that everyone in this county, in this nation, rich and poor alike, can finally realize . . ."

The words grew more political but resounded, in Hermes' rich baritone, with the pathos of Othello. Rosen wanted to listen—wanted his actions justified, but all he could hear were the sobs of the dead girl's mother. He looked to where she'd been, then blinked hard.

"My God."

He broke away from the reporter and ran through the crowd. "Sarah!"

"Daddy?"

"What're you doing here?"

She seemed bewildered, eyes not quite focused. Gripping her hand, he led her down one of the rows. She wore faded jeans and the Georgetown Hoya sweatshirt he'd brought as a present last year. Her thick black hair was cut short and styled into a flip, like her mother's. It made her look far more womanly than a fifteen-year-old should, especially with the earrings and makeup.

At that moment, however, she was the scared five-year-old who'd come running into their bedroom at the sound of thunder, to burrow under the covers between him and Bess. Her hand felt small and damp, as it had those dark nights. Listening to the gentle breathing of his daughter and wife as they fell back to sleep was one of the good memories.

5

"Sarah?"

Her jaw trembled, but she didn't cry. Sarah never cried anymore, Bess said. Not since the divorce.

"We came to see you try the case. I've never seen you in court before."

"'We'? Where's your mother?"

"No, not Mom."

"It's Wednesday. What about school?"

"School's only a half day, because of rehearsal for tonight's performance. Nina and I didn't need to practice, so we took the bus down. Oh Daddy, why did they let those two men go?"

"Your mother never should've let you come."

He noticed another teenager in the row directly behind his daughter. The girl looked about Sarah's age and was almost as pretty, but darker—probably Latino.

She said, "I'm Sarah's friend, Nina Melendez." She smiled shyly, and the dimples made her even prettier.

Suddenly someone shoved Rosen into Sarah. The dead girl's uncle, a burly man with a lantern jaw and eyebrows like scouring pads, pulled Rosen toward him. Another reporter leaned in with his microphone.

"How the hell could you do that!" the uncle shouted. "How could you get those animals off after what they did to my sister's little girl!" He grabbed for Sarah, who shrank against the wall. "What if somebody was to take this here girl and—"

"Leave her alone!" Rosen pushed the man's hand away, and they struggled between the benches, knocking down the reporter. His microphone clattered along the floor.

The uncle suddenly jerked backward, stumbling over the reporter and falling into the aisle. He'd been pulled away by a well-dressed young black man, who had sauntered beside Sarah's friend. He was as tall as Rosen but broader. When the young man smiled and offered his hand, the resemblance was so strong that Rosen could've guessed his next words.

"I'm Jason Hermes, Elgin's son. Nice to meet you. Let me get the girls away from this mess. We'll meet you outside in a few minutes.

My father hasn't finished talking to you." When Rosen glanced at the uncle struggling to his feet, Jason added, "Don't worry. I won't let anything happen to them."

Taking each girl by the hand, Jason walked them from the courtroom. The uncle muttered something to the reporter, then trudged up the aisle toward the twin podiums, where a black minister, surrounded by the victim's family, was holding an impromptu press conference.

Sitting down, Rosen leaned heavily against the wall. His hand trembled slightly. He wanted to get out of there, to close his eyes and, in a cool, dark room, hear his daughter play the piano, as she was going to do that evening. How he'd been looking forward to the evening.

Elgin Hermes sat beside him. "Here, you forgot your briefcase. Was that your daughter?"

Rosen nodded.

"Pretty girl. You must be very proud, like I'm proud of my Jason. That's what we really live for—our children."

"Like Denae Tyler's mother."

Hermes slowly shook his head. "I don't understand why I should have to lecture a civil liberties lawyer about a basic constitutional issue."

"I know exactly what you're doing."

"Maybe what's bothering you is the color of the boys you were defending. If it'd been two white boys who murdered for kicks, like Leopold and Loeb did back in the twenties, maybe you'd feel differently. Leopold and Loeb—weren't they both Jewish?"

"That's not it, and you know it."

"Then what? It seems simple enough to think about the Fourth Amendment."

"What about the Sixth Commandment." When Hermes furrowed his brow, Rosen continued, "'You shall not murder.'"

"That's not the point."

"Isn't justice always the point of law? Leopold and Loeb didn't get away with murder. They were sentenced to life, like those two boys today should've been."

7

"But the police—"

"The police should've been punished too."

Hermes shook his head. "They will be. You saw to that, thank God. And maybe from now on they'll think twice before going after the next two kids who go driving by, just because they're black."

Rubbing his eyes, Rosen repeated what his grandfather had always said, "'From your mouth to God's ear.'" He lifted his brief-case. "Good-bye."

Hermes stood with him. "Wait a minute. You're still going to be in town for a few days, right?"

"Yeah. I'm taking vacation time through next week."

"You brought your daughter with you—that's nice."

"My daughter lives in Arbor Shore with my ex-wife."

Hermes raised his eyebrows. "Arbor Shore, very nice. I'd never have guessed that an underpaid civil liberties attorney—"

"They live with her new husband, who does quite well."

"I can imagine. Where're you staying?"

"In Evanston. My boss's brother, Miron Nahagian, is out of town. I'm using his condo. Why all the questions?"

"I like you, Rosen. You've got two qualities that rarely intersect anymore, intellect and morality. A lawyer with brains like you—I'd wonder why you weren't rich."

"You and my ex-wife."

Hermes laughed heartily. "Yes, I like you. In fact, I've got a business offer. Let's have lunch next Monday. Give my office a call, and my secretary will set it up." He shook Rosen's hand. "Again, con-gratulations. You did a helluva job."

They walked up the aisle together and through the courtroom doors. The hallway was wide; across from the courtrooms were sev-eral county offices. Under the sign "telephones" stood back-to-back conference areas, each with a public telephone, a small table, and two chairs bolted to the floor. Sarah sat with her friend, while Jason leaned against the wall. Seeing his father signal, he said good-bye and followed Hermes toward the exit.

The hallway was quiet. Nearby two lawyers whispered, a policeman waddled by, sipping a cup of coffee, and a woman sat on a bench reading the newspaper, while her little boy crayoned the floor around him. Rosen walked into the conference area and set his briefcase on the table. Sarah's friend quickly stood and offered her chair.

"No, that's all right," he said.

"Please."

He sat beside his daughter. She stared through the glass to the courtroom door, as if waiting for something else to happen.

He turned to her friend. "You're, uh . . . ?"

"Nina."

He hadn't taken a close look at her before. She had deep brown eyes, a generous mouth, and eyebrows that arched when she smiled. Her thick black hair, clasped by a tortoise-shell comb, fell behind her shoulders. Although wearing no makeup, she seemed older than Sarah, maybe because of her simple white blouse and gray skirt. Not just older but old-fashioned as well, reminding Rosen of a delicate señorita adorning a Cuban cigar box.

"You're performing with Sarah tonight?"

"Yes, I'm singing. Sarah's accompanying me on the piano." She spoke with a slight Hispanic accent, saying the "y" like a "j."

"I'm looking forward to it." Checking his watch, he added, "It's after four. I'd better get you both home."

Still his daughter didn't move.

"Shayna?" His nickname for her—"pretty one."

"Daddy, how could they let them off?"

He leaned back in his chair, not knowing what to say. He wasn't arguing in court—that was easy. But during the five years since the divorce, every time he visited Chicago, Sarah was different. She'd grown, put on makeup, pierced her ears, cut her hair, become interested in boys, liked Jell-O and hated chocolate. Each Sarah was different, like a separate photograph in the pages their relationship had become. Each page dated by her birthday, a holiday, or one of his cases that let him visit. Did he really know her anymore? God, it'd been bad losing Bess, but he couldn't stand to lose his daughter.

He waited for her to look at him, then said, "You're old enough

9

to understand there are rules the police have to follow—rules that protect everyone, not just the bad guys who commit crimes, but everyone—you and me and Nina too. Suppose the police started bothering Nina for no other reason than because she's Puerto Rican or Cuban?"

Nina said, "I'm from the Dominican Republic."

"Okay, Dominican." He asked his daughter, "How would you feel about that?"

"That's different. Nina wouldn't do anything bad. But they killed a girl for no reason. They just didn't kill her, they . . . raped her. Just because they didn't have a reason to search. They knew they were bad. So what if they didn't have a warrant. The way they were all crying in there—"

"Just a minute, Shayna. You're getting me confused with all the 'theys.'"

"You know what I mean!"

"All right. Look, you remember your Great-grandfather Raphael?"

She nodded.

"Remember the scar on his cheek? You asked me once what it was."

"He was cut by a sword."

"By a Cossack, who cut him just for being a Jew. The Cossacks were like the Tsar's police, only their job wasn't to protect the Jews, but to terrorize them. You understand what I'm getting at?"

"I know what you're trying to say, but it's not the same!"

"That's like back home," Nina said. "What my mother tells me happened under the dictator Trujillo. He had one of my grandfathers killed, just to take his land. And my mother's aunt—he took her and. . . ." Blushing, she bit her lip. "He did the same thing to her that those men in court did to that girl. The very same thing. Even today the police are only good for taking your money. What's the word?"

"Bribes," Rosen said.

"That's right—bribes. And you should see the way they treat the Haitians who come to cut sugar cane. Your father's right, Sarah. If you saw the things I saw in my country, you'd understand."

10

Looking up at her friend, Sarah nodded. "I guess so. It's just so unfair."

Rosen kissed her on the forehead. "We'd better go."

As they left the conference area, he nodded a thank-you to Nina, who smiled back. Walking down the courthouse steps, they crossed a driveway and entered the main level of the four-tiered parking lot. Rosen stopped suddenly.

"Let's see, was it on this level? Sarah knows I occasionally forget where I've parked the car."

Nina giggled. "She's told me. Just like my mother. She'll start talking and forget where she is. Remember, Sarah, last week when she took us shopping downtown for my birthday present?"

"It's one tier up. Come on."

As they climbed the stairs, he glanced back to see Sarah smiling at her friend's reminiscences. He'd drop them both home, drive back to the condo and shower, grab something to eat, then hear his daughter play. The next ten days he'd be able to spend with her. There'd be the movies, the art museum, the ballgame next week. Just the two of them. Maybe he could learn to be a father again.

He unlocked his rental car, a Ford Escort, and the girls slid into the back seat. "You ladies probably aren't used to such luxury."

Sarah said, "You know, I'm taking driver's ed. Nina already has her license."

"Maybe we could practice this weekend. Would you like that?"

"Uh huh. I'll drive real careful. Anyway, you don't have to worry. It's . . ." Her voice trailed off.

"It's?"

"Only an Escort."

He laughed, and the girls joined in his laughter.

Rosen drove past the courthouse, just as the dead girl's family walked down its steps, trailed by a gaggle of reporters. As Rosen passed them, the uncle ran up to the car and slapped his hand on the hood.

"God damn you! Let two murderers out! How you gonna sleep at night! Damn you!"

Rosen shook his head. What could he say?

11

Running alongside, the uncle shouted, "That your girl in back! What if it'd happened to her! Wish it woulda' been her they'd done a job on!"

Accelerating, Rosen looked through the rearview mirror and saw the uncle whack the trunk, the sound reverberating like a thunderclap. He also saw his daughter's face, eyes wide in fear, but she was no longer the little girl who'd run to him for safety.

"God damn you both!" the uncle shouted, stumbling after them. "I hope they do her next!"

Chapter 2

Bess and her husband Shelly waited for him in the high school parking lot. They stood behind Shelly's metallic blue Jaguar with the license plate "FEET 1ST." Anywhere else the car would have been impressive, but in the suburb of Arbor Shore—amid rows of Cadillacs, BMWs, Rolls Royces, and Mercedes—it was just another Jag.

Bess looked good, and not just because she'd kept her figure. As poor as they'd both been, she'd always understood that real wealth was more an attitude than a stock portfolio. It didn't matter that she taught in the community, and might therefore be regarded as a servant, or that as a Jew she was an outsider, or, worse, that her husband Shelly's success was recent and therefore "new money."

She knew instinctively how to dress—never flashy, never too much makeup or jewelry, and never what their daughter called the frizzy, dyed "shopping mall hair." Yet as understated as it was, Rosen guessed that her outfit—the pink cashmere turtleneck, stone-washed jeans, and blue slicker—cost far more than his best suit. Of course, that wasn't saying much.

Bess crossed her arms. "I want to talk to you about Sarah. She's very upset over what she saw in court this afternoon."

"Murder can do that to people."

She shivered. "I heard about the verdict. A real mess, isn't it."

"You knew I was representing two men accused of rape and murder. How could you let her go?"

"Sarah kept on about it—how she's never seen you in court, how the kids have been talking about the case in school. She had the afternoon off and kept after me. I tried calling you this morning,

13

but you'd already left for court. Sorry—I thought it'd be all right. Was it that bad?"

"About as bad as it can get. The victim's family was ready to lynch me. One man even—" He stopped suddenly.

"What?"

"Nothing. We'd better go in."

She grabbed his arm. "Did something happen to Sarah?"

He didn't like standing so close to her. She still used the same perfume, the kind he'd always bought for her birthday.

"The girl's uncle said something, that's all."

"Said what? Did he threaten her?"

"Not exactly. It was just—"

"Just what?"

"Just blowing off steam. You'd be mad as hell too, if it'd happened to you."

"He did threaten her. My God!"

"Don't worry," Shelly broke in. "If Nate knows the man's name, I can have some people look into it."

"It's nothing," Rosen insisted, staring into Bess's eyes. "I get threats all the time."

"But this is your daughter."

"You never should've let her go."

"How was I to know you'd get off two animals who raped and killed an innocent girl?"

"So it's my fault. Now I really do feel at home."

"Stop it!"

Breaking his gaze, she walked a few steps past him, then a moment later turned back. "Sorry. I should've checked with you first. It's just that Sarah wanted to show you off to her friend Nina. You know how proud she is of you."

He didn't know what to say, and it was Shelly who finally spoke. "If you two want to finish—"

"No," Rosen said. "Let's go in."

He let Shelly step between them as they walked into the auditorium. Shelly didn't have Bess's sense of style, not with his plaid shirt, khaki pants, and Bulls warm-up jacket. He wasn't much to look at either—short, balding, a brush mustache, and eyes that seemed constantly peering in amazement through a thick pair of glasses. In the old neighborhood, where they'd all grown up, he'd have probably been called a "schlemiel"—a goof. Yet now he had one of the most famous faces in Chicago, thanks to the incessant TV commercials advertising his string of podiatry clinics, the Arches of Triumph.

The auditorium lobby looked like an English hunt club, with its oak paneling and tongue-and-groove hardwood floors. Between the two entrances to the auditorium stood a handsome fireplace, logs stacked ready for kindling. Two brightly lit chandeliers illuminated walls filled with framed photographs of the school's musical productions since the 1920's. Glancing at some of the older photos, Rosen recognized a future U.S. senator and a secretary of state. A refreshment stand was set in a far corner, near the public phone.

Bess took a folded piece of paper from her purse. "I found this sheet music on the living room floor. I think it's part of what Sarah's playing tonight. I'd better give it to her. You two go on in."

"No," Rosen said, "let me."

"But you don't know where . . . All right, here. Go into the hallway, then turn right at a long corridor, go past Martin Bixby's office, into the rehearsal room. We'll see you inside."

Following Bess's directions, he entered a narrow corridor, its walls covered with playbills for Shakespeare, *Hair*, and *Phantom* among others, as well as program and scholarship announcements from the theater departments of a dozen major universities. On his left he passed a doorway marked "Bix's Digs," and continued until reaching a large open room. What assailed his eyes and ears, at that moment, might have passed for avant-garde theater or a painting by Hieronymus Bosch entitled *Teenagers*.

A solemn-faced boy tuned his violin with great deliberation, while two others, each dressed as half a horse, tried clip-clopping to a tune played on a tape recorder. A trio dressed as the Andrews Sisters argued over who was coming in on cue correctly, a Cyrano with a long putty nose practiced his fencing, and four "cats" scampered through their Broadway number.

Rosen stepped gingerly around the young violinist, who suddenly shouted, "Take my history teacher—please!" Still he didn't see Sarah. Nearby a flamenco dancer leaned forward and, putting one foot on a stool, adjusted the strap of her pump.

"Excuse me," he said.

The girl lifted her skirt above the knee, then smiled. She was dark like Sarah's friend Nina, but her face was rounder, her lips fuller. A few curls peeked from under the gypsy scarf tied around her hair. As she arched her brow, the girl's eyes seemed about to laugh at him, while she ran a hand languidly over her calf, smoothing her stocking.

Her voice was a half whisper. "You want something, Mister?"

"Have you seen Sarah Rosen?"

"She's over in the corner, by the keyboard."

"Thank you."

"Any time."

Rosen felt his face grow warm as he hurried toward the far corner of the room. Sarah sat at a keyboard, with Nina standing beside her. Both girls wore identical white dresses with chiffon sleeves and long pleated skirts. Both listened attentively to a man who gestured dramatically with his right hand, while his left rested on Sarah's shoulder.

Sarah's eyes blinked in surprise.

Rosen said, "Your mother found this music at home and thought you might need it."

"I've memorized this. Daddy, this is Bix—Mr. Bixby, our drama teacher. He's in charge of the program."

The man shook Rosen's hand; his grip was moist. "Sarah's told me a lot about you. In fact, I saw you on the news this afternoon. Congratulations on winning your case." He had a bedtime story voice, with a slight English accent.

Short and plump, Bixby resembled a teddy bear, with his curly brown hair, bushy eyebrows, and mocha-colored mohair sweater. An impish grin lit his blue eyes as he smiled. Rosen might have guessed the teacher's age at thirty, but the deep creases around his eyes and mouth suggested he was older. Rosen glanced at his watch—8:01. "I'd better get to my seat. Good luck, girls. Nice meeting you, Mr. Bixby."

"Same here, and please call me Bix. Everyone else does. You should be proud of your daughter. She's really quite gifted."

During their conversation, the teacher had kept his left hand on Sarah's shoulder. It was a gesture Rosen had made often, when his daughter was a little girl at the piano and he'd helped her count the rhythm. Was that why he felt uneasy? Was jealousy the reason he wanted to knock Bixby's hand away? Returning to the lobby, he followed a line of parents filing into the auditorium. He checked his seat number, as the house lights dimmed, and found his place, past Bess, next to Shelly in the center section about ten rows up. He'd passed two empty seats in the row; otherwise, the auditorium appeared filled to capacity.

As the curtains opened, Martin Bixby ambled into the spotlight. The audience applauded warmly, a few of the people around Rosen chuckling at the teacher's casual appearance.

"That's Bix," a man in the next row said, laughing.

The teacher said, "Welcome to our annual spring 'Arts in Life Festival,' brought to you by the freshman and sophomore classes of Arbor Shore High School." He went on to thank the administration, his colleagues, the parents, ". . . and, most of all, your wonderfully gifted children. Now, without further ado, on with the show!"

More enthusiastic applause, as the two boys dressed as a horse trotted on stage and tried tap-dancing to "Mr. Bojangles."

Shelly whispered, "I wish Sammy Davis were alive to see this."

After the boys finished, a series of acts followed, as varied as one might expect from a group of teenagers. The violinist's music was far better than his attempt to impersonate Henny Youngman. When "Cyrano" finished his speech about having fallen from the moon, Bess leaned over to congratulate the two people sitting beside her.

The final act listed in the program before intermission was "Margarita Reyes in a selection from *Carmen*."

The flamenco dancer entered the stage. Clicking her castanets, she whirled to a medley from Bizet's opera. Her tight blouse and swirling skirt revealed a woman's body. Eyes half closed, nostrils flaring, she flaunted a sensuality that caused several men in the audience to shift in their seats and loosen their ties. Watching these men as much as the girl, Rosen felt his throat tighten. He thought of the children of Israel dancing shamelessly before the golden calf.

When the girl had finished, there was a long silence, followed by a scattering of applause. Only when the house lights went on to signal intermission did the audience rise from their seats. For a moment, each person seemed ashamed to look his neighbor in the eye. Then the small talk began, rippling through the auditorium like a prairie fire. People spoke about everything—except the dancer.

Again Bess congratulated the couple sitting beside her. "Chip did a wonderful job as Cyrano. He shows the same panache in my English class."

The woman smiled. "'Panache'—isn't that a euphemism for 'pain in the neck'?" She was about forty-five; her figure, in an emerald green jumpsuit, looked trim and lithe as a gymnast's. Her strawberry blond hair was cut short, accentuating her green eyes and generous mouth.

"We're so looking forward to hearing Sarah and Nina. You know the girls practiced at our place a few times. We never realized the piano could sound so beautiful, did we, Byron?"

But the woman's husband was already standing in the aisle and stretching his long legs. The charcoal sweater and gray slacks went well with his silver hair and ruddy complexion. Both walked briskly up the aisle, the man pausing to run a hand through his hair.

Shelly said to Rosen, "That was Dick and Kate Ellsworth. You've heard of Ellsworth-Leary Investments. Nina Melendez lives with them—her mother's their housekeeper." He asked Bess, "You see the empty seats next to the Ellsworths? What do you suppose happened to Mrs. Melendez?"

"I don't know. Nina said both her mother and aunt were coming."

In the lobby Bess moved amiably from one set of parents to the next. Content to let her go, Rosen walked outside and deeply inhaled the cool breeze. He was surprised when Shelly followed him.

"Mind if I tag along?"

"Of course not, but you don't have to entertain me. If you'd rather go around with Bess—"

"I wouldn't. Look, it's not that I don't like being with her. It's just those people she hangs out with."

"Your neighbors?"

"Yeah, my neighbors. She gets along with them, because she teaches their kids and because, Goddamnit, she doesn't give them the choice not to. Talk about chutzpa. Well, you know Bess."

In the moment when the two men shared a brief smile, Rosen finally admitted to himself that he liked Shelly Gold.

"I see your commercials on TV all the time," Rosen said. "I like the new one."

"Which one? Fred Astaire and Ginger Rogers dancing, while the voiceover's singing 'Feet to Feet'?"

"That's good, but I'm thinking of the big lumberjack who can't do his job because of sore feet."

"Paul Bunion."

"Yeah. Very clever."

"People like humor in the face of adversity. Believe me, having fallen arches is no picnic."

"I'll bet."

Shelly nodded curtly toward the people inside. "Even though I'm a doctor, even though I can buy and sell most of those schmucks twice over, I'll always be to them what my grandfather was the day he got off the boat. A dirty little Yid." He winced as if slapped. "Take Ellsworth, the guy sitting by Bess. I was good enough to invest a hundred thou in one of his real estate deals, but not good enough to invite over to his Goddamn house a block away for a drink. I'm not asking for dinner, just one lousy drink. But not even a sip of water from his backyard hose, like the Mexican gardener, for Chrissakes?" He shook his head sadly. "Not even that."

"Look, Shelly, we'd better get back."

"You know, the only other Jew besides Bess who can take on these snobs 'mano a mano' is your brother."

Rosen stiffened. He hadn't expected this; the last people he wanted to talk about were his family.

"Yeah, as God is my witness, one day there's a board of directors meeting at the hospital. A big problem about insurance—some actuarial bullshit. Everybody's arguing—a real 'tsimmes.' All of a sudden, *Dr.* Aaron Rosen takes the elevator from cardiology and walks into the boardroom like Moses coming down from Sinai. He has his say, walks out, and suddenly everyone's nodding 'yes' and meeting adjourned. Some brother you've got."

Rosen bit his lower lip. "The lights are flicking. We'd better get back."

Settling into his seat as the curtain once again opened, he tried not to think about his brother, because that would mean thinking about his father, and the cross-examination he feared most would begin once again. Should he visit the old man? Twenty years had passed since his father had sent him away. Twenty years, and it still felt like yesterday.

His attention was diverted to a grand piano slowly being wheeled onto the stage. The program read, "Nina Melendez and Sarah Rosen—a musical interpretation of the poetry of Gabriela Mistral, Nobel Laureate." Two seats away, Bess leaned forward, her lips parted in a smile.

The girls walked onstage, Sarah sitting at the piano and Nina standing before a microphone a few feet away. They glanced at each other, blushing, then Sarah began playing a piece she herself had written. It was beautiful, and the beauty lay in its simplicity, a soft melody that fluttered on butterfly wings through the auditorium.

After a few minutes, the music grew even softer, as Nina closed her eyes and began singing in Spanish. In her white dress the girl seemed so innocent, almost ethereal, yet her voice carried such longing, that Rosen suddenly felt heartsick for something he wasn't sure of—something lost that could never be reclaimed.

Nina stopped for a moment, then sang in English:

> Because you sleep, my little one,
> the sunset will no longer glow:
> Now nothing brighter than the dew
> nor whiter than my face you know.
> Because you sleep, my little one,
> nothing on the high road do we see,
> nothing sighs except the river,
> nothing is except me.

She continued, the words of a mother's lullaby, while Rosen watched the innocent face of his daughter, remembering how he rocked her to sleep with the old Yiddish songs his mother had sung to him long ago. He felt her in his arms. "Shayna, Shayna." Suddenly he realized that was what he was heartsick for.

It seemed so long ago, but Rosen tried remembering what being a family had been like—the small apartment in Chicago with Bess and little Sarah. He thought, at the time, how secure they were in the old neighborhood, his work, and their marriage. But the neighborhood had grown bad, his practice put him on the road too much for too little money, and the marriage broke apart. And now, Sarah growing up—what protection was there for her, for anyone? Denae Tyler, the black girl taken a half block from her house, raped and murdered—what protection had there been for her?

What was left for her family? To grieve; to curse God and die, as Job had considered; or to strike back blindly in revenge? What had the dead girl's uncle said about Sarah, banging his fist against the car:

"What if it'd happened to her! . . . I hope they do her next!"

His hands gripped the armrests. He heard the applause, saw Sarah walk beside Nina, then both girls bowed awkwardly. As they left the stage, he steadied himself and walked up the aisle. The lobby was empty, except for a boy and girl behind the refreshment stand who stared at him curiously.

Inside the men's room, Rosen leaned against the sink and splashed cold water on his face. He'd told Bess it was silly to worry about Sarah's safety; now he only needed to convince himself. If his daughter couldn't be safe in a place like Arbor Shore, where could she?

He pulled at the cloth towel rack several times, drying his face and hands, then returned to the hallway. Debating whether to return to the auditorium—there were probably another half dozen acts—he was distracted by several voices shouting from the corridor leading to the rehearsal room.

It wasn't just the number of people shouting, or the Spanish mixed with the English. It was the intensity of the exchange, along with a strange litany of accusation and denial.

A woman kept screaming in Spanish. Rosen knew enough of the language from his early "pro bono" work with immigrants to recognize words like "toca"—touch, and "hija"—daughter. The word "diario," which he thought meant "newspaper," was repeated several times. Another woman was translating, but she spoke so quickly that he missed most of what she'd said. Something about touching or hurting the other woman's daughter. A man tried to deny it but was continually cut off, like a dog slapped across the snout for whimpering too loudly.

Stepping into the corridor, Rosen saw that the argument was taking place in Martin Bixby's office, its door ajar. The man's voice was Bixby's, and his protests only made the women's voices angrier. Rosen was about to step back into the hallway when two other voices made him freeze in his tracks.

"No, Mami, no! Estás equivocada! Nada pasó! Nada pasó!"

"That's right, Mrs. Melendez! Nothing happened! Please!"

That last voice—Sarah's!

He walked slowly through the corridor, holding the wall as if he were a blind man, and listened at the open doorway. Sarah and the other voice—Nina's—joined in the teacher's denials, but the cacophony of voices grew too great. He walked into the office.

Two women, their backs to him, were arguing with Nina in front of a desk. One waved a spiral notebook in her hand and shouted, "Tu diario lo dice!"

"No, Mami," Nina sobbed, "nada pasó!"

"Tu diario lo dice!"

The woman next to her looked past Nina and translated, "Your diary says so! Well, Bixby . . . what about it?"

"You both don't understand!" Sarah's voice.

Moving closer to the desk, Rosen saw his daughter behind Nina, protecting Bixby, who had wedged himself into a corner made by the wall and a file cabinet. Hands raised in front of his face, he was shaking violently.

"What's going on?" Rosen asked.

The translator turned. About thirty, she looked remarkably like Nina, the same delicate features and thick black hair, hers tied into a long French braid. Cocking her head, the woman looked Rosen up and down, as if deciding whether this was any of his business.

Finally she said, "This man . . . this teacher Bixby . . . has been molesting my niece. Her mother has Nina's diary that tells everything." Her English was perfect, with just the trace of an accent.

"No, Tía!" Nina shook her head violently. "Nada pasó!"

Nina's mother took a step forward. Her eyes widened and, in the heat of anger, lost their focus. They were terrible, those eyes—searing, yet chilling him to the bone.

"Nada pasó!" she screamed, and with a trembling hand slapped her daughter across the face.

Bursting into tears, Nina ran from the room.

When Sarah started to follow, Rosen grabbed her. She struggled against him, and their eyes locked.

"Not now, Daddy."

"What about this?"

"Not now. Nina needs me."

He let her go. She hurried past several students who had gathered at the door, as well as a slouching man in a blue three-piece suit. He was bald and heavy-jowled, like an old bloodhound.

The man stepped forward timidly. "Uh, is there some sort of problem, Mr. Bixby? Perhaps we could discuss it in my office after the performance."

"Dr. Winslow!" Bixby whined.

Rosen pushed through the crowd and returned to the lobby. He heard laughter from the auditorium, then applause. The performance was still going on. The girls wouldn't have gone in there. Maybe the ladies' room, but he doubted they'd remain in the building.

Rosen walked along the sidewalk, parallel to the parking lot, which ended in a baseball field. He saw the two girls sitting together on the outfield grass, illuminated by a haze of moonglow as if they were fairies. He stopped at the edge of the field and waited.

It was enough, at that moment, to know Sarah was safe. Even though he realized, from what had occurred in court that afternoon and in the teacher's office a few minutes ago, there was precious little he could do to protect his daughter from anything. So Rosen waited and kept his gaze fixed upon her, afraid that if he blinked, like a fairy she might disappear forever.

Chapter 3

The walls were lined with built-in bookshelves, made of the same dark wood as the long table that stretched the entire length of the conference room. The shelves were filled with volumes on educational theory, educational law, and educational curricula, as well as dozens of classroom texts. Once their bindings might have offered a rainbow of colors—perhaps even have made the room a bit cheerful, but over the years they'd faded to dullish green or brown. A coffee urn gurgled in the corner; its aroma mixed unpleasantly with that of lemon furniture wax, like a tropical drink gone bad.

It was Friday afternoon, the time when Rosen had hoped to begin a weekend together with Sarah. The fun he'd planned for them—pizza, their favorite Bogart videos, a Cubs game, even a jazz club. Most importantly, they'd get to talk like they used to. But that was before last Wednesday night and the accusation made by Nina's mother. Now neither of the girls would speak to anyone except each other.

"I don't know anything, Daddy," Sarah kept repeating, like a hostile witness taking the Fifth Amendment. Only that and "Nina needs me."

If Bess hadn't told him of this meeting with the principal, Rosen would have demanded one. Something had to be done.

Dr. Winslow sat at the head of the table, his large body slumped forward like a partially deflated balloon. He was complaining about "those awful nicotine patches" to Kate Ellsworth, whose son had played Cyrano in Wednesday's performance. With her white blouse, black skirt, and leather slipcase, she might have just left her office downtown and taken the train home.

25

Next to her, and across from Rosen, sat Nina's mother and aunt. Mrs. Melendez wore a simple green dress with a white starched collar, but even that couldn't hide her heavy breasts and wide hips. Her lips were fuller than her daughter's and her nose broader, but she had the same beautiful dark eyes. Her face was framed by thick black hair, which curled at the shoulders. Her hands gripped the spiral notebook Rosen had glimpsed on Wednesday evening— Nina's diary.

The other woman's hair cascaded down her back. Two silver barrettes, clipped above each ear, kept it in place. She wore a pair of jeans and a baggy sweatshirt with the emblem of F.A.C.E.—"Fund a Child's Education." It was a stunning logo, which Rosen had seen throughout the country—the silhouette of a long-haired girl with delicate features staring into a book. The silhouette reminded him of someone, but who?

To the principal's right, Martin Bixby curled back in his chair, his hands resting heavily on the armrests. His sport coat, a brown tweed with leather elbow patches, looked tight at the shoulders and was unbuttoned. The teacher's face remained expressionless; only his eyes shifted, like a caged animal's, from one person to the next.

Dr. Winslow kept glancing at his watch. "It's nearly two-thirty. Mrs. Gold should be here any minute—just a matter of having someone cover her last class. I do have another meeting at three. Uh, Mrs. Melendez, whose daughter Nina is a sophomore, has asked for this meeting. She's with Ms. Lucila Melendez, her sister."

"Sister-in-law," Lucila corrected.

"Excuse me. Sister-in-law, and quite an artist, I understand. As for *Mr.* Melendez . . . ?" The principal paused.

"My brother, Nina's husband, has been dead for five years."

"Oh, I'm terribly sorry. The records weren't quite clear. You see, sometimes in cases like these—sponsorship, I mean—the mother comes here with her children to work for a family, while the father stays behind in the country of origin."

"We know exactly what you mean."

His cheeks colored as he turned to his right. "Uh, we have here Mr. Rosen, Sarah's father. I'm not really certain that it was necessary for you to attend this meeting—this really only directly involves Nina. But Mrs. Gold informed us that you'd like to be here, so welcome."

When Rosen wouldn't respond, the principal's smile flickered, then died. "Mrs. Ellsworth is currently president of P.P.A.—Parents for the Performing Arts, and has been a past president of the P.T.A. I thought that, as a parent with a thorough understanding of our school, as well as being Mrs. Melendez's sponsor and employer, she should be here as well. Of course, we all know Mr. Bixby. I'd like to make this quite clear at the outset that—oh, here's Mrs. Gold."

Bess walked around the table and sat beside Rosen. She wore a white blouse with a pleated blue skirt and when she nodded a greeting, he inhaled her perfume. Even with his eyes closed, he would've known she sat beside him.

The principal continued, "Besides being Sarah's mother, Mrs. Gold is one of our most respected teachers. Over the years, she has assisted in several of the school's dramatic presentations and variety shows. As such, she knows Mr. Bixby as well as any faculty member. I'd like to make it perfectly clear that this gathering is . . . uh . . . informal and should be regarded simply as a response to a parental concern, just as this school is sensitive to any parental concern."

He spoke very carefully, pausing to reconsider the implications of each word, as if searching in his closet for the best tie to match his suit. "You do understand."

Lucila shook her head. "What are you saying—that this meeting doesn't really mean anything?"

"Not at all. I'm merely saying that we think this can be resolved informally."

"We?"

"Mr. Bixby, the school board, and myself. Otherwise, Mr. Bixby would have his union representative here. The school's attorney might be present, even the superintendent. My goodness, we might have to use the auditorium." He laughed nervously. No one else did. "Uh, I'd like to say that yesterday I reviewed the matter thoroughly with Mr. Bixby, and he categorically denies any accusation of impropriety."

"What a surprise," Lucila said.

"I did interview separately your niece Nina and Sarah Rosen. Both girls were rather uncommunicative."

"What did you expect? They were scared."

A smile slid across the principal's face. "Certainly not of me."

"Of him." She nodded toward Bixby.

"As a matter of fact, the only thing they definitely said—and they both were in agreement on this—was that Mr. Bixby had never . . . uh . . . acted improperly toward them."

Rosen asked, "Did the two girls actually *say* nothing happened, or did you make that statement and they both agreed with it?"

"I don't really see any difference."

"If you made the statement, they might have nodded agreement, because they were nervous or felt under pressure. It's a big difference."

"Oh really, Mr. Rosen, you're beginning to sound like a lawyer."

"I am a lawyer."

Dr. Winslow grimaced. "Oh, I see. Well, let me think. I suppose the girls did nod their heads when I mentioned Mr. Bixby's statement that nothing happened. But I still don't see the difference. Believe me, I'm not one to frighten children."

Thumping the spiral notebook on the table, Nina's mother said in a heavy accent, "El diario—the diary. You read the diary. It tells you what happened."

"In and of itself, the diary isn't enough to bring . . . uh . . . charges of misconduct against Mr. Bixby."

"No, no," Mrs. Melendez insisted, "you read the diary. Lucila!"

The two women conferred in Spanish, the mother's hands growing more animated. Nodding in agreement, her sister-in-law opened the spiral notebook and began reading.

"'April 2—Tonight at rehearsal he said Sarah and me we're good enough to be professionals. He's putting —'"

"Ms. Melendez," Dr. Winslow protested, "we've already agreed that it serves no purpose to—"

"'He's putting us in the second act with the better groups. In his office he put his hand on my shoulder, like he usually does, but this time it brushed against my breast. Did he do it on purpose? What should I do? Does he do it to Sarah too?'"

Staring at Bixby, whose glance darted away, Rosen felt his throat tighten.

"'April 4—After rehearsal, he picked me up on his way home. We went to the park overlooking the beach. His eyes, so stern with everybody else, looked so gentle tonight. We kissed. He says I'm not a girl to him but a woman. A woman! I think we might make love. Should I tell Sarah? April 6—'"

"Please!" Dr. Winslow rapped his knuckles on the table, as if calling class to order. "I'm afraid if you're going to persist, I'll have to . . . uh . . . adjourn this meeting."

"'April 6—'"

"Ms. Melendez!"

She slapped the diary on the table. "Isn't what I read proof enough! Words don't lie!"

Swallowing hard, the principal shook his head. "Ms. Melendez, if I were to present Martin Bixby's personnel file, you would see literally thousands of words filled with commendations for all the wonderful things he's done for this district. Do you know that, three years ago, he was chosen as Arbor Shore's Teacher of the Year?" Winslow opened his two hands like a scale. "To balance all that . . . ," he dropped his left palm, ". . . against a few sentences in an adolescent girl's notebook . . . ," he lifted his right palm.

Rosen asked, "Why don't you?"

"I beg your pardon."

"Why don't you let us see Mr. Bixby's personnel file? Perhaps among all those accolades, we might find something that might help to substantiate Nina's diary."

"What do you mean?"

"A parent's letter of complaint or an official reprimand. I'm sure you know the term 'negligent retention.' If he's done something like this before, and you've kept him on, the school would be held liable."

From the corner of his eye, Rosen watched Bixby. The teacher appeared unconcerned, but his knuckles, gripping the armrests, slowly whitened.

"Dear me, no," Dr. Winslow said.

Lucila demanded, "Why can't you show us his file?"

"Mr. Bixby's file is . . . uh . . . personal. Even if I was so inclined, I'd have no right to do so. I'm sure Mr. Rosen, as an attorney, understands my position."

Leaning forward, Rosen said, "The only thing I understand at the moment is that this man Bixby may have molested Nina Melendez, and possibly my daughter as well."

"But surely you understand that we must respect Mr. Bixby's privacy, his individual rights."

"I don't give a damn about Mr. Bixby's rights. All I'm interested in is protecting my daughter."

"That's right," Lucila agreed.

She continued arguing for access to Bixby's file, which the principal politely but firmly refused. Rosen stopped listening, going over the words he'd just said. For the first time in his life, he sounded like a prosecutor.

A familiar voice caught his attention; Bess was finally speaking. "I love my daughter as much as any parent, and if there were the slightest doubt in my mind, I'd be in complete agreement with Mrs. Melendez. But I've known Martin Bixby for many years. We've team-taught on a number of occasions and worked together on several drama productions. From what I've observed, his behavior with faculty and students has always been above reproach."

Rosen stared at her; she sounded just like Winslow. The principal smiled and, as if on cue, Kate Ellsworth continued where Bess had left off.

"I must agree with Mrs. Gold." She looked at Nina's mother. "Esther, I know this is awkward because I'm your employer, but I speak to you as one mother to another. My older daughter Megan was in several productions with Mr. Bixby, and there was never the slightest hint of impropriety. I grew up here, attended Arbor Shore High School more years ago than I care to remember, and know most of the families in the community. *No one* has ever had anything but praise for Mr. Bixby."

Esther's face tightened as her sister-in-law translated what Kate Ellsworth had said. Then she shook her head hard.

"I know my daughter. She's a good girl. I don't let her run around with boys. She don't lie. You read the words she put in her diary. You say maybe . . . that she . . ." Frustrated with her English, Mrs. Melendez rattled off several sentences in Spanish, which Lucila translated.

"My sister-in-law says that Nina would never make up something like that. If she wrote it in her diary, then it's true. Esther believes it's true, no matter what anybody says." Leveling her gaze at Martin Bixby, Lucila added, "I believe it's true too."

Esther Melendez nodded at the teacher. "Let him talk. Let him say what he did."

Dr. Winslow began, "Mr. Bixby has already assured me—," but stopped when the teacher cleared his throat.

Hands clasped together, Bixby gazed at Mrs. Melendez. "Dear lady, I give you my word that I've done nothing improper with your daughter or any child in this school. I have no idea why Nina wrote what she did." He shrugged. "She is a very imaginative child."

Esther Melendez almost spat, "Mentiroso!"

"Pardon me?"

"Liar!"

There was a long silence, broken finally by Dr. Winslow's fingers drumming on the table. Sighing softly, he glanced at his watch.

"Mrs. Melendez, I was hoping that we could . . . uh . . . reassure you on this matter. As Mrs. Ellsworth said, Arbor Shore is more than just a community. It's a family. The Learys, for example—Kate Ellsworth's family—go back three or four generations. We know each other, we know our children, and we know our teachers. Perhaps if you'd lived in the community a bit longer, you'd understand—"

Lucila rose to her feet. "We understand. Your lily-white community is looking out for itself. Because my niece is a little brown girl, the daughter of a servant, you don't give a damn."

"No, no," Dr. Winslow protested. "It's completely irrelevant that your niece is Mexican."

"We're Dominican." She shook her head sadly. "That's what we

31

all are to you, us brown people, just Mexicans who do your lawns and take care of your babies so you can go play tennis. Kate, what if *your* daughter had written in her diary the same things Nina had? Would you be so sure of your friend Bixby's innocence?"

Mrs. Ellsworth replied, "I suppose I might feel as you and Esther do. But I know Martin Bixby."

"Yes, like a member of the family."

The principal once again looked at his watch. "I've another meeting due to start here any minute. I don't think there's really . . . uh . . . anything more to say. As a courtesy to Mrs. Melendez, I will interview Nina again on Monday. If necessary, we can talk further. Thank you both for bringing this to my attention."

He stood and, stepping behind them, opened the door. "Good afternoon, ladies."

Lucila stared into his eyes and, as his face turned the color of peeled shrimp, said, "Don't think Esther and I will let this go away. We'll get a lawyer if we have to. Whatever it takes—sue the school board, go to the newspapers—we'll do. Just so you understand."

Winslow's lips trembled, but Rosen didn't wait to hear the principal's reply. He hurried into the hallway after Bess.

"Wait a minute!"

She held up a hand. "Not now. I've got a ton of kids to see after school."

"Don't you think your daughter's a little more important?"

"Don't start, Nate."

"You heard all that doublespeak from your principal—'we will . . . uh . . . look into it.' He wants to bury the whole mess, and you were shoveling right along with him."

"What do you want from me?"

The bell rang. On either side of the hallway, doors sprang open, and students dashed out as if it were the running of the bulls. Bess drew him against the wall. Inhaling her perfume, he forgot for a moment why he was angry with her.

She lowered her voice. "Watch what you say. These kids pick up gossip like radar."

"That's it, isn't it?"

"What?"

"That's why Winslow wanted you at the meeting. He knew you'd stand up for Bixby, because Bixby's part of the school, and the school's part of Arbor Shore."

"You don't know what you're talking about."

"He used you to get at Esther Melendez. Sarah is her daughter's best friend, so if you defended Bixby . . . ," he tapped his heart, ". . . one mother to another, she might buy it. You can't afford to rock the boat with a case involving child molesting in Arbor Shore. Afraid of what your 'goyim' neighbors might think."

"Damn you!" She pulled a necklace from under her blouse to reveal a golden Star of David. "It wasn't me who ran away from my faith."

No, it wasn't, and so what more could he say? As he turned to go, she touched his sleeve.

"I shouldn't have said that. It's just that you don't understand how things work here. If I thought for a moment Bix was involved in anything like that, do you honestly think I'd stand by and do nothing? My God, Nate, what kind of a mother do you think I am?"

He rubbed his eyes, then shrugged.

"I do believe Martin Bixby—I've known him for a long time. But if it is true, you won't get anywhere by pushing these people. They'll just stonewall, especially if it's someone they only see as a cleaning lady. This weekend I want us to sit down with Sarah, Nina, and the two Melendez women. Maybe we can get at the truth that way. I'm also going to talk to Linda Agee, Sarah's counselor. She might be of some help. You can come along, that is, if you can stop being a lawyer for five minutes."

"All right, we'll try it your way for now, but I'm not going to let this be buried. Not until I know for sure."

She was about to say something but caught herself. "I've got to get to my room. I'll call you later."

Bess took a few steps, then turned. Rosen felt that she wanted to come back, but again changing her mind, she hurried down the hallway and around a corner. After taking a long drink from a water fountain, he walked the other way toward the exit.

Arms crossed, Lucila Melendez leaned against a stairway near the double doors. As they ran outside, several boys did a double-take as they saw her; one even stumbled down the front steps.

When she told Rosen, "I was waiting for you," another group snickered behind him.

She stood very erect, like a model, and her crossed arms seemed as much a way of keeping him distant as it was a sign of her impatience.

"Where's your sister-in-law?"

"She went home. She wants to be there for Nina. So what do you think about this Bixby guy?"

Despite Bess's warning, he said, "'Mentiroso.'"

Lucila nodded. "You're the only one at the meeting who gave us any help. Even your wife—"

"My ex-wife." Rosen nodded at her sweatshirt. "Fund a Child's Education—that's a wonderful organization, and a terrific logo." In the corner of the design were the initials L.M. "Winslow mentioned you're an artist. Did you do that?"

She stifled a smile. "Uh huh."

"I knew there was something familiar about the girl's silhouette. It's Nina."

"Who better to represent a beautiful, innocent child. So, are you going to help us?"

Students clustered in threes and fours throughout the entrance-way and outside on the steps.

"I'll walk you to your car."

Rosen had been so worried about Sarah he hadn't realized how beautiful the day was. Feathery clouds wisped across a powder blue sky, and he inhaled the fragrance of white blossoms hanging heavy as Christmas ornaments from trees along the sidewalk. He liked being out on such a day, and he liked walking with someone as beautiful as Lucila Melendez. Liked the sidelong glances of envy the teenage boys gave him. Liked her hair falling down to the middle of her back instead of in a French braid. Should he tell her how much he liked it?

"Are you going to help us?" she repeated.

"You and your sister-in-law handled things pretty well your-selves."

"Esther was terrified sitting with those people. It was only fighting for her daughter that made her strong. She needs help."

"She has you."

"She needs a lawyer. If it's a fee you're worried about, I can pay."

Rosen said, "It's not the fee."

"If you're afraid of those people—"

"No."

She looked him up and down. "I didn't think so. Maybe it's your ex-wife. She wouldn't like you mixing in this." When he hesitated, Lucila smiled. She had dimples just like Nina. "Here's my car."

A Lexus and a BMW appeared to lean away from the old mon-key-brown Chevy station wagon parked between them, as if its rust were communicable. Its back seat had been turned down, and the entire rear of the wagon was filled with paint cans, easels, canvases, and other art supplies.

Rosen opened the door for her. "You didn't lock it, and in this neighborhood!"

He liked the sound of her laughter. Slipping into the driver's seat, she tossed her head like a proud horse and smoothed back her hair. Ripping a piece from a cardboard flap, she wrote her phone number.

"Here. If you decide to help us, give me a call. It was nice meeting you, Mr. . . . ?"

"Rosen. Nate Rosen."

"You said that just like the guy does in those James Bond movies. Well, maybe I'll be seeing you. Bye."

He watched her drive away, the station wagon leaving a trail of blue smoke, then pushed the piece of cardboard into his shirt pocket. Not that Rosen needed it. He'd already memorized her number.

Chapter 4

He'd usually been able to ignore Saturday mornings. They seemed pretty much the same as any weekday—good for researching a case in the law library, interviewing witnesses, running down leads, traveling to and from Washington. But this morning, as Rosen sat in the window seat overlooking the park in downtown Evanston, the loneliness fluttered through his body as gently as the lace tablecloth his mother had spread upon the Sabbath table.

It was nine-thirty. His father would be "davening," rocking in prayer with the few other devoted men still in the old neighborhood, as would Rosen's brother David in his West Bank settlement—no, the Sabbath was almost over in Israel. Aaron and his family were probably at that new synagogue near their house, watching the electronic doors of the Ark silently open to reveal the Torah. Each of them was with someone to share the holy day. Even a Jew alone need only pray to God and then was not alone. But Rosen wouldn't pray.

Instead, he sipped his tea and listened to the radio murmur reassuringly from the kitchen. Sarah should have been with him. They'd planned to watch videos, eat popcorn, and talk, but she'd been too upset to see him.

"Maybe tomorrow, Daddy," she'd said on the phone last night. "I've got to talk to Nina. Call me tomorrow morning."

There was a telephone on a small desk near the window, but he'd wait until ten o'clock. Instead, checking his directory, he dialed another number.

"Polski Dziennik Glos."

"Good morning. Do you speak English?"

"*Polish Daily Voice*," a woman said with a thick accent. "How may I help you?"

"I'd like to speak to Andi Wojecki."

"I'm sorry. She's on assignment in Warsaw."

"Poland?"

"Yes, a photo essay on Polish-Americans who've returned home. Can I be of help?"

"I'm a friend from out of town. Andi's doing well?"

"Oh yes, what a wonderful photographer! She'll be back in . . . uh . . . ten days. Can I take a message?"

Rosen hesitated then said, "No thanks. Good-bye."

He'd met Andi last year in South Dakota, helping clear her Lakota friend of a murder charge. After she'd moved to Chicago, they'd kept in touch, although lately the phone calls had been less frequent. Rosen had been too busy to mind. He'd called, planning to ask for help gathering information on Martin Bixby. But the real reason was just loneliness.

He returned to the window seat. It was another fine April day. Across the street, mothers pushed their baby strollers, children played on the swings, and old men jogged around the park's perimeter. A young couple passed the swing set and stood by a flower bed filled with yellow, blue, and pink petals. Putting his hands on her shoulders, the boy pulled the girl close, and they kissed for a long time.

They might have been alone beside that beautiful garden, and Rosen remembered a favorite passage from The Song of Songs:

Rise up, my love, my fair one, and come away,
For winter is past, and the rain is over and gone;
The flowers appear on the earth;
The time of the singing of birds is come,
and the voice of the turtle is heard in our land . . .

He vaguely recollected a woman in a dream last night. Andi—no. Someone with long, dark hair.

Could Lucila Melendez have been the woman? To dream of a woman was bad, his old rabbi had told the yeshiva boys. Did not the Talmud state that ". . .whoever sleeps alone in a house will be seized by Lilith," the female demon with long hair? Rosen almost laughed aloud, but then he didn't really know Lucila.

The condo where he was staying belonged to his boss's brother, a wealthy pharmacologist whose wife patronized the fine arts in Chicago. Their living room resembled a gallery, one wall containing shelves filled with art books and sculptures. The figures were Third World in origin—bronze or wooden African statuettes and squatting pre-Columbian gods. Across the polished wooden floor, past a white leather sofa and matching chairs, the opposite wall displayed a collection of paintings. They had in common broad strokes, bold colors, and a glorification of the peasant.

Rosen took, from the bottom shelf, an oversized volume entitled *Daughters of Frida Kahlo: Art of the Latin American Woman.* He found a reference to Lucila and turned to a page with two paintings—a sickly barrio girl clinging to an old "Dick and Jane" reader, and a pregnant woman being crucified. The woman resembled Lucila's sister-in-law, Esther.

The accompanying text read, "Lucila Melendez, Dominican-American, whose work deftly combines two themes—the social injustice of her homeland with the radical feminism of her adopted country."

Returning the book, Rosen wondered if any of the galleries in the Chicago area displayed Lucila's work. He could ask her when he called.

"Oh?" he wondered in the same quizzical voice his rabbi had used when asking a Talmudic question, "and how did you know you were going to call her before you knew you were going to call her?"

He started to smile, then checked his watch. Sarah. He went to the phone.

Just then the radio announced, "And tragic news from the northern suburb of Arbor Shore. A listener's call-in tip sent our WMAQ reporter Dean Grodin to a small park on Lake Michigan, where a girl has died. Dean, what have you learned so far?"

"Jim, police haven't released many details yet. What's clear, however, is that sometime last night a teenage girl fell to her death from the edge of Ravine Park, an area that overlooks the beach."

"Do you know the victim's name?"

"No, but she apparently attended Arbor Shore High School and lived in the immediate area—at least that's what one of the police officers said before being called away by Police Chief Otto Keller. Chief Keller's handling the investigation himself and says he'll have a statement later this morning."

"The reason for the girl's death?"

"Police are still examining the area and, of course, an autopsy will have to be done. According to neighbors who've gathered here, teenagers come to the park at night, as well as the nearby ravines, to drink. You may remember I reported last year about a boy who got drunk and fell into a ravine, breaking an arm and both legs."

"So it may have been another tragic accident."

"It's possible, but at this point we're just speculating. I should know more within an hour or two."

"Stay with it, Dean."

Rosen gripped the receiver. He kept telling himself it wasn't Sarah. What would she have been doing out there at night? Besides, if it'd been Sarah, Bess would've called long ago.

He dialed her number. The phone rang for a long time, but he refused to hang up. Finally someone lifted the receiver.

"Hello." Bess sounded tired.

"What happened?"

"Oh, Nate, you heard. I suppose by now everybody—"

"Sarah's all right!"

"Sarah, oh yes. We've got her sedated." Bess's voice tightened. "It was bad for a while. I've never seen her like that, but Shelly got her to take something. I feel like hell. We're all sick over the whole thing."

"What are you talking about?"

The other end of the line grew quiet. Then she said, "You don't know, do you?"

"Know what?"

"Oh, Nate, the girl who died was Sarah's friend Nina."

"I'll be right over."

He drove north on Sheridan Road, through a half dozen of Chicago's most affluent suburbs. Thirty minutes later he reached Arbor Shore. Its downtown was a long avenue shaded by a bower of giant oaks. Side streets were cobblestoned and the solid square stores gentrified with their red bricks and copper-colored shingles.

Rosen continued north past Sarah's high school. A few blocks ahead, three police cars and a TV news van had parked on the shoulder of the road near a side street. Dressed in a gray jogging outfit, Shelly stood among a small crowd. Parking on the next street, Rosen walked back to join him.

Shelly asked, "You heard about this?"

"I talked to Bess. The radio didn't name the dead girl. How did you know it was Nina?"

"I was jogging in the park when the police arrived. They brought out Esther Melendez, I guess to identify the body. If you'd seen the woman." He shivered. "I went home and told Bess. Sarah overheard. She went nuts—don't worry, we calmed her down—just a mild sedative. Funny. She screamed but didn't cry—the kid never cries. Bess stayed with her, and I came back."

"Did you find out anything more?"

"Everybody here's been saying it's just another kid who got drunk and fell down hard. There's a helluva lot more of that happening in this neighborhood than anybody lets on." Blinking hard through his big glasses, he glanced at a reporter and lowered his voice. "I don't believe it. Not a kid like Nina. You think Sarah would've snuck out and gotten so shit-faced drunk that she fell off a cliff?"

Rosen shook his head.

"Well, Nina was the same way. I saw a lot of those two together. Good kids, both of them. Goddamn shame, with all the crazies running around in the world—a good kid like her dies."

"If she wasn't out drinking, then what happened?"

"Who the hell knows?"

Rosen noticed a girl in the crowd. "Isn't that the flamenco dancer?"

"Uh huh. Margarita Reyes. 'Ita,' the kids call her. You just walked past where she lives, on the corner. Her mother's the housekeeper. Just like Nina and Esther." He shook his head vigorously. "You wanna find out what happened to Nina? C'mon."

They walked down a short street that led to a wooden bridge. A squad car was parked at the end of the cul-de-sac. A young policeman leaned over the bridge, idly dropping stones into the ravine below. At their approach, he straightened to attention.

"Sorry. Nobody can come across until we're done on the other side. Been a death here."

He had a scarecrow kind of body and a pinched face that peered at one man, then the other, then back again—as if not sure whom to address.

Shelly said, "I'm a friend of the Ellsworths, as well as Esther Melendez. We'd like to see them."

"I'm sorry, sir. Like I was saying, after —"

"I'm a doctor. Mrs. Melendez may need medical attention."

"I don't know." The policeman stared even more intently at Shelly. "You look really familiar. Where've I seen you?"

Shelly began humming softly, then broke into song, "'And we're out together dancing feet to feet.'"

The policeman's eyes flashed, like a Zen Buddhist suddenly hearing the sound of one hand clapping. "Of course, the commercial on TV. You're the Arches of Triumph guy!" He finished the jingle, "'Call today, the first visit's free; 933 F-O-O-T!'"

"That's right."

"You drive that cool Jag around town. I like the license plate."

"Thanks. We'll just go on ahead."

He walked onto the bridge. Rosen followed.

The policeman called after them. "I better call the chief to let him know!"

"You do that!"

By then they were halfway across the bridge. Shelly stopped to look into the deep ravine, which twisted its way through a dense tangle of trees, bushes, and creepers.

"My older boy took a tumble about a half mile up. He was seventeen. Drinking malt liquor with his friends in the middle of the night. Fell down and broke his leg. Took his friends fifteen minutes to find him. He still walks with a limp. I asked him why he'd do something so stupid, and you know what he told me—'I don't know, Dad. Guess I was bored.' Bored? When I was a kid, I didn't have a Mustang, video games, my own credit card, phone sex for Chrissakes! A Davey Crockett cap and a hula hoop—that's what I had. And I wasn't bored. Go figure."

Rosen shrugged. "I guess you were just a fun guy."

Shelly looked at him for a moment, then burst out laughing. "Yeah, guess I was."

"You handled that policeman pretty well. We're not supposed to have access to a crime scene while it's still being investigated."

"You know in the movies, when the cops have to walk on eggs around some rich guy, because he owns the town's saw mill? Well, in Arbor Shore that describes just about everybody. The cops here could give the UN a lesson in diplomacy."

Stepping from the bridge, they walked along a gravel path through a heavily wooded area. Suddenly Rosen blinked at the sunlight and found himself on the edge of a park, stretching far to his left. Closely clipped grass interrupted by an occasional tall tree holding very still, like an old man waiting for pigeons. The park ended at a double-rail fence about a quarter mile ahead. Past the fence, white sky met the azure blue of Lake Michigan.

Continuing along the park's perimeter, the path was bordered on the right by a tall gray stockade fence. As they walked closer toward the lake, Rosen saw, above the fence, the dark roof and sharp gables of a mansion.

"The Leary estate," Shelly said, "where Byron and Kate Ellsworth live. Leary is Kate's maiden name."

"I bet it's some house."

"The whole place is probably bigger than Monaco or Lichten . . . schmuck, whatever it's called. She inherited it all—an only child. Not bad, huh."

"And her husband?"

"A real tight-ass. I mean, what kind of a name is Byron; something you'd call your Great Dane. 'Here, Byron, here boy!' I think the guy started out as some pretty-boy tennis player. When he married Kate Leary, her father bought him a seat on the Exchange as a wedding present. Guess the old man thought it would give the guy something to do besides hitting tennis balls. Thing is, Ellsworth turned out to have quite a head for business. Made a pile of dough in his own right, so Leary took him into his investment business. Now that the old man's dead, guess who's in charge?"

Again Rosen looked up at the estate. "Big place for one family. They have two kids, right?"

"Uh huh. Girl's away at college. Of course, Esther Melendez stays in the coach house with Nina. And there's that creepy body-guard who hangs around."

They passed a gate in the stockade fence, then came to a small wooded area, where the gravel road ended and a squad car was parked. Rosen smelled fresh grass and saw a pile of clippings dumped over a few dead branches. They walked into the park until they reached an area of grass yellowed-taped into a square under the wooden railing.

"This must be where it happened," Shelly said.

Rosen studied the top railing, which looked undisturbed except for a sliver bent like a hangnail. The police had laid sheets of clear plastic over the grass, holding them in place with small rocks. The sheets covered something more than grass—scattered bits of red. Both men knelt beside the plastic.

"What do you make of it?" Rosen asked.

"Something broken—no, they're too delicate. You know what they look like—flowers. Maybe petals off a rose."

"I think you're right. They go all the way to the edge of the bluff. And see there, where the grass is all torn up and that bush is flattened. She must've hit the ground hard before starting her fall."

The two men walked around the tape and stood at the railing's edge. It was a steep slope of fifty feet to the beach below where jagged rocks lay strewn along the beach. One policeman stood between the rocks, while another wandered, like a beachcomber, up and down the water's edge.

"You wanna go down there?" Shelly asked.

Rosen nodded, and the two men followed the rail fence to their left, where it ended in a winding wooden staircase. They clattered down to a dirt path which, in turn, led to another set of stairs, this one made of railroad ties fanning out like a deck of cards on a gradual incline two feet apart.

They passed a heavy policeman huffing his way back up to the park. Pausing to wipe his forehead with his sleeve, he tapped a two-way radio hanging from his belt.

"Jay called from the bridge. Chief's expecting you gentlemen."

Another gravel path had them skittering down to the beach. Rosen knew this was Lake Michigan; nevertheless, he seemed to be standing within a postcard of a Caribbean island. He shielded his eyes from the sunlight glinting off the gently lapping water, while his feet rippled through sand the color and consistency of cream.

Shelly said, "Pretty, huh. In another month, you could go swimming. Then it really is a slice of paradise." Waving his hand at the man standing beside Nina's body, he called out, "Chief Keller, how are you!"

The police chief was a small man about sixty, his gray hair cut very short in contrast to his bushy eyebrows. His right hand held a pipe to his mouth, the left gripping his right elbow like a marionette waiting to have its strings jerked.

After an awkward moment of silence, Shelly said, "Hope you don't mind us coming down here. I'm Shelly Gold. I live a few blocks away."

The policeman nodded, taking a few deep puffs and sending a trail of gray smoke into the air.

"This is Nate Rosen. His daughter—Sarah's also my step-daughter—was Nina Melendez's best friend. We're naturally concerned, not only about what happened to Nina, but how this might affect Sarah."

The police chief took the pipe from his lips. "I thought you came to give medical attention to Mrs. Melendez. Isn't that what you told Jay?"

Shelly scratched his head. "Guess I did say something like that."

"Aren't you a podiatrist?"

"Uh, yes."

"I don't think her feet're bothering her at the moment, but I can understand your concern. You'll just need to stay clear of any evidence."

"What evidence?" Rosen asked.

Keller looked from one man to the other. "What you'd expect to find, when something like this happens. Up on the bluff a thread snagged on the top rail—could be from the girl's blue jeans, as she fell over the fence."

"What else was she wearing?"

"Sweatshirt, sneakers."

"Underwear?"

"We didn't look to see if she had on any panties."

"What about a bra?"

Keller hesitated, then shook his head. He pointed to a jagged rock near the body.

"Blood and hair—sure it'll match the girl's. She might've survived if she hadn't cracked her head on that. Looks like a lot of cuts and bruises while she was falling."

"What else did you find up on the bluff?"

"We found a gold necklace, at least its chain. Pendant broke off—we're still looking for it. You ever see a necklace on her, Dr. Gold?"

"Jeez, I don't know. Didn't her mother recognize it?"

"Maybe your step-daughter would know."

Rosen asked, "What about those bits of red in the grass?"

Keller clicked his tongue. "Didn't they bag that stuff yet?"

"Petals from a flower?"

"Roses. There were more petals clutched in the girl's right hand."

"Any stems?"

"Huh?"

"Did you find the flower stems?"

"No."

Rosen shook his head. "Did the roses come from Nina's house?"

"According to the mother, no. There were a couple empty beer cans and a broken whiskey bottle near the bottom. We're checking them for prints."

Shelly asked, "What do you think happened?"

Keller took a few more puffs, his eyes narrowing behind a veil of smoke. "Can't say for sure yet. Of course, it was a Friday night. Kids come out here regularly to drink. Sometimes they get pretty wild."

"How do you know she snuck out last night? Anybody see her?"

"We found the body about nine this morning. Only her face and jaw were stiff. Means she probably died around eleven P.M., give or take a couple hours. We can narrow that down a bit. Her mother says Nina took a phone call, about ten, from your stepdaughter Sarah. You know anything about a call, Dr. Gold?"

"No. I mean, it's possible."

"The mother went to bed about that time, and when she woke up this morning, Nina was gone. Her bed hadn't been slept in. Mother walked around the neighborhood looking for her. By the time she told her employer, Mrs. Ellsworth, one of the fellas at the yacht club had found the girl's body and reported it to us."

At that moment, the young policeman who'd been walking up and down the beach joined them. He had curly brown hair, a little longish for a cop, round cheeks, and a turned-up nose.

"Nothing on the beach, Chief. No pendant, flowers, beer cans, or anything."

Shelly shook his head. "Nina wasn't the kind of kid to sneak out and get drunk."

Keller said, "I've found that parents don't always know what their kids will or won't do. Plenty of teenagers been hurt around here while their parents thought they were tucked safely in bed."

Shelly reddened and looked away.

"Still, kids don't go off alone. There's usually at least one other drinking buddy."

The young policeman laughed. "Sure thought we had another one—huh, Chief. The mother kept saying 'Lamato . . . Lamato.' Thought maybe the girl had some Italian boyfriend."

Keller's jaw set tight. Then he said, "Get up on the ridge and see those rose petals are bagged." To Shelly, "Are you sure your step-daughter was home last night?"

"Uh, yes. Nina spent the evening over at our house. She left around nine-thirty. Sarah watched a video in her room until about eleven. Then she came downstairs and played the piano for awhile, before going to bed. I was in my study for another hour or so after that. Everything was quiet."

"And that phone call Nina supposedly received from your daughter around ten o'clock?"

"Maybe. She's got her own phone in her room. Look, if you're thinking that Sarah snuck out with Nina, forget it."

Keller paused to draw on his pipe, but it had gone out. "If you're right, and the girl went out alone . . . Well, it's awful strange. What with the flowers—it sort of reminded me of a grave."

"You're not saying it was suicide?"

"No, sir, I'm not saying anything yet. Of course, in a case like this, the victim's state of mind is awfully important. I'm afraid we'll have to talk to your stepdaughter. She was the victim's best friend."

"Of course. Of course."

Rosen almost smiled. Shelly had no idea how right he was; Keller was a master diplomat. During their conversation, the policeman had given away nothing that he wouldn't be announcing soon to the media. He had avoided the questions he wanted to avoid—had Nina's mother recognized the girl's necklace or had the police found any witnesses to her death? He'd put Shelly on the defensive with that comment about teenagers drinking without their parents' knowledge. Most importantly, Keller had carefully turned the discussion to Sarah, because he needed her help. In a community like Arbor Shore, that meant getting the parents' cooperation, and Shelly was ready to do anything to help.

Rosen asked, "Is there any other reason to believe it might've been suicide?"

"No," Keller said, "but kids get moody, especially girls. This area has more than its share of teenage suicides. What the hell, it's a tragedy either way—accident or suicide."

"Sure. We've taken enough of your time. Thanks."

"Not at all." He tapped his pipe bowl against his shoe. "I'll need to talk to your daughter soon."

"Of course."

Rosen and Shelly walked quietly across the beach. Rosen shaded his eyes and looked far into the horizon. Sunlight danced on the water.

Shaking his head, Shelly mumbled, "Accident . . . suicide. I just can't believe it."

"Neither can I. We need to talk to Mrs. Melendez."

"Why?"

"Remember what the other cop mentioned her saying?"

"Uh . . . yeah. About some Italian boyfriend . . . Lamato, wasn't it?"

"You know what 'la mató' means in Spanish? 'He killed her.'"

Chapter 5

Blessed with holy water and covered with a white pall, the coffin rested in the church nave. Behind the casket, melting wax slid like tears down the tall paschal candle, reminding Rosen of the small "yahrtzeit" candle he lit each year to commemorate his mother's death. As Proverbs stated, "The spirit of man is the candle of the Lord."

The candle burned clean and steady, the brightest illumination in the old Gothic church. Light painted the stained glass windows in brilliant colors then, like a brush's dirty water, dribbled its muddied brown into the dark arches overhead.

The young priest looked down from the altar. His shadow of a mustache made him appear even younger, as did his eager blue eyes. However, his voice carried the funeral mass with surprising authority, and he began the service in Spanish.

After a few minutes he said, "I have been referring to the Gospel of John, Chapter 11: 'And when he thus had spoken, he cried with a loud voice, Lazarus, come forth. And he that was dead came forth, bound hand and foot with graveclothes: and his face was bound about with a napkin. Jesus said unto them, Loose him, and let him go.'

"These verses remind all of us that, while Nina Melendez has given up her earthly body, she lives eternally with our Lord and Savior. Just as the white pall draped over her casket reminds us that she is now clothed with Christ and the paschal candle reminds us that she has risen with Christ."

As the priest lapsed into Spanish, Rosen saw himself reciting the kaddish alone before his mother's grave, his tears hot as the wax melting down the paschal candle. "What higher act of goodness was there," his rabbi would ask, "than to attend the dead?" Yet his own father hadn't sent word to Rosen of his mother's death. So he came alone, days later, to pray beside her grave as he was praying now. And as he had then, he realized, "I'm more dead to my father than my mother is. At least he burns the yahrtzeit candle for her."

The priest continued in Spanish, and more from the cadence than the words, Rosen recognized the Twenty-third Psalm of David: "Only goodness and steadfast love shall pursue me all the days of my life, and I shall dwell in the house of the Lord forever." He grimaced, looking down at the casket. Had goodness and love followed Nina Melendez, an innocent girl? And if not her, could they follow anyone?

The priest said, "At this time, it is customary for family members to read a passage from the scriptures. Nina's Aunt Lucila, however, has chosen to read from one of Nina's favorite poems."

Wearing a long black dress, her hair twisted into a bun, Lucila Melendez walked from the first pew. She looked down at the coffin, as if standing beside Nina's bed, and spoke in Spanish with the lilt of a lullaby. Then in English,

> "'Sleep, my little one,
> sleep and smile,
> for the night-watch of stars
> rocks you awhile.
>
> Look at the bright rose,
> red as can be.
> Reach out to the world
> as you reach out to me.
>
> Sleep, my little one,
> sleep and smile,
> For God in the shade
> rocks you awhile.'"

Lucila kissed the head of the coffin, then returned to her seat. Several women, including Nina's mother, were crying loudly. After the priest finished the service with a fervent prayer in Spanish, the mourners walked slowly down the aisle and through the church doors. Blinking back the sunlight, Rosen stared at his daughter, who looked as white as the paschal candle. He wanted to comfort her, but what was there to say?

Shelly touched his arm. "I'll put the car into the funeral procession, then pick you up in front of the church."

Shelly joined the others walking down the steps—Lucila helping a sobbing Esther Melendez; the Ellsworths with their son Chip and a big man, wearing ice-blue sunglasses, who walked with a military bearing and took out a dark cigarillo from a silver case. Dr. Winslow led several teachers and students from the high school. Among the latter, Rosen recognized the flamenco dancer, Margarita Reyes. Halfway down the steps, she slipped her hand into Chip's. The boy blushed but didn't let go.

A line of cars turned the corner, headlights blinking on, and slowly moved past the church. Sarah and Bess slid into the back seat of their blue Mercedes, while Rosen sat in front beside Shelly. They drove in silence, except for Sarah's stuttered breathing.

Both church and cemetery were in Logan Square, an old German and Norwegian neighborhood on the North Side that was now heavily Latino. It was late Monday morning; streets were congested with lunch-hour traffic. The funeral procession drove past Mexican restaurants, discount houses, jewelry stores, and fashion shops with mannequins wearing cheap, flashy dresses. A skinny man pushed an ice-cream cart along the sidewalk; another vendor scooped shaved ice into a paper cone, then poured syrup over it from an old liquor bottle. On the brick wall of a corner liquor store, someone had painted a large mural of an eagle, wings outstretched, covering a young mother with an infant in her arms.

Turning north on Kedzie Avenue, the motorcade drove around Logan Square itself, a grassy knoll from whose center rose a tall white concrete monument topped with an eagle. From a park bench a scraggly old man, drinking from a paper bag, saluted as the cars drove by.

A few minutes later they arrived at the cemetery. Rosen reached over the seat to take his daughter's hand. It was warm and moist.

"Shayna?"

She didn't look up.

He said very softly, "Maybe it would be better if you stayed in the car. I'll stay with you, or your mother—"

"No, I want to go."

That was the most Sarah had spoken to him since her friend's death. They followed the others down a tree-lined path that meandered toward an ancient oak. Under its largest branch lay Nina's casket beside a freshly dug grave. A trellis filled with white lilies leaned against the tree; the breeze carried the flowers' delicate fragrance among the mourners.

Rosen remembered the lines from The Song of Songs he'd read to Bess the day they'd become engaged: "His lips are like lilies; They drip flowing myrrh." The priest recited some prayers in Spanish, Nina's mourners responding to the litany, but not Rosen. Even when the priest lapsed into English, Rosen merely sighed. Not just for Nina, but for the pain within Sarah and for what he himself still felt for his mother.

What had Lucila said in church? "'Look at the bright rose, red as can be.'" He'd brought red roses, her favorite, to his mother's grave that first time, then come back a week later with fresh flowers, knowing the old ones had wilted and the petals scattered. Scattered rose petals on the matted grass beside her grave, just like the murder scene.

He'd seen Nina's death in Sarah's eyes every moment since it had occurred. The piece of fabric caught on the top fence rail, the girl's skull crushed against the jagged rock, the scattered rose petals on the ground and clutched in her hand. He'd wanted to look into the case but couldn't leave Sarah. So he'd remained in Bess's house the whole weekend, like sitting shivah for the dead, while his daughter entombed herself in her room.

"Time to go, Shayna."

Rosen pulled her away as the service ended, but she stiffened against him as Nina's mother was dragged screaming from the casket.

"Oh, Daddy!" Yet still she didn't cry.

He was about to say, "It's all right," but it wasn't. It would never again be quite all right for her. She deserved the truth; they all did. "La mató," Esther Melendez had said.

Returning to their cars, the mourners talked quietly in small groups. A plump Hispanic boy, wearing a madras suit and a tie that was too long for him, gave directions to Lucila's apartment, where lunch would be served.

"Just three blocks over—that way." He pointed north. "Above the Mercado Jimenez."

Shelly nodded. "I know where it is. One of my clinics is on the same block."

Dr. Winslow said to Bess, "The other staff members and I are returning to school. It's very good of you to stay and comfort Mrs. Melendez." He clicked his tongue. "Tragic way for this to end."

"What makes you think it's over?" Rosen asked.

"Well, what I meant was . . . uh . . ."

"Dr. Winslow," Bess said, "I know how much it means to Nina's mother for you to be here."

"Not at all. It's my duty. Someone representing the administration . . ."

As the principal babbled on about his responsibilities, Rosen watched Byron and Kate Ellsworth standing beside their silver BMW.

"Can't you come over for a few minutes?" Kate asked.

Her husband shook his head. "I've already had to reschedule one very important meeting to this afternoon, and I can't afford to miss it. I'm lining up several investors for a significant project. You know how tenuous these things can be. If you don't strike while the iron is hot—"

"Spare me the clichés."

"My God, Kate, it's not like she was an actual member of the family. Her mother's only our housekeeper."

"What?"

"I'm sorry. I didn't mean that."

"No, of course not. She's anything but *only* a housekeeper."

"Look, Kate—"

"You'd better hurry. You have promises to keep."

When he took her in his arms, she presented her cheek.

He winced as if slapped, but kissed it. "You can get a ride with either Soldier or Chip."

"I'll be fine," she said, and walked away.

Ellsworth watched her go, then turned away. For a moment, his gaze locked on Rosen's. He suddenly brushed back his hair then checked the soles of his shoes for dirt. Stepping into the BMW, he drove onto the grass, glided past the line of parked cars, and disappeared through the cemetery gates.

A few minutes later, the rest of the cars slowly followed. A few turned on Fullerton, which would eventually lead to the Kennedy Expressway and the long drive north to Arbor Shore. Most, however, continued in a straight line past a few more streets filled with small shops and vendors.

Shelly pointed to a building in the middle of the street with a sign in large black letters, "ARCHES of TRIUMPH." Underneath, in smaller letters, "Se Habla Español."

"You'd be amazed how difficult it was for these people to find affordable podiatric care before my clinic opened. We'll park in back. That store the boy mentioned is down on the corner."

Mercado Jimenez was a small two-story building of red brick. The grocery occupied the first floor, with a large picture window, protected by iron mesh, displaying all sorts of odds and ends—espresso makers, audio tapes of Latino music, some Bart Simpson sweatshirts with sayings written in Spanish. Salsa blared from a radio inside. Two windows on the second floor, their sashes raised halfway, stared intently into the street.

Inside the store, three narrow aisles were filled with packaged goods. Along the walls, large open crates offered a variety of produce, including several exotic fruits he'd never seen before. In the corner hung rows of dried "bacalao"—codfish. Rosen smelled its pungent odor from the doorway.

Wearing a gold necklace with the name "Inez" and a tight red blouse, a young woman perched on a stool behind the register.

She asked, "You from the funeral for Luci's niece? Go around back and up the stairs. Hey, you wanna buy a lottery ticket?"

Walking around the corner, Rosen was startled by a large mural covering the store's entire brick wall. Lucila had painted the logo of F.A.C.E., with a long-haired girl reading a book. The long-haired girl was Nina.

Sarah stared wide-eyed at the mural, but Bess quickly led her behind the building and up two flights of clacking wooden stairs. Shelly and Rosen followed, helping an old woman carry a large pot of rice inside.

The doorway opened into a narrow corridor, flanked by the bathroom and kitchen. There was no real wall separating the kitchen, only a white Formica counter that horseshoed around the sink and appliances. Large dented pots filled with all sorts of steaming meat and vegetables elbowed one another for space along the counter. Still more pots pushed their way in, as well as platters of flan and cookies.

The corridor led to one enormous room, which served as Lucila's studio. Except for a small bedroom, which appeared to be an alcove between the kitchen and far corner of the room, everything else was open space. At least two dozen people sat in clusters of folding chairs throughout the room. Six or seven children sprawled on Lucila's bed watching a portable TV on a rickety stand.

Lucila sat with her sister-in-law at the opposite corner, as people approached in single file to pay their respects. Esther sobbed softly into a handkerchief, barely glancing at those who passed by.

When Sarah stood before her and said, "I'm so sorry," the woman trembled and, looking up, drew Sarah to her.

"Mi hijita. Una angelita, como mi Nina. Quédate conmigo. Quédate conmigo."

Sarah dropped to her knees and hugged the woman.

"Quédate conmigo," Esther repeated, wrapping Sarah in her arms. Bess stood over them, her hands resting gently on the other woman's shoulders. Unsure of what to do, Shelly thrust his hands in his pockets and stepped behind his wife.

Rosen moved to one side, next to the man who had accompanied the Ellsworths to the funeral. He wore a pinstripe suit tailored both for his muscular shoulders and thick waist. The sunglasses lay folded in a coat pocket, and his gray eyes didn't seem to blink. His jet-black hair was cut short, accentuating a flattened nose and puglike face. His wide mouth balanced a thick mustache that ended precisely at the corners. "Quédate conmigo," Esther murmured once again.

The other man said to Rosen, "She's asking your daughter to stay with her." He spoke softly for a big man and with a slight New England accent.

"Thanks. My Spanish isn't so good. You're . . . ?"

"Ed Masaryk." His grip was what Rosen expected from a hand nearly as big as a fielder's glove.

"Aren't you the Ellsworths' bodyguard?"

"I'm chief of security for Mr. Ellsworth's firm."

"But I understand you live on their estate."

"I do have quarters there."

"So your duties are split between the family and the company."

Masaryk stared at Rosen, his eyes still unblinking. "I like to do a thorough job."

Just then Chip Ellsworth and Margarita Reyes walked up to Esther Melendez. The boy had his mother's green eyes and slim build. His blond hair was a little too long; he kept brushing it back.

In contrast, everything about the girl was dark—thick curls reaching her shoulders, her dress a little too tight around the bust and hips, and the sheer stockings. The only bit of color was her makeup, too red, and a gold necklace with the name "Margarita."

Chip mumbled his condolences, then the girl took Esther's hands and, speaking softly to her in Spanish, hugged her tightly.

"Gracias, Ita, gracias," Esther said, still holding Sarah tightly.

Chip and the girl walked to Masaryk.

Chip said, "Soldier, we're probably going to split."

"Probably?"

"Well, yeah, I mean, we've paid our respects, so we're going."

"What about lunch?"

"I don't like all this soupy stuff. We'll just grab something at McDonald's."

Keeping his gaze on Chip, Masaryk said to the girl, "He doesn't know what he's missing, does he, Margarita?"

Smiling, the girl took Chip's hand. "He knows what's good for him." Then she rattled off several sentences in Spanish.

Masaryk responded in Spanish, speaking with an excellent accent. They spoke too quickly for Rosen to follow, and the big man's face betrayed no emotion.

Finally the girl laughed and said, "No te preocupes."

Masaryk's eyes suddenly narrowed. Rosen sensed something was wrong, but what was it? She'd only told the other man not to worry.

Masaryk said to the boy, "I know you two will have lunch, then drive over to school in time for your afternoon classes."

Chip swallowed hard. "You're not gonna have us followed?"

Laughing, Margarita pulled him away. "That makes it more fun. C'mon." She saluted. "Adiós, Soldado."

Nodding curtly to Rosen, Masaryk walked to the kitchen counter, where Kate Ellsworth served food to a line of men carrying their plates before them like a religious procession. She glanced at the door and seemed about to follow her son. Masaryk, however, put a hand gently on her shoulder and whispered to her. Her face made a tight smile, but she nodded and continued ladling something thick and steaming onto the plates. He stayed, watching her the whole time.

Someone suddenly screamed—a child by the television set. Other children began shouting, while pointing toward Esther and Sarah.

"Dr. Foot, Dr. Foot!" the children shouted.

Shelly blushed and nodded shyly. One of the little boys pulled him toward the TV set, as the other children sang in harmony with the commercial:

"Call today, the first visit's free, 933 F-O-O-T!"

Jumping up and down, the children grabbed at Shelly as if he were Santa Claus. A matron hobbled over and slapped the children on the head, pulling one boy's ears until he screamed. However, several men eagerly shook Shelly's hand; one of them kept pointing to his left foot.

"Such is the price of fame."

Rosen turned to see Lucila standing beside him. She held a bowl heaped with some sort of chicken stew. A big spoon had been pushed into the steaming mass.

"Here. I thought you might be hungry."

"Thanks. What's it called?"

"Sancocho. Chicken, carrots, plátanos, onions, and rice."

"Potatoes too."

"That's plátanos—plantains. You've seen them—they look like big bananas, only they're like potatoes. Starchy."

Rosen shook his head. "I saw these little bananas in the store downstairs."

"Those are called niños."

"And they're . . . ?"

"Little bananas."

They both laughed. Lucila's came brittle as broken glass. She rubbed her eyes, already raw from crying.

Rosen said, "I'd better sit down. You'll join me?"

"There're a couple chairs over there by the wall. I'll get you something to drink. Is iced tea all right?"

"Perfect."

Tasting the first spoonful of sancocho, Rosen realized how hungry he was. For the next few minutes, he was absorbed with his food, pausing only to sip the iced tea.

Lucila said, "So the food doesn't displease you."

"It's delicious. Did you make it?"

"Uh huh."

"I didn't realize you were so domestic."

"I'm not. When I'm working, I usually throw together some rice and beans or fix a salad."

Putting down the empty bowl, Rosen thumbed through several canvases stacked against the wall. The last one depicted an older woman placing her hand on a younger woman's pregnant belly.

"These are wonderful paintings," he said.

"Thanks. They're usually on the wall, but I took them down today. Too much of Nina. They're interpretations of Gabriela Mistral's poetry. You've heard of her?"

"Sarah and Nina used a poem of hers at school the other night."

"That's right. Mistral was Chilean, a Nobel Prize winner who wrote of her love for children. That last painting is based on a poem in which a young woman, afraid of her first pregnancy, seeks comfort from her mother." Lucila recited something in Spanish, then translated, 'I fell on her breasts, and all over again I became a little girl sobbing in her arms at the terror of life.'"

Rosen said, "Mistral must've had a large family of her own."

"She was childless—never married. There was a broken love affair, in which the man committed suicide."

"How terrible."

Lucila stared at the painting. "I'm not so sure. If she had married, he probably would've chained her to the house—bearing children, washing clothes, cooking beans and rice. It might've killed the poetry within her."

"Is that really fair to say?"

Blinking hard, she turned to Rosen. "You don't know what it's like for a woman in a Latin American country. It's a kind of slavery. First she obeys without question her father, who passes the manacles and chains to her husband."

"But there must be women in your country who are doctors, lawyers, and writers."

"And here there's a black Supreme Court Justice. Does that mean your blacks are really equal? I tell you what I know—what I saw in my mother's life. I won't be put in those chains."

"So instead, you've chained yourself to your work."

Crossing her arms, she nodded slowly. "My own choosing."

"I'm not being critical. It's just, with your obvious love of children, I'm a little surprised you're not married."

"But now you understand."

"I may be a little thick, but the lesson's sunk in."

Lucila said, "You're anything but thick. I'll get you some more iced tea."

Watching her walk to the kitchen counter, Rosen felt something stir within his heart. He wanted her sitting close to him, yet was ashamed to have those feelings at such a time, in such a place—a house of mourning. His face growing warm, he turned back to study the painting.

Lucila seemed to have been away for a long time. Finally she returned, handing him his drink. She also held a notebook.

"What's that," he asked, "more poetry?" Then he looked at the notebook more carefully. "Nina's diary."

Moving her chair closer—he smelled the fragrance of her hair, Lucila opened the diary. "This is Nina's first entry, dated about a month ago. 'On my way home he drove by and gave me a lift. He said today for the first time he really noticed how pretty I was. I'm keeping this diary, because I can't tell anybody, not even Sarah—at least not yet. She's still a child, doesn't understand what I feel inside when I see him.'"

Lucila flipped ahead several pages. "This is about a week before Nina died. 'When Mami was asleep, I slipped out and met him in the park. We just held hands and watched the moon over the lake. He said he's going to give me a special present for my birthday. I wanted him to kiss me, but he didn't. Maybe next time.'"

Closing the notebook, she stared at the cover for a long time.

Rosen asked, "Did you show Nina's diary to the police?"

"Yes, but they won't do anything about it. The police chief says it's not evidence, not if there's nothing else to go with it. Besides, Nina was just a little brown girl from the city. They're going to bury the case, just the same as we buried my niece today." She looked up at Rosen. "That teacher killed her."

"Maybe, but the police are right about needing more evidence."

"They have to keep the case open to do that, and they won't for Esther or me. But if you, a lawyer, or Mr. Gold insisted, they'd listen. After all, if Bixby was after Nina, he might've been after your daughter as well."

Rosen grimaced. That's what had bothered him all along.

She said, "I'm not going to let this thing go."

"I understand. She was your niece."

"It's more than that. Two years ago, I met Kate Ellsworth through our mutual interest in art. When she needed a new house-keeper, I sent for my sister-in-law and Nina from the Dominican Republic, mainly to give Nina a better chance in life. I brought her here, and that's what killed her."

"You can't blame yourself for what might've happened."

"He's going to be punished, no matter what."

Lucila's eyes flashed with that same terrible righteous anger Rosen had seen so often in his father's eyes.

It frightened Rosen, but he also saw the swell of her breasts as she leaned toward him and asked, "Will you help us?"

For a moment the word stuck in his throat, cold as iron drawn by a magnet.

"Yes."

Chapter 6

Leaving Lucila's apartment about one in the afternoon, Rosen walked a few blocks down Diversey and caught the Jefferson Park "L" that would take him downtown. The el was nearly empty at that time of day. A blond wearing too much makeup held a large box in a brown Marshall Field's bag, while a young couple in DePaul University jackets crammed for a political science exam.

Rosen watched neighborhoods repeat themselves with the same regularity as the clackety-clack of metal wheels against the rails. The train passed so close to the backs of tenements, he could almost touch the flapping laundry strung from the third-floor landings. He wondered how people could live like that—not so much the poverty, but the daily exposure to a thousand voyeurs, each eye blinking like a camera before moving on to the next back porch. What passion or crime could go undetected for long? No wonder people like the Ellsworths built walls and locked their gates to strangers.

The "L" slipped underground, as it reached the north end of the Loop. It seemed to move faster, roaring through the darkness into the sudden greenish glow of each stop. The young woman left the train at Washington Street for Field's. Rosen exited with the two students at Jackson. Climbing up the stairs, the boy and girl turned east toward DePaul, while he walked west into the heart of the financial district, LaSalle Street.

Although it was sunny and about sixty degrees, the lake breeze put a chill into the air. Still, Rosen enjoyed the walk; the sancocho had been delicious but lay heavily in his stomach. Men carrying leather briefcases checked their watches, women in gray blazers and swishing skirts hurried past in sneakers, and deliverymen balancing packages bounded from their trucks. Young traders or their runners, each wearing a colored jacket and large ID on the lapel, gesticulated as if still trading on the floor of the exchange. Turning at the Board of Trade, he walked up LaSalle, passing the Federal Reserve and a dozen other banks with their Corinthian columns, the great temples to capitalism. The Leary Building was a few blocks north. An old squarish structure of ten stories, its brick had darkened to squirrel gray, and its top floor windows were crowned with Gothic arches.

Past the lobby, to Rosen's right, stood the Leary Gallery. Although Kate Ellsworth was probably still at Lucila's apartment, he walked into the gallery.

The art was Eastern—landscapes with distant mountains shrouded in clouds, pagodas secluded in the wilderness, and barefoot pilgrims crossing tiny bridges. Potted palms and hanging plants with scented flowers reinforced the theme. Sculptures of East Indian goddesses reminded Rosen of the Nahagian home in Evanston, where he was staying. He wondered if Mrs. Nahagian was a customer.

"I'll be right with you, sir."

A young Asian woman in a green knit dress and copper-colored scarf sat across the desk from a heavily jeweled dowager. "Now, Mrs. Seton, by next week we'll have for you two more Nagashimas to perfectly complement the one you purchased today."

He walked through a narrow entranceway into a large room devoted to Latin American art. More plants and rocking chairs beside small round mahogany tables topped with dominos and bowls of tropical fruit. A corner table offered coffee, tea, and a plateful of oatmeal raisin cookies. No Lipton, so he chose "Passionate Papaya."

Although more than a dozen canvases hung on the four walls, one painting dominated the others in both size and intensity. Even from across the room, Rosen knew it was Lucila's. Walking closer, he studied it intently, trying to understand why it moved him—no, why it frightened him so.

The painting was called *Flowers of Madness*. A mountainside of the most vibrant greens and browns, with a threatening sky of Prussian blue. A young girl in a flowing white gown knelt before a woman who looked, not at the girl, but straight ahead. The girl, delicate with long black hair falling below her shoulders, was Nina. The woman held crimson roses that dripped blood down her dress and into a stream. She was incredibly sensual, with pouting lips and heavy breasts; her thick hair was cropped below her ears as if by a knife. Above all her eyes, big and dark and burning, struck Rosen like a brand.

"I see it's enchanted you too." The Oriental woman stood beside him. She held a white folder. "That figure in the center—so intense."

Rosen nodded.

"The artist is Lucila Melendez, extremely talented. We're giving her first Midwestern exhibit next month. All her paintings in the show are based on the poetry of Gabriela Mistral. Most deal with children."

"This one?"

"Well, there is the kneeling girl, but it isn't at all like the others." She opened the folder. "Here's what Ms. Melendez included in the gallery notes for this painting—verses from Mistral's poem, which is called 'The Flowers of the Air.'"

Rosen read the verses:

> "I scaled the rocks with deer
> and sought the flowers of madness,
> those that grew so red they seemed
> to live and die of redness.
>
> When I descended happily trembling,
> I gave them as my offering,
> and she became as water
> that from a wounded deer turns bloody."

Handing her the folder, Rosen asked, "Do you know anything more about the painting—if the artist based the two characters on anyone in particular?"

The woman shrugged. "Ms. Melendez will be here next month at the showing. You could ask her then. If you're interested in purchasing this painting, I could arrange—"

"No, that's all right."

"Perhaps you'd like to look at some of these others. They're all by young female artists, all of whom, like Melendez, are establishing quite a reputation."

"I don't think so."

"In our other rooms, just through that entrance, we have some very striking—"

"No, thank you."

She frowned slightly. "Perhaps if you told me the type of painting that interested you, I could be of better service."

"Actually, I have business in the building, and Mrs. Nahagian told me to stop by."

"Ana Nahagian! She's one of our most valued patrons. See over here."

She led Rosen back into the first room. The bulletin board behind her desk was filled with snapshots from various gallery shows.

"Mr. and Mrs. Nahagian," she said, pointing to a statuesque lady with silver hair beside a dark thickset man who resembled Rosen's boss.

"Oh, yes," he said. "And the couple beside them—the Ellsworths."

"You know them as well? Then of course you know this is Mrs. Ellsworth's gallery. Mr. . . . , uh?"

"Rosen." He studied the photograph. "That's quite a choker Kate's wearing," he added, referring to the large diamond pendant hanging from a gold chain.

The saleswoman sniffed. "Hardly her taste." Realizing what she'd said, the woman added, "It was a gift from her husband. Very generous, I'm sure."

"Just not very tasteful."

She started to smile, then bit her lower lip. "I understand that Mr. Ellsworth is a very fine businessman."

"Yes. Well, I'd like to thank you for—" Suddenly Rosen noticed another photograph.

"The man standing beside Mrs. Ellsworth."

This time the woman did smile. "That's Martin Bixby, a teacher at the high school Mrs. Ellsworth's son attends. He comes quite often to our shows."

"He comes by Mrs. Ellsworth's invitation?"

"Oh yes. Bix is quite charming. Such a way with words. I'm sure he'll be attending Lucila Melcndez's show."

Studying the bulletin board, Rosen found Bixby in several other photographs. "Does he ever show up with a companion?"

"I don't believe so. Why do you ask?"

"No particular reason. I just see him with different people in each of these photos."

"That's Bix. As I said, he's quite charming. He's really on such good terms with the Ellsworths and our patrons, even if he is only a teacher. What I mean to say is—"

"I've taken up enough of your time. Thank you."

"Not at all. It was a pleasure meeting you, Mr. Rosen. I'll tell Mrs. Ellsworth you stopped by."

Waiting for the elevator, Rosen realized how important his visit to the gallery had been, and it made what he was about to do even more necessary. After checking the directory, he rode to the top floor.

The doors opened to a small reception area with a door on either end. Across Berber carpeting of hunter green stood a white wrap-around desk, like an airport information counter. Behind the desk hung the company logo—a large sun, the letters "EL" in its center, with eight beams radiating from its center. He stared a long time at the logo. In Hebrew, "EL" was another name for God.

Two people sat behind the desk—a pointy-chinned woman of about twenty-five, wearing a white blouse with a frilly collar, and a man a few years older in a gray suit, gray tie, and white shirt.

Having the look of an IBM executive or an FBI agent, he stood as Rosen approached the desk.

"Yes, sir?" the secretary asked.

"I'd like to see Mr. Ellsworth." He anticipated her next question, "I don't have an appointment."

"Then I'm afraid—"

"Please tell him that I'm an attorney investigating the death of Nina Melendez."

"Your name, sir?"

"Nathan Rosen."

As she picked up a phone, the security guard asked, "May I see some identification?"

Rosen took out his driver's license, which the other man scrutinized, jotting down the license number.

"Out of state," he muttered.

The secretary said, "Mr. Ellsworth can spare you ten minutes. Walk through the door on your right. His office is just past the fountain."

The guard reached under the desk to press a button, allowing Rosen to open the door.

He had expected a long corridor with a water fountain. Instead, he entered a large circular lobby with a half-dozen offices along its circumference. There was the same expensive carpeting, as well as nature prints along the walls. In the center of the room was what the receptionist had mentioned—an artificial fountain that bubbled through a rock garden.

Directly past the fountain sat a gray-haired secretary with a face as round as a grape well on its way to becoming a raisin. She had draped a pink cashmere sweater over her shoulders, and a small watch hung on a gold chain from her neck.

"That's really something," Rosen said, nodding back at the fountain.

The woman smiled. "Old Mr. Leary put that in back in the fifties. Said it reminded him of his favorite vacation spot in Colorado, and that if he couldn't go there all the time, he'd bring it here. Quite an eccentric—that's what they call crazy people with money. You're Mr. Rosen?"

"That's right."

"Go right in. He has a meeting at two, which gives you only ten minutes."

Ellsworth's office turned back the clock fifty years. Desks and bookshelves of dark wood, leather chairs, leather-bound books, and liquor in decanters on a portable bar in the corner. Rosen could almost smell the aroma of a good cigar. On the rear wall hung the portrait of a silver-haired businessman in a double-breasted suit, with the same green eyes and generous mouth as Kate Ellsworth. Eyes that seemed to bear down upon the man sitting directly below him.

Leaning sideways from his mahogany desk, a spectacled Byron Ellsworth faced his computer monitor. A can of diet Pepsi rested precariously on a stack of papers. Phone cradled against his ear, he was punching a series of figures into the computer.

Waving Rosen into a chair across from his desk, Ellsworth continued speaking into the receiver. "Fax me the latest figures with the adjustments Brenner made last night. . . . No, Brenner's figures are more accurate. And you've included Marinetti's report? . . . Good. I want all our ducks in a row. We'll probably put you on the conference line about two-thirty—two forty-five at the latest. . . . Okay, I've got to go—somebody's in the office."

Hanging up, Ellsworth continued working at the computer. "Excuse me, but I have a very important meeting in a few minutes. My secretary said you're from the state's attorney's office investigating Nina's death."

"That's not quite right. I'm an attorney from out of state who's looking into her death."

"I don't understand." He became absorbed in his figures.

"Mr. Ellsworth?"

The other man kept glancing at Rosen but always returned to his computer, like a dog protecting his bone. "If you're not with the authorities, I'll have to ask you to leave."

"Are you aware that Esther Melendez believes her daughter was murdered?"

"What?"

Ellsworth pushed away from the computer. He took a slow drink of Pepsi, then asked, "What's your name?"

71

"Nate Rosen."

I've seen you before."

"We were both at the high school performance last Wednesday night, as well as the funeral this morning."

"The funeral, of course."

"Nina was my daughter's best friend. Sarah went to school with her. You know Sarah's mother Bess—my ex-wife. She teaches English at Arbor Shore. Her husband's Shelly Gold."

Ellsworth thought for a moment, absently brushing back his hair. "Gold—you mean the foot guy. I still don't understand why you're here."

"As I said, Esther Melendez believes her daughter was murdered."

"Good God, we're talking about Arbor Shore."

"People don't die in Arbor Shore?"

"Sure. Old age, heart attacks—"

"A fifteen-year-old girl?"

"She fell off a cliff. Kids are always fooling around in the ravines or in the park after hours. They get liquored up, start seeing cross-eyed, and take a tumble. It's happened before."

"Her mother says Nina wasn't that kind of girl."

Ellsworth leaned back in his chair and sighed. "Who understands kids these days?"

"Are you speaking from experience?"

"What do you mean?"

"Is your son Chip that kind of kid?"

"That's none of your business."

"Because if he is, maybe he was in the park Friday night, when Nina died. Maybe he knows what happened to the girl."

"Chip was home. He turned in early."

"On a Friday night? Come on."

Ellsworth slapped his hand on the desk. Cola spurted through the pop-top, dribbing onto the papers. "He wasn't feeling well . . . look, the police have already asked Chip these questions. I certainly don't have to go over them with you."

Of course Ellsworth was right, yet he'd said so much already and seemed likely to say a good deal more, despite his protests. Rosen glanced at the portrait of "old Mr. Leary," who would've thrown out Rosen on his ear. But Ellsworth wasn't his father-in-law. Something worried him—his two o'clock appointment, or did it have something to do, after all, with the circumstances surrounding Nina's death?

Rosen asked, "What do you know about Martin Bixby?"

"The teacher? Why, nothing."

"I understand he's a very good friend of your wife."

"They're . . . He's a very talented teacher and knows a lot about art. Hell, Rosen, your ex-wife works with him. I'm sure she knows him much better than Kate. Haven't you asked her?"

"I'm not referring to Bixby's professional qualifications. What about him personally?"

Ellsworth sipped his drink. "Do you think Bixby's somehow involved in Nina's death?"

"At this point I'm saying no such thing."

"Of course not. You're a lawyer, and you know that Bixby could sue your ass for defamation of character. Come to think of it, you didn't say that the girl was murdered, only that her mother thought so."

"Do you have any reason to doubt Esther Melendez?"

"My God, her daughter's just died. I'm sure she's hysterical. Who can blame her?"

"How well do you know her? Do you think that, under these circumstances, she might—"

"For Chrissake, how would I know! She's the Goddamn housekeeper!"

"But Nina's diary indicates that Bixby was taking advantage of her."

"'Taking advantage'—what does that mean? Just some sort of misunderstanding. I'm sure Police Chief Keller gives as little credence to this diary as I do."

Rosen nodded. "That's really why I'm here. I think Keller is likely to ignore Esther Melendez's accusation, especially if Bixby has friends in high places, like you and your wife. I'm asking that you encourage him to pursue this investigation."

"It's none of my business."

"You have a daughter, as well as a son."

"She's away at college."

"She had Bixby as a teacher. Aren't you afraid that if he did molest Nina, if he was involved with her death, he might also have molested other girls? Perhaps even your own daughter?"

"Of all the filthy—"

The intercom buzzed. Blinking hard, Ellsworth finished his drink, then put the glass and stack of papers in a drawer. "Yes?"

"Mr. Erskine and Mr. Izui are here for their two o'clock appointment."

"One minute, please."

Dabbing his forehead with a handkerchief, he removed his glasses and brushed a hand across his hair. Then he turned to the computer, typed in a few more figures, and pressed a key that set the printer softly humming.

Studying the screen, Ellsworth said, "I suggest you leave any police work to Chief Keller. You know, the Golds are very nice people but fairly new to the Arbor Shore community. I'm sure they wouldn't want to get the reputation of being . . . well . . . pushy, because of your actions. They already have to endure so many stereotypes."

Rosen's cheeks grew hot. He stood, hands balled into fists, but before he could respond, Ellsworth buzzed his secretary.

"Please show the gentlemen in."

Ellsworth and the two businessmen chatted amiably, ignoring Rosen as if he weren't there. And, of course, he wasn't. He was as alien to their corporate world as Ellsworth intimated Bess and Shelly were to Arbor Shore. Jews, new money, "the foot guy." Someone like Ellsworth could make them feel even more isolated, make their lives intolerable.

Rosen found himself standing outside Ellsworth's office, the door closing hard behind him. His face still felt warm, as if slapped.

"Mr. Rosen, are you all right?" the secretary asked. "Can I get you a glass of water?"

"No, thank you."

"If you're ready to leave, I'll notify security."

He nodded. "You really have tight security for an investment firm."

"It wasn't like this under old Mr. Leary, but over the years the business has gotten so global, they're always worried about leaks. Then there was that kidnapping attempt about ten years ago."

"Kidnapping?"

"Oh yes. Some terrorists grabbed two of our executives off a Greek cruise ship. Mr. Ellsworth—he was a vice president then—hired a group of professionals to rescue the two men. Worked out very well. The men were returned. I guess some money changed hands—I'm not sure about that. Ever since, the company's been much more careful."

"Isn't Mr. Masaryk in charge of security?"

"Uh huh. He was the one who rescued our two executives. A very capable man, our Soldier. That's his office, right next to Mr. Ellsworth's. Good afternoon."

As Rosen walked through the reception area and stepped into the elevator, the security guard reached for the phone.

Rosen had a feeling that whatever had caused Nina Melendez's death was in some way connected with the Ellsworth family. He needed to investigate further, and he needed help. A recessed area across from the elevator contained a series of public phones. He looked up the number in his notebook.

A woman answered. "Mr. Hermes' office. How may we help you?"

"This is Nate Rosen. Elgin Hermes asked me to stop by this afternoon. I'm at the Leary Building—that's only a few blocks away."

"Let me check with Mr. Hermes." After a minute she said, "He'd like you to come right over."

As Rosen hung up, Kate Ellsworth walked into the lobby, followed by Edward Masaryk. Removing his blue sunglasses and resting a hand lightly on her arm, Masaryk said something while she slowly nodded. They looked at each other for a long moment, before she entered her gallery and he stepped into the elevator.

Back on the street, Rosen wondered about the relationship between Mrs. Ellsworth and Masaryk. It seemed more than just the boss's wife and an employee. Even so, what could it possibly have to do with—

"Hey, buddy, spare some change?"

A short, big-shouldered man in a frayed suit blocked the way. Disheveled and smelling of whiskey, he had eyes that glinted like jade. Other pedestrians stepped into the street to avoid the beggar.

"Sure," Rosen said, reaching into his pocket.

Closing his hand into a fist, the man struck Rosen in the stomach, then pulled off his watch. The beggar punched him twice in the side before running down the street.

Straightening slowly, Rosen took a deep breath, which caught in his rib cage. The second breath came easier.

An elderly gentleman with a cane stepped beside him. "Are you all right?"

The old man wore a Seiko with a gold band, easily worth several hundred dollars. Why bother stealing Rosen's fifty dollar Timex when the old man was hobbling along right behind him? And something else.

"Young man, are you all right?"

Rosen nodded.

"Can you imagine, being mugged on LaSalle Street in broad daylight? Such riffraff!"

"Not riffraff," Rosen said, remembering the beggar's hand as it lunged for his watch. A hand with manicured nails.

Chapter 7

Brushing himself off, Rosen buttoned his jacket and walked slowly up LaSalle Street. The crowds had thinned considerably, but near the entrance of each building, a few sad-eyed men and women puffed a last cigarette before returning to their smoke-free offices. He cut over to Wells and continued north under the clattering "L" tracks until reaching Hermes' offices.

Inside the small gray building, a hallway led between two marble staircases to the directory and elevators. Beside the directory hung the portrait of a handsome old black man in a double-breasted suit. His large eyes smiled as much as his lips, and Rosen was sure he'd seen the man somewhere before. A small engraved nameplate read, "Oliver Jones, 1890–1972."

After scanning the directory, Rosen climbed one of the staircases to the second floor. The offices of Hermes Communications stretched along either side of the wide hallway, each door with an old-fashioned window of frosted glass. The third door on the right read "Elgin Hermes."

Hermes' secretary sat behind a desk in the small outer office. Tall with coppery skin, reddish hair sculpted to the contour of her head, and obviously pregnant, she looked like the statuette of an African fertility goddess.

"You're Mr. Rosen," she said, her teeth a perfect string of pearls. "Go right in."

Ignoring the computer on his right, Elgin Hermes hunched over his desk while writing on a yellow legal pad. On the rear wall hung the same portrait as downstairs. Hermes leaned back and smiled broadly, showing an obvious resemblance between himself and the portrait.

Motioning to a chair across the desk, he declaimed, "Nate Rosen, good of you to stop by. Make yourself comfortable."

"I hope I haven't come at a bad time."

"Not at all. I was just working on a piece for Sunday's edition."

"Wouldn't it be easier on the computer?"

"That's what my secretary tells me, but it's hard for an old dog to learn new tricks. Besides, I can't picture Lincoln or Hemingway sitting in front of one of these, plunking out their prose onto little data disks."

Rosen said, "I didn't picture you as such a traditionalist."

"Some people think I'm ass-backwards on just about everything." He tapped the legal pad. "Like this follow-up to my editorial yesterday concerning the Denae Tyler case."

Rosen's stomach tightened. Whatever Hermes wanted from him must have something to do with that case.

Hermes continued, "There's a real division in the African-American community over the verdict."

"I can understand why."

"Of course. Who wants to see two murdering rapists get acquitted? But the larger issue—they've got to understand the larger issue. Tell me what you think of this."

Hermes read from the page, "In his autobiographical novel, *Night*, Elie Wiesel recounts the story of the Holocaust, which took his father's life and put Wiesel in a concentration camp. He writes, 'We were without strength, without illusions.' Today, many people within the African-American community feel the same way—that we are a people without strength, without illusions. In that sense, others would do to us what the Nazis did to the Jews. Not content with a physical ghetto, they would create a ghetto of the mind."

Hermes looked up. "Well?"

"I don't quite follow where you're going with it."

"I want to use the Denae Tyler case to differentiate between those fighting for a level playing field versus all those gimme-gimme crybabies."

"I still don't—"

"The police fucked up—right?"

"Yes."

"And they fucked up because they rousted two young black men as just a couple niggers instead of following proper police procedure. So what do we do about it?"

Rosen cocked his head slightly. The way Hermes phrased it—like a Talmudic question.

The publisher continued, "We can demand that the police treat us fairly and kick-ass until they do, or we can blubber about the city hiring 15.5 percent more African-Americans as cops. Which would you do?"

"I don't think it's really an either-or question. Can't you do both?"

Hermes shook his head. "I say no. You can't stand like a man and whine like a child at the same time."

Staring at Rosen, his eyes grew hard. This wasn't merely another editorial position; something had touched Hermes deeply.

Rosen cleared his throat. "You're obviously not planning to run for office in the near future."

"No. I've been called lots of names by my own people, but like somebody once told me, it's what you call yourself that's important."

"That somebody sounds like a wise man."

A smile spread like butter over Hermes' face, and he nodded at the portrait behind him. "My grandfather, Oliver Jones."

"You resemble him a great deal."

"You've probably seen him a dozen times without realizing it."

Rosen studied the portrait, then shrugged.

Hermes laughed. "Ever see *Gone With the Wind*?"

"Sure. You mean . . . he was in it?"

"That and *Birth of a Nation* among others. You've seen him shuffle, tug at his hair, 'yowsa,' and roll his eyes in dozens of movies—and never knew his name. 'Bug-Eyes' is what they called him. That and 'coon' and 'nigger.' But he endured without a whimper. Whenever we young'uns would complain about something, he'd say, 'Do what the Bible tells you—clap your hand over your mouth.' That's what he did."

"'Thus the Lord blessed the latter years of Job's life more than the former,'" Rosen replied.

"Yeah, from the Book of Job. That isn't a very popular attitude either. You know what Richard Wright said in *Black Boy*: 'The white South said that it knew "niggers," . . . Well, the white South had never known me.'" Well, nobody knew my grandfather—not the white filmmakers who cheated and debased him, or the civil rights groups that called him an Uncle Tom. Nobody knew that he supported thirteen people, organized free theatrical performances for black people throughout the country, or that he gave money to help establish the very civil rights groups that later attacked him."

Rosen asked, "How would your grandfather feel about your views?"

Hermes' eyes hardened once again. "He said being black was like wearing God's brand. You should wear it with pride, but it's a brand just the same. He didn't think things could ever really change. In that respect he was wrong. In fact, that's why I asked you here. A group of civic organizations has formed a citizens' committee to monitor the police departments of Chicago and its suburbs. I've been asked to chair the committee."

"By 'monitor,' you mean—"

"Keep track of police harassment, put pressure on government bodies to end it, offer legal assistance to those who've been harassed—that sort of thing."

"And you want my opinion as to its feasibility."

"No, I want you to be its chief counsel."

Rosen leaned forward. "What?"

"Don't act so surprised—you'll make me want to rethink the offer. This is important work, Nate. As important as what you're doing for the Committee to Defend the Constitution."

"There must be a few hundred attorneys right here in Chicago who'd do a good job. Why me?"

Hermes tapped his pen on the legal pad, as if ticking off reasons. "The very fact that you're not involved in local politics—nobody's got a grudge against you. Also, you're smart, tough, and have a moral quality refreshing in a lawyer. There's something else, something harder to explain." He nodded at his grandfather's portrait. "The way you acted in court—the way you felt for the victim's family, even though they were on the other side. Like I said, it's hard to explain, but I think you carry God's brand, just like my grandfather did. You'll do an excellent job for us."

Rosen rubbed his eyes. "I don't know. I've been with the CDC a long time."

"The longer in one place, the harder to change. You're not getting any younger. Stay at the CDC a few more years, and you won't ever be able to leave. This job in Chicago will give you lots of exposure and a lot more money. Maybe your last chance to really make something of yourself. Besides, you'd be with your daughter. Shouldn't you be thinking of her?"

"Sarah," he half whispered. Hermes was right. Rosen shouldn't be thinking about anyone except her.

"I need a favor."

The other man nodded. "If it involves facilitating your move to Chicago—"

"Not that. What can you tell me about Byron Ellsworth?"

"You mean Ellsworth-Leary Investments? Already planning to invest the extra salary we're going to pay you?"

Maybe he'd meant it as a joke, but Hermes wasn't smiling. His pen beat a tattoo on the yellow pad, while he waited for Rosen to explain himself.

"I know it's a big company."

The other man snorted. "Like a dinosaur was a big animal."

"You know much about it?"

"Not so much the international sphere, but we ran a series on Chicago development over the past few years, and EL has played a big part. It's gentrified several neighborhoods, displacing quite a number of 'poor folk,' as my grandfather would've said. Its name has come up during discussions about a new stadium, a third airport, casino gambling—just about every big project that's considered for the city. You've seen its logo?"

"The sun symbol?"

"One of our writers described it more accurately as an octopus.

Not just because its tentacles seem to reach everywhere, but that it covers all its questionable dealings with a heavy supply of ink."

Rosen had figured as much. Corporations like EL kept their dealings well hidden from the public eye. And what was true for a business was even truer for its owners. He'd been lucky to see Byron Ellsworth once. He might never have that chance again.

He asked, "What do you know about the Ellsworths—I mean their personal lives?"

"The same thing you'd know by reading the business section and society page. Ellsworth constantly surprises people—they don't expect a tennis pretty boy to be so sharp and tough."

"And his wife?"

"Big money, big heart. Into art and charity. I've seen her at lots of functions." He leaned back and slowly rubbed his jaw. "She's got that way about her."

"What way?"

"The way certain rich people have—people who've been rich all their lives, so they don't think about it. So they can have breakfast with the Queen of England, then eat lunch with some welfare mother, and treat them both the same. You know what I'm talking about?"

Rosen remembered the way she'd spoken to Esther Melendez in the principal's office. "Yes, I know exactly what you mean. How do the Ellsworths get along?"

"How the hell would I know? One thing for sure, he doesn't sit around the house in his undershirt drinking beer." Hermes leaned forward, his hands clasped together. "What's this all about?"

Rosen told him about Nina's death and her mother's suspicion about Martin Bixby.

He concluded by saying, "Bixby's a friend of Kate Ellsworth. Then there's the negative publicity a murder in Arbor Shore would cause—her husband wouldn't like that."

"No he wouldn't. Is that why you're asking about their personal life—trying to pressure them to keep the case open?"

"Not just that. Something's strange about that house. After all, Nina was a beautiful, vulnerable girl. And Ellsworth—I don't think he and his wife are close."

Laughing, Hermes slapped his desk.

Rosen asked, "You don't believe something could be going on in that house?"

The other man shook his head slowly. "I was in journalism school with a guy from Arbor Shore. He told me that, at cocktail parties, car keys were thrown into a hat, and the wives would go home with whoever's keys they pulled out. Of course I believe something's going on—I'd be surprised if there wasn't."

"Then why—"

"I laughed, because you think you can get something on them. It's been tried. Believe me, to block some of Ellsworth's real estate deals, I've tried. No luck. The dirty laundry's hanging safely behind that big wall of their estate."

"Did you have no luck because of Soldier?"

Hermes' eyes narrowed. He held perfectly still, even after the pencil in his hand cracked. "What do you know about Masaryk?"

Rosen wanted to say, "Not half as much as you just told me," but instead replied, "That's part of the favor I need."

Staring at his broken pencil for a long time, Hermes finally pressed his intercom. "Sherry, please come in here."

His tall secretary stood in the doorway. "Yes, sir?"

"Nate, you've met my secretary. She's also my daughter-in-law. Going to give me my first grandchild in about three months. Don't you think she should be home resting?"

Sherry laughed. "You'd be helpless without me."

"Well, that's the truth. Punch up our file on Edward Masaryk. You know how this damn machine hates me."

She worked over his shoulder, putting in a series of access codes. "There. You know how to scroll the screen."

"Once it's up, I'm fine. Thanks."

Hermes waited for his secretary to close the door behind her. Tapping his broken pencil on the edge of his desk, he studied the screen.

"Masaryk was a Green Beret, first in Vietnam and then in Latin America. Rumored to have been with the Bolivians who killed Che Guevara in '67. A few years later he was reported to have been in Uruguay advising government troops in counterinsurgency."

"That's where he must've learned his Spanish."

"We don't know anything about him during the next ten years, before he helped Ellsworth deal with the kidnapping of his executives."

"I heard about that."

"Did you also hear that a few months after Ellsworth's men were returned, one of the suspected kidnappers was killed in Egypt? Of course, the Israelis were suspected, but they denied it."

"You think Masaryk was involved?"

Hermes nodded and, for a moment, looked down at his desk. "Now Masaryk's head of security for EL and reports directly to Ellsworth. The two of them are very close. He even lives on the estate, like part of the family."

He switched off the computer, and the two men sat quietly. Rosen grew uneasy, not because of what Hermes had said, but because the editor himself was afraid. Behind him the portrait of his grandfather looked down with calm assurance, the way Hermes himself had always appeared. Until now.

Rosen asked, "What about Masaryk's personal relationship with the Ellsworth family?"

"I was only interested in EL's business dealings."

"Would you look into it?"

Hermes rubbed his jaw. "You haven't told me if you're interested in my offer."

"Chief counsel? I don't know. It's something I'll have to think about."

"You think about my offer, and I"ll look into Masaryk and the Ellsworths. Call me at the end of the week. I'd like your acceptance covered in the Sunday papers."

"If I accept."

"You will. It's too good an offer to pass up. I'll have the package ready for you on Friday—job description, salary, the works. I can tell you, with perks it'll be about $90,000. That might not be much to a corporate attorney, but for someone in civil liberties—."

"It's a very civil figure."

84

Chuckling, Hermes stood and extended his hand. "I'm looking forward to working with you, Nate. Talk to you soon."

Back on the street, Rosen walked toward the "L" station vaguely dissatisfied. Hermes had promised to help, but as a parent might reluctantly agree to "think about something" to assuage a petulant child.

Then there was Hermes' offer. Rosen's present job with the CDC was more a way of life, one he'd chosen even over his marriage. It was important work, but maybe not any more important than what he'd be doing in Chicago. And he'd be with Sarah, especially now. After all these years, could he really change?

He should've taken the underground Howard Street line straight north to Evanston and the Nahagians' condo. But it was still early. Instead he climbed up the clanging metal steps above the street to ride the Ravenswood "L." It clattered through the Loop—past the State of Illinois Building, shiny as tinfoil; the huge Merchandise Mart; and the red brick beehive ghetto of Cabrini Green—then jogged northwest in successive right angles that took him into his old neighborhood. Kimball and Lawrence Avenues, the end of the line, intersected a few miles directly north of Lucila's Logan Square, but the two neighborhoods were worlds apart.

He walked west on Lawrence Avenue where, as a little boy, he had held his mother's hand while she shopped. The kosher butcher, the kosher baker, the fresh fruit and vegetable stands, old women wearing babushkas chattering in Yiddish to one another were all gone, buried with his mother years ago. Now the shop signs were written in Greek, Spanish and, most of all, Korean. The old Jewish delicatessen had been renamed Aristotle's.

Turning up Pulaski, he passed a series of well-kept apartment buildings and two flats, all with front porches and neat postage stamp–sized lawns. As a boy leaving heder, he'd walked these same streets dozens of times while struggling to balance the books under his arms. The times he should've gone straight home, but his father was working at the tailor shop, and his mother wouldn't tell.

He crossed Foster Avenue and walked into Gompers Park, a gen-

tly rolling green expanse with a branch of the Chicago River mean-
dering through. As others had done so many years ago, young boys
on their way home from school played catch or stood on the bridge
talking to the wizened fishermen who came every day to catch their
catfish dinner. Older boys walked with their girlfriends, stopping
under a tree to kiss. Back then, he'd watch them shyly—knowing
that for a boy to be alone with a girl was wrong and that his having
stolen the time from his studies to watch them made him equally a
sinner. Yet he could never stop looking, or lying to his father about
where he'd been. He'd watch them, inhale the aroma of freshly
mown grass, hear the splashing water, and remember the Song of
Songs:

> A garden locked
> Is my own, my bride,
> A fountain locked,
> A sealed-up spring.
> Your limbs are an orchard of pomegranates
> And of all luscious fruits . . .

It was the place, years later, where he'd first kissed Bess.

An old man sat on a bench. Nearly bald and peering through
thick glasses, he wore an old gray suit with large lapels. When the
old man swiped at a fly, the thumb and forefinger of his right hand
pressed together as if holding a needle, and Rosen remembered. It
was Hyman, another tailor who had sometimes worked for his
father.

"May I join you?" Rosen asked.

Hyman squinted, then smiled and patted the bench seat. "It's
nice to have company besides these farshtinkener flies. You from
around here?"

"I know someone who used to live here."

"Then I know him too. Who is he?"

Rosen hesitated. "Aaron—Aaron Rosen."

The old man nodded deeply. "Of course, Isaac's son—the great doctor. No, Aaron doesn't live around here no more. He's up in the suburbs. That's what happened to all the Jews around here. Either they moved to the suburbs or to the cemetery."

"Not my . . . not his father."

"Old Isaac—no. The Angel of Death wouldn't bother, for fear of getting into an argument with him."

"Is he all right?"

"All right? At our age, if you look in the paper and don't see your name in the obituaries, you're all right. He comes here sometimes with Aaron and the grandchildren."

"Aaron wasn't his only son."

Hyman ran a hand over his bald pate. "No. There was another son . . . David . . . that's right, he has the same name as my boy. David. He went to Israel. I think maybe he's a rabbi. That's what Isaac wanted—his boys to be rabbis. He never became one himself, though he was a real Talmud Torah man. He was hard though, harder than God. Oh look." He pointed to a fisherman. "He caught a big one. Mazel tov!"

Watching the man pull in the fish, Rosen felt the same shortness of breath the fish must have felt. "Wasn't there a third son?"

"Hmm?"

"A third son."

"I don't know . . . so long ago. Maybe there was. Yes, the one who went to live with an uncle."

"The one who was sent to live with an uncle."

"I'd almost forgotten. Isaac never speaks of him. The boy could be dead, for all I know. Now what was his name? There's Aaron and David and . . . ?" The old man furrowed his brow. "What was his name?"

He used the past tense, just as Rosen's father would have done. His jaw trembling, Rosen stood and walked away.

Hyman repeated, "What was his name? It's gonna drive me meshugge all day trying to think of it."

Elgin Hermes had almost been right. Rosen did wear a brand, but it wasn't God who had branded him.

Chapter 8

Rosen reached the office of Sarah's counselor just as the bell rang. Classroom doors opened like rodeo shoots, and the students stampeded out—shouting, jostling, and grabbing one another. Yet three minutes later, with their return to class, the hallway once again was deserted, except for the laughter echoing faintly off the metal lockers. He checked his watch and remembered the mugger had taken it. The clock on the wall read 9:42.

Yesterday, after taking a cab home from the old neighborhood, he'd driven into Arbor Shore to see his daughter. Sitting on the edge of her bed, idly paging through a book, Sarah said very little but mentioned one thing that confirmed his suspicions.

Bess turned a corner and walked briskly toward him, her heels clicking loudly in the corridor.

"Sorry, I was with a student." She opened the doorway. "Hello, Linda. Nate, this is Sarah's counselor, Linda Agee."

"It's nice meeting you, Mr. Rosen. Sarah's spoken often about you. Please have a seat."

She was younger than Rosen expected, maybe thirty, with long straw-colored hair and a handful of freckles scattered under the bluest eyes. She wore a Levi dress that buttoned up the front, and wooden clogs. He expected love beads, a roomful of Peter Max posters, and a mouthful of "like."

But her office was tidy, with a potted palm in the corner, cut flowers in a vase on the desk, and one print on the wall—Edward Hopper's *Nighthawks*. In her line of work, it was probably a great conversation starter.

"Mrs. Agee said, "I noticed Sarah's name on the absentee list. How is she?"

Bess took a tissue from her purse. Her face was a mask, but the lines at the corners of her eyes and mouth were beginning to crack.

"I stayed with her as long as possible this morning—I was late for school. Shelly's with her today. Our doctor prescribed some medication to help her sleep. That's all she does—sleep. Oh, she eats a little and reads in her room."

"Has she spoken much about Nina's death?"

"She doesn't talk about anything. That's why I wanted to see you. It must be like poison festering inside her. I can't . . ." Bess choked on the next word and swallowed hard.

Mrs. Agee said, "I know what you're going through."

"No, you can't."

"Believe me, Bess, I've dealt with dozens of families with this same problem, the death of a loved one. Grandparent, parent, sibling, close friend—it's always difficult. We adults have gone through it, and we know each person mourns in his own way. Last year I worked with a boy whose father committed suicide. The boy took his father's credit card and went to a dude ranch in Colorado, a place they'd gone together ten years before. He said it was the place he'd felt closest to his dad."

"But at least he did something, instead of keeping it all inside."

"I agree, she's got to talk about it. If you want, I'll come by after school to see her."

"That would be wonderful."

"I can't guarantee anything. Our relationship has become fairly casual. As you know, she's technically no longer part of my caseload. You may want to contact a private psychologist. I'd be happy to refer you to several whom we use."

Rosen cut in, "What was your relationship with Sarah?"

Mrs. Agee shifted to face him. "Last year, when Sarah enrolled at Arbor Shore, Bess was planning her second marriage. Sarah still had some unresolved feelings about the divorce. Her junior high recommended I see her during her first semester, to ease her transition into high school. I believe you were aware of this. I noted in Sarah's file that you were sent copies of all the pertinent information."

Rosen nodded but said nothing, waiting for her to continue.

"I'm not at liberty to detail our conversations, but it's no secret that Sarah was deeply upset about the divorce and the physical separation caused by your moving to Washington, D.C. She was also worried about how the divorce would affect you personally. We discussed that a great deal."

Rosen looked away for a moment. Maybe he should've stayed in Chicago. If he hadn't been concerned so much about his own pain, would his daughter have needed a stranger's empathy?

He cleared his throat. "But your report indicated she was all right."

"I think so, in part because you seemed so accepting of Bess's remarriage—didn't make it a contest in which Sarah would have to choose sides."

"Then why continue seeing her?"

"It's what we call an 'as needed basis.' It's not unusual for a girl like Sarah to want to talk to someone occasionally."

"What do you mean, 'like Sarah'?"

The counselor smiled. "I didn't mean to categorize her, but in some ways—especially intellectually, she's quite mature. She'd come in once or twice a month to discuss something she'd read, or go over a disagreement with her mother or something you might've said on the phone. Certainly nothing out of the ordinary."

Rosen leaned forward. "But she didn't always see you alone."

He'd phrased it as a statement, not the shot in the dark that it was.

Mrs. Agee hesitated, then replied, "No, she didn't."

"They were best friends, so Sarah brought Nina Melendez along."

"A few times over the past few months. Again, it was all very informal."

"Did you take notes?"

"No."

"But you do remember what they talked about."

Her smile melted but didn't quite disappear as she turned to

Bess. "I think it best to concentrate on how we can help your daughter over her grief."

Rosen said, "I want to know what you talked about in those sessions."

"Although I understand your feelings, I must respect Sarah's right to privacy. Surely as an attorney, you understand my position."

"No, I don't. You're not some $150-an-hour psychiatrist. You're a public employee dealing with a kid in trouble, and I need to know what you know."

Bess's hand struck the armrest. "Nate!"

The counselor spoke slowly. "Mr. Rosen, your daughter talked a great deal about the case you just finished—representing two boys who raped and killed that girl. It must've been very difficult to defend two murderers because of a point of constitutional law. But you did what was right, based upon the tenets of your profession. I'd like you to understand that, in Sarah's case, I'm only doing the same thing."

Rosen knew the woman was right. Yet this time—this one time—he didn't give a damn about professional ethics.

"I'm not talking to you as a lawyer, but as a father."

Mrs. Agee looked down at her desk, as if reading an imaginary file. "Nothing Sarah and I discussed has any bearing on Nina's death."

"How can you be sure?"

"Our conversations were casual. Nothing—"

"You know that Esther Melendez thinks Martin Bixby murdered her daughter."

Bess grabbed his arm, but he shook her off.

"Arbor Shore's a small town. You must've heard."

The counselor nodded. "Nothing Sarah and I discussed could have any bearing on Nina's death."

"What about Nina? You spoke with her too."

"I can't reveal that conversation either."

"Why not? The girl's dead."

"Perhaps if Mrs. Melendez made a formal request—"

"I'd call an accusation of murder a formal request."

Bess said, "That's enough."

"Last night Sarah admitted that, on the evening of Nina's death, she hadn't called Nina. Nina lied to her mother. That could mean she slipped out of the house to meet someone. Someone who might've killed her."

Mrs. Agee stared back at him for a long time. Finally, she replied, "Nothing either girl told me lends the slightest credence to your theory. If you'll both excuse me, I have a meeting in a few minutes."

"Of course," Bess said.

"I'll be over about four. I'd like to call Sarah first, to make sure she's agreeable to my visit."

"I"m sure she will be. I can't thank you enough, Linda."

"Not at all. It was nice meeting you, Mr. Rosen." As he turned to leave, she added, "I know it's difficult not to worry about Sarah, but she's quite a resilient young lady with a good sense of values. There's no need for you to feel . . ."

When she hesitated, he said, "Guilty?"

"I was going to say overly concerned."

"Sure."

Outside the counselor's office, he said to Bess, "I'll be over after school."

"No you won't. I don't want you anywhere near the house when Linda Agee's there."

"Why not?"

"Linda's coming over on her own time to help Sarah, not to subject herself to another cross-examination."

"If Martin Bixby killed—"

"For God's sake, lower your voice." She looked up and down the deserted hallway.

"If he killed Nina, Sarah may know something about it. He may even have pushed himself on her."

"You sound like one of those Kennedy conspiracy freaks. The police are handling the investigation, and I haven't heard the word 'murder' from anyone but you and that Melendez woman. I care about Sarah getting over her best friend's death. That's all."

"But—"

93

"If you want to call later, fine. Just stay away from the house. I have to get ready for my next class. Good-bye."

She walked down the hallway and turned the corner. He started in the other direction, toward the main doors, thinking about what Mrs. Agee had said about her sessions with Sarah. Maybe the position offered by Elgin Hermes wasn't such a bad idea after all. He'd be able to make up to his daughter for all the time they'd missed together.

Rosen shook his head. What would they do—take long walks in the park on weekends? Go to the ballgame? Of course he'd love to be with her, but only because he loved being with her, not that their being together would undo all the hurt. There was only one sure way of helping her, and that was to find the truth.

He turned and walked through the hallway, which ended at the auditorium lobby. He heard the teacher's voice from inside the auditorium.

Taking a seat in the last row, Rosen watched Bixby conduct a class. Two students, Chip Ellsworth and another boy, were improvising on stage, while a dozen others sat along the first row.

One foot resting on the stage steps, Bixby said, "Remember that caricature is an essential part of improvisation. Now get into character . . . *really* get into character, and let yourself go!"

Chip nodded then, slumping forward on a stool, muttered to his companion, "I have here a . . . uh . . . note of reprimand from your P.E. teacher. It seems you've . . . uh . . . been peeking through a hole into the girls locker room. Is this true?"

The other boy shook his head as if on a spring. "Oh no, Dr. Winslow, sir!"

"But your . . . uh . . . saliva was found dribbling through the hole."

"There must be some mistake. I have two dozen witnesses who say I was in Aspen at the time."

Chip lifted one hand, palm upward. "Well, taking your teacher's eyewitness account . . ." he lifted the other, ". . . against the testimony of your drunken unreliable friends whose fathers hired me . . . " He shrugged. "I apologize for any inconvenience I may have caused you."

The other students applauded loudly, as did Bixby.

"Well done!" the teacher said. "Time for one more. Ted and Hayley, you're next. Let's do the door-to-door salesman."

The girl, a pretty blond with a ponytail, stood in front of an imaginary door, which the boy approached, stamping on the floor to simulate a knock. He tried selling her "an artificially intelligent, user-friendly, solar-powered potato peeler." The more adamantly she refused his sale pitch, the more frustrated he became.

Finally he walked away. "That's not fair!"

Bixby led the boy back to the girl. "Don't give up so easily. You were making headway."

"No, she wasn't cooperating."

"Well, you're such a dork," the girl complained.

Bixby stood between them, putting an arm around each of their shoulders. "The most important rule in business is that anybody can be sold anything—it just takes the right approach. The same is true of acting. You just have to decide upon your approach. Watch me."

He took a step back, closed his eyes for a moment, then approached the girl. "Now, Miss, young as you are, you may not consider how important it is to maintain your beauty. With all the other lovely young ladies trying to catch that certain someone's eye, you can use every edge. Our remarkable potato peeler can keep this hand . . ."

He paused to take the girl's hand in his. Blushing, she giggled nervously.

". . . forever beautiful as it is right now."

Bixby gushed over the girl, while continuing to hold her hand. Reddening even more, she stood very still, not knowing how to respond.

Watching Bixby insinuate himself with the girl, Rosen imagined the teacher touching Nina Melendez. It would've been easy to start innocently like this, in front of twenty other students. And last week, while the students rehearsed their performances behind the auditorium, hadn't Bixby touched Sarah's shoulder?

Rosen was disgusted yet fascinated by the teacher's performance. For those few minutes, Bixby was the perfect salesman. The way his lips oozed the pitch and wheedled the product made a sale inevitable. What had he said—". . . anybody can be sold anything—it just takes the right approach." Bixby was such a good actor; had he been acting during the meeting last Friday, when he'd protested his innocence? The principal, Kate Ellsworth, even Bess had been eager to "buy" his protests, just as the girl at that moment was nodding as he rang up a sale.

"That's how you do it!" he declaimed.

The bell was barely heard above the class's applause. Rosen waited at the center aisle, where the students passed him on their way out.

"Chip."

The boy stopped and kicked at the worn carpeting.

"Chip, I'd like to talk to you."

"Who are you?"

"I'm Mr. Rosen. You know my daughter Sarah."

"Mrs. Gold's kid—sure."

"She was also Nina Melendez's friend. I'd like to talk to you about Nina's death."

The boy looked at his friends, who waited at the door. "I gotta get to class."

"This will just take—"

But Chip ran past him, banging the door open.

"Can I be of help?"

Bixby sat on the stage. He wore an old gray Northwestern University T-shirt, blue jeans, and sneakers. He ran a hand through his curly brown hair and grinned. Like a teddy bear on a toy shelf.

Rosen walked down the aisle.

The teacher held out his hand, which, after a moment's hesitation, Rosen took. "I missed Sarah in class today. How's she doing?"

"She's very upset over Nina's death."

"Yes, Sarah's a sensitive child, and so talented. I can't tell you how impressed I was with her performance the other night."

Again, Rosen remembered the teacher's hand on Sarah.

"I want to discuss Nina's death."

"Yes?"

"Esther Melendez thinks you killed her daughter."

"Absurd. I mean, I can understand the woman's grief, but really."

"Do you have an alibi for the night of her death?"

"Not really. I'm single and live alone. That Friday night I was home watching a video, *My Fair Lady*. One of my favorites—yours too?"

Rosen shook his head impatiently.

"I thought not. Something more brooding. More . . ." He stopped and, for a split second, broke into a grin. ". . . analytical. You're the kind of man who, like the Apostle Thomas, would say, 'Except I shall see in his hands the print of the nails, . . . I will not believe.' Come along."

Bixby led Rosen behind the stage, through the large rehearsal room, and down the narrow corridor into the teacher's office. He opened a desk drawer.

"Before I forget." He handed Rosen two baseball tickets. "The students who participated in last week's festival are going to Wrigley Field tomorrow afternoon. Those are Sarah's tickets, in case she's feeling better. She'd bought an extra one for you—said you're quite a Cubs fan. Do sit down."

Rosen remained standing while the teacher opened his file cabinet's top drawer and rummaged through the papers.

Bixby said, "I can understand why you, as a parent, would be concerned about the innuendos made against me. And then, poor Nina's death under . . . well, less than clear circumstances. Ah, here we are." He pulled out a sheet of paper. "These erroneous allegations—that I was personally involved with Nina—stem from that diary of hers."

"Erroneous?"

"Yes." He handed Rosen the paper. "This is an assignment sheet I gave the students about a month ago."

The paper, titled "Relationships," listed four possible topics as homework. Number 4 read,

Pretend you're carrying on a friendship with someone much older. First write a diary recounting how that friendship began and, later, how it developed. Next, write a one act play based on your diary. As your final project for this course, you may wish to present your play to the class (as director, actor/actress, or both).

97

Rosen stared at the other man. "Are you saying that Nina's diary was based on this assignment?"

"I believe it was. Nina came to me shortly after I'd given the assignment, and asked if she could write about a relationship between a girl and an older man. I don't believe in censorship, but I realized such a diary, and subsequent play, might be viewed with disfavor by the administration."

"What did you tell her?"

"To give her idea serious thought and, if she still wished to pursue it, we'd talk further."

"Did she pursue it?"

Bixby shrugged. "The assignment is due at the end of this week. Nina didn't speak to me about it again. I think the diary Mrs. Melendez found is a fictional account. To be honest, I hadn't thought about the assignment as a possible explanation until a day or two after Mrs. Melendez's sister read portions of the diary at our meeting last week."

"Have you shared this information with the authorities?"

"Yes—with Dr. Winslow and Chief of Police Keller. Both men seem quite satisfied. Of course, as regards Nina's death, it's a moot point."

"What do you mean?"

Bixby smiled. "I didn't think you'd heard. Dr. Winslow called me into his office first thing this morning. He was nice enough to inform me that the police have arrested one of those Mexican landscapers. Yes, some Mexican."

"For what?"

"Why, for murdering Nina."

Chapter 9

How often had his boss, Nahagian, with that acute sense of irony, said, "Sometimes the gods punish by giving us what we want"? Driving through Arbor Shore, Rosen could almost hear him chuckling.

Rosen had been pushing to keep the murder investigation open. He'd thought either Bixby was guilty or that the murderer might be someone in the Ellsworth home. But the teacher had said an outsider, "Some Mexican," had been arrested. Most murders were for simple reasons—money, vengeance, lust—and so were the solutions. He hoped that's what it was, an outsider. Better for everyone—Esther Melendez, Bess and Shelly, and especially Sarah.

Stopping at a red light, he watched a black man carrying an armful of sweaters cross the intersection. Built like a line backer, the man resembled Denae Tyler's uncle who'd threatened Sarah after the trial. Threatened her because two murderers had been released on a technicality. Would Keller follow proper procedure with the man he'd arrested? Just because the accused was some poor Mexican, that didn't mean there could be any slip-ups. No smart lawyer had better get him off.

Gritting his teeth, Rosen shrugged off a second irony. It was the first time he'd ever gone to a police station hoping the defendant was guilty.

The police and fire departments shared the new Public Safety Center, a long one-story building with the corporate look of red brick and glass. In back, a parking lot filled the right angle made by a line of police garages and one of fire trucks. Several firemen, sipping coffee beside their engines, nodded hello. Entering the building, Rosen walked through a corridor leading into the lobby.

"Is Chief Keller in?" he asked through the narrow opening of a glass window.

The receptionist, whose figure resembled a buoy with too many cherry Danishes as ballast, leaned forward. "Is he expecting you?"

"No, but this is important. My name is Nate Rosen. The chief knows me."

Rocking back, she picked up the phone and engaged in a brief conversation.

"Chief Keller's in conference but will see you in a few minutes." She nodded at the lobby. "There's a pot of coffee in the corner. Please help yourself."

He sat on a leather chair and glanced at the magazines fanned across the polished coffee table—*Time, People, Business Week,* and *Architectural Digest.* On the wall behind him hung two large photographs, aerial views of Arbor Shore in 1947 and 1994. The opposite wall displayed several plaques honoring various police officers, including Chief Keller, for their civic duties. All very clean and nonthreatening, like a bank rather than a police station.

Rosen had just finished thumbing through *Time* when a door beside the receptionist opened. Chief Keller walked into the lobby, followed by Edward Masaryk.

They were an odd couple. The police chief, whose small body fit together in tight angles, nervously thumbed the bowl of an unlit pipe. Masaryk towered over him, the tailored camel hair jacket complimenting his broad shoulders and thick arms. His blue sunglasses were tucked into the jacket's breast pocket.

Something about Masaryk was reminiscent of Clint Eastwood. Not looks, rather the way he carried himself with the quiet confidence of the mythic Western hero. A man who had no weaknesses and, therefore, was more than just a man.

Rosen stood as they approached. After Masaryk's nutcracker grip, the police chief's hand seemed like a glop of warm dough.

Keller asked, "What can I do for you?"

"I'm here for the same reason as Mr. Masaryk."

Masaryk looked at him without really looking, the way some

people see waiters. "As chief of security for the Ellsworth estate, I regularly discuss questions of mutual interest with the police."

"Such as what happened to Nina Melendez?"

"She was living in the Ellsworth home, and her body was found next to the estate."

"So we are both here about Nina's murder. 'Murder'—we can use that word now."

Glancing around the lobby, Keller said, "This isn't the place to discuss the girl's death."

"Then your office? I'd like you to tell me about this Mexican landscaper you arrested."

"I really can't—"

"Go ahead, Otto," Masaryk said. "Mr. Rosen does have a legitimate interest—his daughter was a good friend of Nina Melendez. Besides, you can show off your department to a very important attorney, from Washington, D.C. no less. You deserve to crow a little—very efficient the way that man was located."

Rosen said, "Efficient, or just convenient."

Masaryk almost smiled, or maybe that was the way he smiled. "I'll leave you in Otto's capable hands. Good morning."

Reaching for his sunglasses, he walked away.

Left hand on right elbow, Keller again thumbed his pipe. "We'd better go into my office."

Past the doorway to their right, a young policewoman sat before a state-of-the-art communications unit. Above her stretched an electronic map of Arbor Shore. An icon shaped like a running boy flashed in the center of town.

Rosen asked, "What's that signal mean?"

"A sixth grader playing hookey. He was waiting for the ice cream shop to open. The owner's holding the boy until we can take him to school."

"Do you have icons for everything?"

"Just about. Broken window for burglary, car with a crumpled fender for an accident . . . "

"What about a murder?"

Eyes widening, the woman shook her head.

101

"This way, Mr. Rosen," Keller said.

As they were about to enter his office, the dispatcher called out, "Mrs. McAllister's on line one. The usual reason."

The police chief sighed. "Try to handle it."

Keller's office was paneled in dark wood, his large desk in the middle of the room. There were no windows. A small glass-enclosed cabinet held three shelves of books. The other walls were bare, except for a gigantic stuffed bass mounted on the rear wall.

Keller settled behind the desk, his leather chair emitting the faint aroma of pipe tobacco. On the desk top rested a manila folder and a rack with a half dozen pipes.

Sitting across from the police chief, Rosen asked, "You catch that fish?"

"Three years ago in Wisconsin. I have a summer place there. Probably where I'll retire." Nodding at the fish, he grinned. "I keep hoping he's the runt of the family."

"Did you catch another big one this morning?"

The smile froze on Keller's face as he reached for the folder.

"The file on your suspect?"

"Uh huh."

"And you were just going over it with Masaryk."

"As Mr. Masaryk explained, there are certain things that occur in the community—"

"Crimes," Rosen said.

"Yes, and the possibility of crime, that make it wise for us to collaborate. There's nothing unusual about this. I deal with private security firms all the time."

"And you've collaborated with Masaryk on this case."

"He explained the reasons for that."

"He also suggested that you share your information with me."

Keller sucked his empty pipe. "Damn city ordinance about smoking."

"I won't tell."

Cocking one eye at Rosen, the police chief took out a tobacco tin, lit his pipe, then leaned back contentedly. The room slowly filled with the strong aroma of tobacco cured in a particularly sweet liqueur.

Rosen cleared his throat. "Now, about this man you arrested."

"He hasn't been formally charged with a crime."

"Do you suspect him of murdering Nina Melendez?"

"As far as I know, the state's attorney has no plans to charge him with murder."

"But the state's attorney might change his mind."

Keller took a long puff then waited for the smoke to clear. "I understand your interest in this case, but I have to respect this man's privacy. I sure don't have to tell you. It's your job to defend guys like him."

"You discussed this man with Masaryk, as well as with Dr. Winslow."

"So you've already been to the school. All I told Winslow was that Al . . . that this man was in the park about the time of the girl's death and that he saw nobody, including Martin Bixby."

"How do you know he was there?"

Keller's intercom buzzed.

"Yes."

The receptionist said, "Mrs. McAllister's here. It's about her neighbor's dog."

"Already? She just called a few minutes ago."

"From her car phone. Should I send her in? Oh, she's on her way."

Keller put down his pipe and reached the door just as someone knocked. He nodded to an elderly woman, no more than five feet tall, wearing a full-length mink coat.

"Chief Keller, I hope I haven't disturbed you." Her voice whispered like a crackling leaf.

"Not at all, Mrs. McAllister. Won't you sit down."

"Oh no, I can see you're busy. It's just that I'd like you to do something about those new neighbors of mine. You know, the woman who wears what looks like old drapes."

"You mean Dr. Saraswati and his family."

"Yes, I can never remember their name."

"They're very nice people."

"I suppose, but that dog of theirs—always barking and scratching. I actually saw the creature's paws under the fence this morning, so I had to see you. What if it gets into my flower bed? I'm just preparing it—we're supposed to have such a lovely spring."

"Have you spoken to the Saraswatis?"

"Oh, I just couldn't. Ann Jenson, who used to live there . . . we'd have tea together. She knew so much about azaleas. Oh, why did she have to die?"

She trembled and, as Keller put his arm around her, started to cry.

"Sergeant Fuller!" he called.

"Yes sir!" a booming voice replied from down the hall.

"I want you to accompany Mrs. McAllister home and personally inspect her fence to make sure it's secure against any encroachment, especially by the neighbors' dog." To the old woman, "Is that all right?"

Sniffling, she nodded.

"When you get home, I'd like you to go next door with the sergeant and introduce yourself to the Saraswatis."

"Oh, I couldn't."

"Yes, you can. You know, their oldest boy is quite a cellist."

"Sometimes, over the fence, I hear him playing."

"Now you go along with the sergeant. I'm sure everything will be all right."

She gripped his hand with hers. "Thank you so much. I hate to be such a bother."

"Not at all, Mrs. McAllister."

Closing the door, Keller sat down and relit his pipe.

Rosen said, "You handled that very well. I suppose you get that a lot."

"I don't mind—not the old timers like Mrs. McAllister. She goes back to the days of butlers and chauffeurs and the low-slung roadsters you couldn't have dreamed to look any better. Old money. Real . . ." He scratched his head, searching for the right word.

"Proper?" Rosen offered.

Half closing his eyes, Keller blew a thick smoke ring. "No, I guess 'helpless' is the best way to describe it. They couldn't do a damn thing and really appreciated whatever you did for them. Nowadays, it's different. New money that orders you about. You know, brokers who strike it rich, computer jockeys—"

"And podiatrists?"

Keller blinked hard, then sat up straight. "I don't want you getting the wrong idea. I treat everybody the same."

"Sure. How did you know that this landscaper was in the park about the time Nina Melendez died?"

The police chief thumbed his pipe bowl. "Last Saturday morning, when you and Mr. Gold came to the park, remember seeing a pile of branches and grass clippings?"

"Yeah. At the end of the road, beside the Ellsworths' fence."

"The landscaper who takes care of the Ellsworth home is supposed to haul the clippings away, but when he's behind schedule, he sometimes gets rid of it in the park. He's already paid one fine for illegal dumping."

"I don't follow you. He wasn't cutting their lawn in the middle of the night."

"No, he'd done that Friday afternoon, but he was in the park that night. Claimed he came back to clean up the clippings before anybody had a chance to complain. Didn't want to pay another fine."

Rosen shook his head. "You got him to admit that?"

"He didn't have much choice. When my men looked over the area on Saturday morning, they found a McDonalds bag in with the clippings. It had the landscaper's fingerprints on it; the date and time of purchase were printed on the receipt. Friday, 10:16 P.M."

"So he was there, but he didn't pick up the clippings. Why not?"

"He said he wasn't feeling well—something he ate. He left and drove right home."

"And you believed him?"

Keller shrugged. "No proof to the contrary."

"That's it? No mention of the rose petals scattered on the ground by the fence, or the missing pendant that goes with the gold chain you found?"

"No." Keller took another long draw on his pipe.

"Why didn't you pick up this man over the weekend?"

"He wasn't at home until this morning. Said he was at a friend's."

Rosen stared at the policeman a long time, then shook his head. "There's got to be something else. You must suspect the guy, or you wouldn't have bothered going over his file with Masaryk. What is it? Does the man have a criminal record? Was he seen hanging around the neighborhood? Did he make a pass at Nina?"

"I'm really sorry, Mr. Rosen. What I've already told you is a courtesy. I can't say anything more."

"What about his name?"

"No. He's not charged with a crime. In fact, I expect him to be released very shortly."

"Are you treating Nina's death as a murder?"

"We're open to whatever conclusion the facts indicate. At this point, there's still no reason to believe the girl was murdered." Keller stood. "I want to thank you for stopping by."

"Sure."

Back inside his car, Rosen waited. Fifteen . . . thirty . . . forty-five minutes passed, and still he waited. Nowhere to go; nothing to do. Thinking about his conversation with Keller, although what the police chief had said was less important than the simple fact of Masaryk having been there.

He rubbed his eyes, leaned back, and sighed. Nothing fit together. All the offices he'd been to—Ellsworth's, Hermes', Mrs. Agee's, Keller's—and what had they told him? Nothing he could grasp, despite all their computers and papers and folders that flashed before his eyes. He remembered in college reading a story by Franz Kafka. A man is sentenced to death, not knowing why he's condemned. Tied to the bed of a horrible machine, he is slowly turned, hour after hour, while needles write the punishment on his body, until he bleeds to death. That's the way Rosen felt, his body struck by thousands of letters spelling out the reports he'd seen or been told about. Reports revealing nothing about how Nina died, let alone if she had been murdered. And if he couldn't discover that for his daughter—with all his training and cleverness, what could he do for her?

An old green pickup truck, mottled with rust, pulled into the edge of the parking lot, as if afraid to approach the police cars.

Jumping down from the cab, a short, stocky woman wearing a beat-up Chicago Blackhawks jacket over a shapeless dress walked slowly toward the station. Her dark, round face and curly black hair were the same as those of the peasant women whose portraits hung in Kate Ellsworth's gallery. Hesitating at the door, she finally stepped inside.

The side of the truck read, "Hector Alvarez, Landscaper" and a phone number. While copying the name and number into his notebook, Rosen felt his heartbeat quicken and almost smiled. He waited, his breathing growing steadier.

The woman returned twenty minutes later, followed by a man with shaggy black hair and a thin mustache. His jeans jacket hung loose on his scarecrow frame; he had to fold back the sleeves before lighting a cigarette. Then he and the woman climbed into the truck and drove away.

Rosen had to stop himself from following them. No need, not when he had the name and phone number tucked in his pocket. Time enough this evening. He could go home now, because it was all right. He'd think about the case, knowing there was, after all, something to do.

Chapter 10

It was just after seven and getting dark as Rosen left his condo and drove a few miles north, passing under the lizard green ironwork of the Davis Street "L." He pulled over beside a fire hydrant across from the station and studied the commuters leaning against the wall. She hadn't arrived yet; he'd better find a parking spot, walk back, and—

A young woman broke from the crowd, hurrying across the street. It wasn't until she'd slipped into the passenger seat that he recognized Lucila. She unbuttoned her long green coat. She was dressed like a schoolgirl—a brown jumper with white blouse, white stockings, and black patent leather shoes. Her hair was tied back with a thin white ribbon. Only her eyes were a woman's, dark and still brooding over Nina's death.

He said, "Glad you were home when I called this afternoon. You had to go downtown for a meeting?"

"Uh huh."

"With Kate Ellsworth?"

"How'd you know?"

"I didn't, but you do have a show coming up."

"It wasn't just about me. Kate and I met with representatives from the Art Institute. They're thinking of putting together a special exhibit on contemporary Latin American art, with an emphasis on younger artists." She smoothed her jumper and smiled. "I wanted to look young. What do you think?"

His face grew warm. The way she dressed, that little-girl softness and vulnerability, made her irresistible. The more he thought of her jumper and long white stockings, the warmer his face became. Not from embarrassment, but shame. What was there about a woman's innocence that stirred a man? Did the same feeling motivate someone like Bixby? Rosen shivered in disgust.

She said, "I guess you're not crazy about my outfit."

"You look very nice. I just sort of picture you in jeans."

"Me too. Anyways, I'm glad you called."

"I don't know how well this Mexican landscaper speaks English."

They reached the north end of Evanston, a tired old section of factories and warehouses. He took Green Bay Road, which traveled straight through Chicago's North Shore. To their right, nearly hidden by a low ridge of trees and bushes, ran the Northwestern commuter railroad.

"How's your sister-in-law?" he asked.

"She's back at work."

"The funeral was just yesterday."

"She's back at work, and waiting."

"For what?"

"For Bixby to be brought to justice. That's why she could walk away from Nina's grave. She still has to see justice done. Because I told her you would help, that you would make Bixby pay. Otherwise, I think she would kill him herself."

Rosen shook his head slowly.

"What is it?" Lucila asked.

"She shouldn't make certain assumptions."

"Assumptions?"

"That Nina was murdered, and that Martin Bixby is the murderer."

"But you said—"

"I'd help you by trying to discover the truth, and that's what I intend to do. That's why we're going to see Alvarez, to find out what he knows about Nina's death."

"Her murder."

"It may not necessarily lead to Bixby."

"It will."

Rosen shook his head harder, as if to toss off her smugness. "I spoke with Bixby this morning at school. He said that Nina's diary was just a class assignment."

She clicked her tongue. "And you believed him?"

"I'm going to ask Sarah if Bixby really did give such an assignment."

"And if he did? He teaches theater, which means he's an actor. What are actors but professional liars. Bixby did it. You'll see."

The road suddenly swerved left, as if it had seen a rabbit, and Rosen slowed to keep from skidding. A few minutes later it curved again, and they entered downtown Winnetka, its exclusive shops wearing their brightly colored awnings like millinery.

Lucila said, "It hasn't been easy—what happened to Nina."

"Sure."

Looking out the window, she smiled. "Lifestyles of the rich and famous. I suppose you and your ex-wife lived like this."

"Bess and I had an apartment in Rogers Park about half the size of your studio."

"But now you're a successful lawyer."

"I live in a place so small I can't eat and read at the same time. I can illuminate the whole place with my daughter's old night light. I can—"

She laughed, and he loved how it softened to a ripple.

He added, "Don't get civil liberties confused with corporate law. The money, I mean."

"But you help people—there must be many compensations."

"At times."

They drove through Glencoe and Highland Park, under a bower of tall trees lining either side of the residential area. It was beautiful, like the place where Bess and Sarah were living. Quiet and safe; how could these people not be happy?

Rosen almost smiled, remembering the saying his old rabbi had loved to quote: "'Do not look at the jug. There are new jugs filled with old wine and old jugs without even new wine.'" What was behind the façade of these homes?

He said, "Arbor Shore is just past Highwood. After seeing Alvarez, we could visit your sister-in-law."

"I don't think that would be a good idea."

RONALD LEVITSKY

"Why not?"

"She'll expect you to tell her something about Bixby. What can you tell her, unless this Alvarez says something?"

"I'd like to talk to her anyway."

"She has nothing to say."

"She can tell me about the house."

"What house?" Lucila turned to stare at him. "What the hell are you talking about?"

"The Ellsworth house. The house where your sister-in-law lived with Nina. The house where Nina received a phone call that sent her out to the park, where she fell from a cliff and died."

"That house has nothing to do with my niece's death."

"Edward Masaryk was with the police chief this morning. They were discussing Alvarez. Why would Masaryk be there if the Ellsworths weren't somehow involved?"

"I don't know. Maybe because Bixby's a friend of Kate Ellsworth. Maybe she sent Masaryk there."

"Don't you know?"

Lucila narrowed her eyes. "What?"

"You saw Mrs. Ellsworth this afternoon. Didn't you ask her about Bixby?"

"What would she know about Bixby—about that part of his life? They share a mutual interest in art, that's all. Like I said before, he's an actor. I've seen him at exhibits. Oh so charming. He paints his face with layers of lies."

He asked, "What can you tell me about the Ellsworths, as a couple?"

"That doesn't have a thing to do with what happened to Nina."

"I get a sense that Kate and Masaryk are pretty close. At the funeral, for example—"

Lucila turned to face him, her eyes flashing. "You leave Kate out of this. I don't want her name dragged in the mud. You understand?"

Rosen nodded. He understood that there was something wrong in the Ellsworth house.

He slowed the car as they entered Highwood. The poor relative among North Shore suburbs, the town was a mixture of old Italian families, who still played boccie ball and fed Pavarotti when he sang at the Lyric Opera, and Hispanics tending rich people's lawns or working in nearby factories. Bisected by the railroad, Highwood's small square and rectangular buildings lined the street like a toy train set. Yet interspersed with the bars and auto repair and barber shops were some of the most expensive restaurants in Chicagoland.

Glancing at the street signs, Rosen said, "I found Alvarez's address in the phone book, then checked a map. He lives off Maple Avenue, which should've already intersected Green Bay. I'd better ask directions."

He parked the car and crossed the street. From up the block two young women walked toward him. They wore short, tight skirts and leather jackets. Both smelled of liquor, and the taller one was smoking.

"Well if it isn't Mr. Rosen," the shorter woman said.

He looked at her closely. "You're from the high school. The dancer."

She nodded. "Margarita Reyes. This is my cousin Francisca."

"Do you know where Maple Avenue is?"

Francisca pointed behind her. "The next corner, where the bar is."

Margarita said, "Hello, Luci."

Lucila had crossed the street to join him. "I thought it was you, Ita."

"Yes, it's my mother's night off, so we're visiting my cousins." Looking Rosen up and down as if examining a horse before a race, she added, "I didn't know you two were dating. You're always so busy with your painting, I didn't even know you liked men."

Rosen asked, "Isn't it late for you girls to be out alone?"

Her cousin laughed as Margarita said, "We don't plan to be alone for long." Watching Rosen, she scratched the inside of her thigh, letting her skirt ride up another three inches. He looked away.

"Goodbye, Ita," Lucila said and, taking Rosen's arm, led him past the two girls. It wasn't until they'd reached the bar that she released him, half whispering, "Puta." Whore.

Turning the corner they crossed an alley that led behind the bar and continued under the streetlights down Maple Avenue. Rosen felt a great sadness—both for Margarita, a girl giving up her child-hood for much less than Esau's bowl of stew, and for Sarah, whom he could no longer shield from such things. Strange, but Lucila's anger comforted him. It was harsh and unyielding, just as the Old Testament anger of his father had always been. Rosen didn't want any mercy when it came to his daughter's welfare. Yes, strange, because his father had probably felt the same way toward him.

"Is this the street, Nate?"

He looked up at the signpost and nodded. Checking the address-es illuminated on each side of the street, he said, "Alvarez's number is 1185—should be on this side."

The homes were small two-story dwellings, mostly frame, with peaked roofs and concrete stairs. There were as many pickups as cars parked in the street, including Alvarez's landscaping truck.

Eleven eighty-five, in the middle of the block, appeared more tired than the others. Chipped and peeling, its forest green had long ago faded to the color of a worn dollar bill. The windows needed caulking and the gutters cleaning.

Rosen knocked on the door, which was opened by the woman he'd seen earlier at the police station. She wore the same baggy dress but her earrings and necklace were gold. She held the door-knob tightly and waited—no greeting, no questions. From some-where inside, the television blared a baseball game.

"Mrs. Alvarez?" Rosen asked.

She nodded.

"We'd like to see your husband."

"Por qué . . . why?"

"We're looking into the death of Nina Melendez and want to ask him some questions about last Friday evening."

She looked at him helplessly. "I don't . . ." Then she held up her hands.

Lucila spoke to her rapidly in Spanish. Alvarez's wife blinked sev-eral times, and her reply was slow and tentative. The two women continued their conversation with the same rhythm until Lucila stopped to translate.

"Her husband has had a long day, and she'd like us not to bother him."

Rosen said, "Tell her we know her husband has spoken to the police."

The women started, as if the word "police" had pricked her. A man shouted something from inside the house, and the woman's voice scurried like a mouse to reply.

"Es la policia?" he demanded.

She shook her head, then, remembering he couldn't see her, replied, "No!"

Lucila quickly added something, and for a few moments the house grew silent.

Alvarez said, "Okay. Come in."

"What did you tell him?" Rosen whispered to Lucila, as they followed the woman into the house.

"Just that we're friends of the Ellsworths."

The living room was as worn as the house's exterior, with peeling wallpaper and a big water stain in the corner above a window. However, the furnishings looked new, including a foldout leather chair and matching sofa. A big-screen television was hooked to four-foot stereo speakers, and three racks filled with compact discs stood beside a state-of-the-art sound system.

Hector Alvarez sat in the leather chair in front of the TV, one hand holding a beer and the other a bag of "chicharrones"—fried pork rinds. A sleeveless T-shirt and baggy pair of work pants hung loosely on his body. His dark face with its wide cheekbones and thin mustache seemed so typical. Lucila had accused Dr. Winslow of seeing all Hispanics alike, yet Rosen couldn't distinguish this man from the dozen others he must've encountered each day—grass cutters, busboys, fast-food clerks, or even the migrant workers he'd defended a few years before.

Taking a long swallow of beer, Alvarez squinted over the can. Wiping his mouth with the back of his hand, he motioned them to the couch, Rosen sitting kitty-corner to him.

Rosen asked, "Mind lowering the volume?"

Alvarez pressed the remote control until the game was barely audible.

On the TV was a large framed photograph of Alvarez, his wife, and several others, including a girl who looked familiar.

115

"Isn't that Margarita Reyes?" Rosen asked.

Alvarez nodded. "Ita—my wife's cousin. She got me some jobs up in Arbor Shore. House where her mother works, and the Ellsworths." He pointed at Lucila. "Sure, I know you. I see you at the Ellsworths when I work on the lawn. You do know them. Good. I like people who tell the truth."

"Me too," Rosen said. "Tell us what happened last Friday night."

He took another swallow of beer. "I already told the police."

"Tell us."

Crinkling his eyes, Alvarez repeated what he'd told Keller that morning. Then he fished a cigarette from a pack on the floor, leaned back, and puffed contentedly.

Rosen said, "So, after dark you returned to the park for the grass clippings, to avoid paying another fine?"

"Yes."

"Do you work alone?"

"Me—I'm the boss. I got three men working for me."

"Why didn't you send one of them?"

"It was too late. I have to pay them overtime."

"And then you became sick?"

Alvarez made a face. "That *McDonald's*—qué malo. I ate something bad."

"So you were pretty sick."

"Just for the night."

"Yet the police couldn't find you for two days."

"I was at a friend's." He grinned, cupping his hands around a pair of imaginary breasts.

"Or maybe you went on a trip."

Alvarez leaned forward in his chair. "Why would I go away?"

Rosen locked his eyes on the other man's. "Maybe you went to buy something."

"Like what?"

"Look around this house. It's falling apart, yet you've got all this electronic hardware. You know . . ."

"Despacio!" Alvarez shouted. "Slow down."

"You know who lives like this. Drug dealers."

116

"Drugs? You crazy, man! You watch what you say."

"Maybe you went to pick up your supply. Just a little business trip."

"I said you're crazy! I don't mess with drugs. I got my own business." He slapped his chest. "Comprende, I'm the boss. I tell other people what to do."

"But you didn't tell somebody else to take care of the grass clippings last Friday night."

Alvarez crumpled back in his chair, his jaw set tight.

Lucila spoke. "Maybe he didn't understand you."

She spoke rapidly in Spanish. Reaching for his beer, Alvarez pretended to watch the ballgame, but his face grew darker until he could no longer bite back the words.

"Cállese, mujer!"—Quiet, woman!

The exchange became more heated until Alvarez suddenly stopped, his lips twisting into a grin.

"Me gustas, chica. Te deseo."

Lucila froze, as if a spider had crawled onto her, but said something to melt his grin and make him wipe his mouth hard.

"Hell, I'm gonna get me another beer."

Alvarez strode past them, through the hall and into the kitchen. A few moments later, Rosen heard the murmur of conversation; either the Mexican was talking to his wife or someone on the phone.

Rosen asked Lucila, "What was all that between you and Alvarez?"

Her shrug was almost a shiver. "He started saying things."

"What things?"

"Oh, the kind of things men in my country say to women they see walking down the street. 'I want you, baby,' things like that."

"How'd you get him so upset?"

"I said if he ever tried anything with me, I'd tie his balls into a necktie."

"I guess his wife doesn't talk to him like that. I knew something was wrong when he used the word 'te' with you. That's pretty familiar."

"Too familiar. I should've slapped him right then."

"Sure. He'd probably . . ." Rosen stopped, trying to catch a thought flitting through his memory. Something Lucila had just said. But not about Alvarez.

"Nate?"

He rubbed his eyes. What was it?

Sauntering into the room, Alvarez sat down while popping open another can of beer. He turned up the television's volume and said, "I had a long day. You better go."

Rosen raised his voice to match the TV. "You said before that you recognized Lucila when she visited the Ellsworth home. Did you get to know the people living in the house?"

Alvarez snorted into his beer can. "Yeah sure, man. Me and my wife, we go partying with the Ellsworths all the time. I even let him use my lawn mower sometimes, just for kicks."

"I was thinking about Esther Melendez, the housekeeper."

The Mexican shook his head.

"You must've seen her. Didn't she come out with water for you and your men?"

"Maybe. I don't remember."

"And maybe sometimes you saw her daughter Nina come home from school."

"No, man."

"She was very pretty. Maybe you whistled or said something to her, like you said a few minutes ago to Lucila."

Pretending to concentrate on the ballgame, Alvarez didn't answer, but his fingers slowly crushed the beer can.

"And maybe you came back at night looking for her, and when she wouldn't play with you, maybe—"

Alvarez threw the can onto the floor. "Maybe you should go fuck yourself! Get out! Get the hell outta my house!"

"But we haven't finished talking."

Alvarez stood and, reaching deep into his pocket, thrust a business card into Rosen's hand. "You wanna talk, talk to my lawyer! Now get out!"

The card read "Nelson Harding of the firm of Tyler, Estes, and Webb," with a Chicago address in the downtown financial district.

Rosen asked, "How did you get a firm—"

"Get the hell out!"

Leading them into the hall, Alvarez flung open the front door so hard it snapped back and struck him in the shoulder. Putting his hand on Lucila's arm, Rosen followed her from the house. The door slammed behind them.

Rosen's hand remained on her arm as they walked quietly up the street. Nearing the corner, they crossed the alleyway and passed three workmen gabbing in Spanish. One man, smelling of whiskey, stumbled into Rosen.

"Excuse me," Rosen said.

Staying low, the man pushed him into the dimly lit alley, while the other two dragged Lucila after. Rosen wrestled with his assailant while watching the other two. One stood behind Lucila, his hand against her mouth, while the other pulled off her coat. She stood still as a statue, offering no resistance. The men starting laughing.

"No!" Rosen shouted.

His attacker struck him hard on the side of the face, then another fist rocked him. His head swinging like a signpost in the wind, Rosen grappled for the other man's leg and pulled him to the ground. He couldn't get up—could only watch what the other two men were about to do.

Pulling down the straps of her halter, the man facing Lucila grinned and took a step forward. The grin froze on his face and his eyes popped wide as her knee flashed between his legs. He screamed and doubled over. Before he fell, she twisted free of the third man, and reaching into her purse, sprayed a half can of Mace into his eyes. He also screamed before falling beside his companion.

She walked over to Rosen, still entangled with his assailant. Taking the lid off a garbage can, she smashed it over the other man's head. Kicking him away, she helped Rosen to his feet.

Gripping her tightly to keep from falling, he asked, "Are you all right?"

"Am I all right?" She shook her head.

"The police—"

"No. I did more to them than the courts would. Come on."

She helped Rosen across the street and into the passenger side of his car. Sitting behind the wheel, she asked, "Would it hurt your ego if I drove home?"

"No," he said, wincing.

She touched his cheek. "Are you okay?"

"Sure, just give me a couple minutes."

He leaned back, closing his eyes, as she made a U-turn and drove down Green Bay Road. He thought about buckling his seat belt, but it hurt to move. Besides, what did he have to worry about? He was with Lucila.

Chapter 11

"Careful," Lucila said, leading him through the darkened corridor into her apartment. "The switch is just around the corner. Here."

Blinking back the flash of light, Rosen looked into the enormous room, which was far different now from the way it had looked the afternoon of Nina's funeral. Open space, except against the long wall to his right, where a frayed cloth sofa, metallic floor lamp, and overstuffed chair hunkered around an old captain's chest. Filled with paints, brushes, and paper plates smeared with whirling colors, a large pushcart stood beside a half-finished painting near the corner window. Unframed canvases hung along all the walls. Fluorescent light, reflecting off the gray tile, gave the room a greenish glow that didn't make his head feel any better.

Tossing his jacket and tie over the chair, he eased onto the couch while Lucila went into kitchen. A few minutes later, she laid something cold against the left side of his head.

"Hold this compress for a while. It should help the swelling go down. You'll be good as new in a few days."

"Will I be able to play the violin again?"

"God, I hope not. I hate the violin. It always reminds me of a cat in heat. I'll make some coffee."

"Do you have any tea?"

"I'll check."

Cabinet doors banged open in the kitchen, and she called from somewhere under the counter, "Got an old package of Lipton!"

"That's fine!"

Resting his cheek against the compress, Rosen was about to close

121

his eyes when he felt a vague uneasiness—the sensation of being watched. No one else was in the room—

Then he saw their faces.

The afternoon of the funeral, Rosen hadn't taken much notice of Lucila's paintings. They'd been hidden from view, much as their subjects in real life, poor campesinos and their children who were ignored by the rest of the world. But now in the naked green light, the children gazed at him. They were dark with soft dark eyes and, had they smiled, their smiles would have been gentle. The children reminded him of Nina and, although he never knew her, of the murdered black girl, Denae Tyler. Their gaze hardened, as if he were a criminal in the interrogation room. The questions about to be asked—the demands. What did they want?

"You don't look so good. Are you okay?"

Sitting beside him, Lucila placed a tray of tea and cookies on the captain's chest.

"Sure." Reaching for the cup, he sloshed some of the tea onto the tray.

"You're not okay. You're very pale. . . ." Her fingers felt cool against his forehead, ". . . and a little warm."

"I'm fine—really."

"Drink your tea. These cookies are very good—made by an old woman down the street. Do you want an aspirin?"

Afraid to shake his head, he half whispered, "No."

She turned on the lamp, which glowed softly, then walked to the kitchen and switched off the overhead light. Returning to the couch, she asked, "Better?"

"Yes, thanks."

"The tea okay?"

"Yes."

"It's pretty old. I don't know if tea can go bad. Drink it while it's hot. We don't have to talk."

He sipped his tea, glad Lucila was sitting beside him. She idly played with her long tresses, just as Bess used to do. How many evenings had he spent like this with Bess? He'd be working on a brief while she graded papers, and hours might pass without a word between them. But it was a good silence, warm like a blanket around them both. He felt that way with Lucila now, and so he nursed his tea, thinking somehow the feeling would last as long as the liquid in the cup.

When he finally finished, Lucila asked, "More?"

"No, thanks. I'm feeling better."

"Good." She touched his right hand. "How'd you get the scar? A duel over a lady's honor?"

"Shattered glass from a shopkeeper's window. A bombing involving a case I was working on."

"You've got another scar on your inside left wrist."

"Someone with a knife went after a client and got me instead. You're pretty observant. Having an artist's eye, you would be."

She smiled. "I bet you're pretty tough."

"Not half as tough as you. Remember, I've seen you in action. Besides, real tough guys don't get any scars."

Her smile slowly faded. "I have scars."

"You mean Nina."

"Yes, Nina and my parents who worked themselves to death back home, so I could get an education. And my brother . . . my dear stupid brother."

"Nina's father?"

Lucila nodded, biting her lip.

"What happened to him?"

Hands balled into fists until her knuckles whitened, she stared past Rosen, as if something terrible was being replayed in her mind.

Finally she said, "I thought that was all behind us, when we left the Dominican Republic. But maybe violence is genetic in certain families, like cancer. To be so alone. You don't know what it's like." Her eyes glistened. "Oh, Nina."

She wasn't tough anymore, but Rosen liked her better this way. He hadn't seen Lucila cry, not even at the funeral, and wanted to think she'd touched some protective instinct of his. But it was more than that. He watched her tremble, watched her breasts heave against the white cotton blouse. If he touched her, would she tremble that way?

Then he noticed how her halter straps were torn where only an hour ago two men had attacked her.

He looked away, disgusted with himself. "I'm sorry."

"What?"

"I wasn't thinking about what happened to you earlier this evening. Those men could've hurt you badly. What they were trying to do."

Lucila blinked hard, then looked down at her torn halter. "What they were trying to do they could've done only to my corpse. You understand?"

She took his teacup. Slowly walking to the kitchen and returned with a steaming refill. She also sopped, with a sponge, the tea he'd spilled earlier.

"These clothes are dirty," she said. "Do you mind if I take a few minutes to clean up?"

"Of course not. It's getting late; maybe I'd better leave."

"No." The word came at him like a foot in a closing door. More softly, "I won't be long."

"All right. Can I use your phone to call my daughter?"

"It's on the wall in the kitchen."

Lucila walked into the bathroom and a moment later, the shower began hissing. Bracing himself against the dull pain lapping inside his head, he walked into the kitchen.

"Hello." Shelly's voice.

"This is Nate. Can I please talk to Sarah?"

"She's in bed. Just a minute."

In the background he heard Shelly and Bess arguing. Then a long moment of silence.

"Sarah's taken a mild sedative," Bess said. "We were expecting you earlier this evening."

"Sorry. I had an appointment."

"Did it have to do with Nina's death and your fixation on Martin Bixby?" When he didn't reply, she continued, "I don't want you to bring that up anymore, especially with Sarah."

"How did it go with Mrs. Agee this afternoon?"

"They talked for nearly an hour, alone in Sarah's bedroom.

Afterward, Linda said that Sarah's emotional state is pretty typical for an adolescent who's lost someone very close, but she's got to get on with her life. Linda suggested private therapy and gave me a few names. Maybe tomorrow we can discuss it."

"Sure. I'd like to talk to Sarah."

"Now?"

"Just for a minute. Something important I need to know."

"About Bixby, isn't it? Didn't I just tell you—"

"The questions surrounding Nina Melendez's death didn't get buried with her body. You don't know all the answers, and neither does your psychologist friend. Finding out what really happened to that girl is going to help Sarah—"

"Stop it! This isn't about Sarah. It's about you. This drive for 'Justice,' like some avenging prophet, even when the innocent are as likely to be struck down as the wicked. Your father would be very proud of you."

The throbbing inside grew so intense Rosen had to shut his eyes. Sweat slid down his neck, and blood pulsed in his ears.

"Nate?"

Taking a deep breath, he replied, "We have joint custody of Sarah. I can come over right now and talk to her."

"A lawyer's answer. Why don't you try acting like a father."

"I am." His head was splitting. "Look, I don't have to talk to her. Ask her something for me. It's about some schoolwork."

"What?"

He explained Bixby's contention that Nina's diary was only a homework assignment, an assignment she'd begun but never completed. "Just ask Sarah if it's possible. I'll wait."

"All right."

He was about to splash some cold water on his face when Shelly picked up the other receiver.

"How's your investigation going, Nate?"

"Okay."

"You know, if you need any help, just ask. I can make some calls, do some legwork for you. Maybe we could go over to see Chief Keller."

"So you like playing detective."

"Don't get me wrong—the human foot is an exciting thing, but anything to help Sarah. She's a good kid."

"I . . ."

Rosen's voice cracked, not because of the pain in his head. Ever since Bess had first met Shelly, Rosen had only ridiculed the podiatrist. And what was Shelly—a loving husband for Bess, and for Sarah a stepfather who was always there.

Before he could try again, Bess said, "Sarah remembers the assignment. Nina did hers as a dialogue with a famous person, Joan of Arc."

"Did Nina talk about the other assignment? Maybe start it, then put it aside?"

"No."

"You asked Sarah that?"

The second Bess hesitated before saying, "Yes," told him she was lying. She just wanted him off the phone, and he was hurting too much to argue.

"I'll come by tomorrow afternoon. Tell Sarah I love her. Bye."

He dabbed cold water on his face while waiting for the pain to subside. The sink held a tin can filled with paintbrushes, as well as an old rag. He looked closer; the rag was a torn pair of Lucila's pantyhose. They were pink. Settling back into the couch, the soft glow of lamp light snuggling around him like a cat, he barely noticed the portraits staring from the wall.

Rosen touched the spot where Lucila had sat, and his imagination drew another portrait. The steam rising from his tea was like the steam in her shower, and looking through one, he tried to imagine the other. How she'd appear stepping from the bathroom—her hair damp and clinging to her shoulders; moist skin scented with some delicate perfume; and a long silken robe tight around her body, split by her long legs as she walked. She'd be smiling; those lips would be smiling at him. And she'd ask him to stay, just like in the movies. He felt the teacup tremble in his hand.

"There now. That wasn't long."

Blinking hard, Rosen stared from the bathroom door to the couch where Lucila was sitting. He blinked again, then burst into laughter. Wincing, still he laughed.

"What is it?" she asked.

"Nothing . . . nothing really."

"Do I look that funny?"

She wore a baggy canary yellow sweat outfit, and a turquoise towel had been wrapped like a turban around her wet hair. He liked the way she smelled, of soap and shampoo, and the way she was almost laughing with him.

"You look just fine," he said.

"That's what comes from living alone. You don't have to impress anybody."

He ate one cookie, then another.

"So you are feeling better. That guy really laid into you."

"Just a slight headache." He nodded at her paintings. "Are these for your exhibition?"

"Three of them."

"I stopped by Kate Ellsworth's gallery and saw one of your paintings—quite remarkable. What's it called?"

She waited a long time before replying. "The Flowers of Madness."

"From a poem by Gabriela Mistral. The woman in the gallery read it to me. Something about climbing the rocks, wasn't it?"

She almost whispered,

> "'I scaled the rocks with deer
> and sought the flowers of madness,
> those that grew so red they seemed
> to live and die of redness.'"

He asked, "The girl in the painting is Nina?"

"Who else could show such innocence?"

"The other woman in the painting, the mad woman with fire in her eyes. Whom did you use as a model?"

Lucila shrugged.

"The reason I asked—she looked familiar. Not so much the face, but her expression."

"Nobody special."

"But—"

"Why does it have to be anybody special? You see them everywhere, don't you—in the dirtiest streets of Santo Domingo or the richest houses in . . . !" She shook her head hard. "Anywhere there's not enough food in the belly or love in the heart. Anywhere."

Massaging her face, she tried to smile, her lips tight as a mask. "Did you call your daughter?"

He nodded.

"How is she?"

"Making progress, I suppose."

"She's a wonderful girl, like Nina. Did you discuss Bixby and his story about Nina's diary?"

"Yes. She doesn't remember Nina writing the diary as a class assignment."

"Of course not. We both know Bixby's lying. What'd you think of Alvarez?"

"He's lying about something."

"Do you think he saw what happened to Nina?"

"Maybe, or he might just be lying because he's dealing drugs." Rosen remembered the jewelry Alvarez's wife was wearing, then the scene of the crime. "I wonder if he's the kind who'd bring a girl roses and a necklace."

"You don't think that Nina would take up with somebody like Alvarez."

"I doubt it. Still, he had access to the estate and probably a lot of money to flash around."

"She'd never dirty herself with scum like that!"

"All right," Rosen said, "but why did Masaryk talk to the police chief about Alvarez? What's a landscaper to the Ellsworths? And how did Alvarez retain the services of some law firm in downtown Chicago? Something's not right. Another thing."

"What?"

"Those men—the ones who attacked us. Was it just a coincidence that, a few minutes before we left his house, Alvarez went into the kitchen?"

"You think he arranged it over the phone?"

"I don't know."

Lucila clicked her tongue. "This is getting us nowhere. You're supposed to prove that Bixby killed Nina, but all you've been doing is sitting around."

"We went to see Alvarez."

"And what happened—you got knocked on your ass. If it wasn't for me, they'd be selling your body parts to the local hospital." She looked at her lap and, hands balled into fists, struck her thighs. "Sorry, it's just—you're not doing anything."

He laughed.

"Glad I'm amusing you."

"It's not—" He winced at the pain still nipping inside his head, then picked up the sponge from the tea tray. "Let me try to explain. When I was a boy studying scripture, my rabbi said there were four types of students."

"Oh, this is interesting."

"One is like a sponge, a fool who collects everything; another is a funnel, an even greater fool who forgets everything as soon as he learns it. A third is a strainer, who ignores the good and collects the bad; he's an evil one."

"Are we coming to the punch line?"

Rosen nodded as patiently as his old rabbi once had. "The fourth is like a sifter that collects only the good."

"And that, no doubt, is you."

"I hope so. I'm trying to piece together what really happened to your niece, and at this point the best way to do that is to sift through the evidence without any preconceived notions as to who's guilty."

"I see." Lucila thought for a moment, then stood. "I want you to spend the night."

The breath caught in his throat. Feeling his face grow warm, Rosen looked away. She walked behind him, and he waited—for her hand to touch his shoulder, for her lips upon his neck. Suddenly a pillow fell upon his lap, followed by a blanket.

"The couch is pretty comfortable."

Narrowing his eyes, he looked up.

Lucila was smiling, her dimples showing. "You didn't think I meant . . . ? It's not that you aren't cute, but this isn't even a first date. I'm just worried about you. It's a long drive into Evanston, and you don't look so good, though a little of your color's come back."

Switching off the lamp, she kissed his cheek. "Tomorrow morning I'm going to show you how to get things done without using a sifter. 'Night."

Rosen listened to Lucila's feet paddle along the floor to her bed in the corner by the kitchen. Too tired to wash up, he lay beneath the blanket and remembered another one of his rabbi's sayings: "A woman spins even while she talks." So she'd been planning something all along, something she wanted to drag him into.

He should have been angry but was too busy listening to the slight creaking of her mattress as she shifted in bed. Only a little mental exercise, he thought, like disputing a Talmudic passage. He wondered how she slept, on her back or side, did her sweatpants ride up her calves as she stretched out, and did her hair fall like a silken veil across her cheek? Only a mental exercise, yet he grew so warm that he had to throw off the covers before falling asleep.

Chapter 12

Rosen awoke to some Latino radio station blaring from the kitchen. A female singer jabbered over and over, like a gerbil turning a wheel in its cage. As he sat up slowly, the aroma of espresso smacked him in the nose. Massaging the kink in his neck, he waited for the pain to stop running circles in his brain like another gerbil.

"Buenos días!" Lucila said from behind the kitchen counter. "Almost nine—time you got up. Breakfast will be ready in five minutes."

Eyes half closed, Rosen walked into the bathroom. He almost forgot to put up the toilet seat before urinating. How different a woman's bathroom was. Not just the pantyhose over the shower door, the bath sponge, or the comb placed diagonally in the thick brush. He inhaled a fragrance, a lotion or maybe just the soap, that reminded him of Lucila. Did every woman's bathroom carry her scent? What had Bess's been like? It had been so long. He washed and patted his sore face with a towel, sorry he couldn't sink into a warm bath for a few hours.

Lucila worked over the stove as he sat on the other side of the counter. She had laid out dishes, coffee cups, glasses of orange juice, and a basket of small, round rolls.

"Just in time," she said, lowering the radio and sitting across from him with a skillet of eggs.

Her long hair in a ponytail, she wore a white fisherman's sweater, blue jeans, and sneakers. She looked like a teenager and almost could've passed for Nina.

"Feeling better?"

"Yes, thanks. Breakfast looks good."

She served the fried eggs. "I bought the rolls this morning from a Dominican baker down the street. They're as good as the ones back home."

Rosen spread butter over the warm roll, but before he had taken his first bite Lucila had nearly finished eating. She bent over her plate, as if reading it, using her fingers to manipulate bits of egg between two pieces of bread.

"What's the matter?" she asked.

"I've never seen anyone inhale a meal before."

"'Get it before the cockroaches do'—that's what my grandfather used to say. Grandfathers always say things like that, don't they?"

Rosen smiled. "Yes, they do."

"Ready for coffee? I know you like tea, but you're eating Dominican-style this morning."

"It smells great."

Lucila returned to the stove, where an old tin pot was boiling. Putting on a pair of oven mitts, she lifted a coffee can from inside the pot and tipped it through a lung-shaped piece of cheesecloth, pouring the rich black espresso into another can.

"This is the way the old-timers do it—makes the best coffee." Once again she poured the espresso through the cheesecloth, into the first can. "We call this strainer a collador—it was my grandfather's and still works great." She laughed. "What did you tell me last night—that a strainer was wicked, because it collected the bad and let the good escape?"

"My rabbi never made coffee."

"No, not like this."

Sitting down, Lucila poured two half cups and placed the sugar bowl between them. She inhaled deeply.

"This is my best memory—a little girl sitting on my grandfather's lap in his big rocker. He'd hold out his cup of coffee and let me spoon in the sugar. Two teaspoons," and she put that many into her own cup.

Rosen did the same and sipped the espresso. "This is good."

As quickly as Lucila had eaten breakfast, she now lingered over her coffee, savoring the taste of each memory.

"You miss your home, don't you?" Rosen asked.

"This is my home."

"You know what I mean."

"I told you once before, it's not the place for a woman like me. Some people have to go their own way, no matter how much pain it causes. Maybe you don't understand."

"I understand." Rosen stared into his coffee cup and saw his father's face carved in ebony, stern and unforgiving as a pagan god. "I understand."

They sipped their coffee for a few minutes.

Finally Lucila said, "You're pretty strange. I mean . . . you don't talk much."

"I suppose that is strange for a lawyer."

"Not just a lawyer, but for a man. All the guys I've ever known can't wait to talk about themselves, and the divorced ones, they're the worst. All they do is bitch about their ex-wives. Not you. I don't know a thing about your background. Only what Sarah talked about when she was with Nina and me."

Rosen leaned back in his chair. "What kind of things did she say?"

"What a smart lawyer you are, and how good you are to her."

"Then anything I say could only detract from your image of me." He watched her hands holding the coffee cup. "I suppose you're speaking from experience—that you go out with a lot of men."

"What kind of a woman do you take me for?"

"I mean—you're attractive, very bright and creative. I assume you date a lot."

"Why all the interest? Are you asking me out?"

"I . . . uh."

Laughing, Lucila said, "I'm just teasing you. Maybe that's why you don't talk much. You're shy. I like that. Well, I'd better do these dishes."

"Let me help."

"No, Señor. This morning I'm the lady of the house. Sit back and enjoy it while you can."

133

Trying to smile, Rosen felt the dull ache in his head and remembered something he had to do.

"Can I use your phone?"

"Sure. You know where it is."

After checking the address book in his coat pocket, he lifted the receiver on the kitchen wall.

"Good morning—Hermes Communications." Hermes' secretary Sherry was speaking.

"Good morning. This is Nate Rosen. Could I please speak to Mr. Hermes?"

"I'm sorry, but Mr. Hermes is in Atlanta until tomorrow. May I take a message?"

"Actually, you can do more than that. As I recall, you're the brains of the outfit when it comes to computers."

She laughed. "I do what I can."

"I wonder if you'd check your files for any information on a law firm called . . ." Rosen pulled the card from his pocket. ". . . Tyler, Estes, and Webb. In particular, Nelson Harding, a member of the firm."

"I really can't share any information without Mr. Hermes' approval."

"I understand. It's just that Mr. Hermes promised me his help, and it is rather important."

"Hold on a moment."

As he waited, Lucila said over the dishes, "You're not so shy after all. Not when it comes to getting something you want."

Sherry came back on the line. "I've spoken to Mr. Hermes' son Jason, who says it's all right to release the information. I've got the *Tyler, Estes, and Webb* file on the screen. What do you want to know?"

"I suppose, first of all, why you have information on the firm."

"Let's see." She paused to scan the file. "Over the last ten years it's been involved in a number of real estate dealings downtown, as well as in certain minority neighborhoods scattered throughout the city."

"By any chance, has it represented Ellsworth-Leary Investments?"

"Oh yes, on numerous occasions."

"What about one of their attorneys, Nelson Harding."

"Let's see. He represented Ellsworth-Leary in a request for a zoning variance last year. They wanted to bring a shopping mall into a residential area on the South Side."

Rosen asked, "Any record of Harding doing criminal law—drug trafficking, for example?"

She laughed. "Tyler, Estes, and Webb is pretty diversified, but I'd be surprised if it'd dirty itself down in the criminal courts. It's kind of like week-old bread—white, dry, and stale."

"Thanks. That's all I need to know. And thank Mr. Hermes' son for me."

"I will. I believe Mr. Hermes is expecting to hear from you on another matter."

"Right. I'll call him in a few days. Good-bye."

Rosen hung up the phone as Lucila finished drying her hands on a wash towel. He told her what he'd learned from Hermes' secretary.

"So," she said, "something's not right."

"No. Why does a high-priced law firm, with connections to Byron Ellsworth, bother with a drug-dealing Mexican landscaper?"

"A payoff to keep Alvarez's mouth shut. He saw something that Friday night."

"If that's true, it probably eliminates Martin Bixby as a suspect. Why would Masaryk go to all this trouble to protect him?"

"No, Bixby did it. Maybe because he's such a good friend of Kate's. Maybe she's helping to protect him."

Rosen was about to disagree—to say how unlikely Lucila's theory was, but he didn't. He wasn't going to get into an argument; besides, he didn't really think she believed it herself.

Lucila twisted the towel, then threw it on the draining board. "We better get going."

"Going—where?"

She put on a jeans jacket, then handed him his coat and tie. Grabbing her purse and tucking a sketch pad under her arm, she smiled. "Trust me."

Back in his car, Lucila had him snake through the North Side of

Chicago, moving toward both the lake and Evanston, where he was staying. He should've asked where they were going, but he enjoyed just being with her. Regaining her good humor, she chatted about her involvement in the Logan Square neighborhood—wall murals and other art projects, an early childhood center, and a battered woman's support group.

When Rosen steered the conversation to her upcoming show at the Ellsworth Gallery, she grew pensive. Her paintings, tied so closely to the poet Mistral's words about children, must have reminded her of Nina. It was Nina who had so often modeled childhood innocence.

They reached Howard Street, in a Latino neighborhood that divided Chicago from Evanston, and drove under the "L."

"Turn left on Sheridan," she said.

He drove north on Sheridan Road, the same street that led through the North Shore and, if they traveled long enough, would take them to Bess and Sarah's home, the Ellsworth mansion, and the cliff where Nina had fallen to her death. But they'd only gone a few blocks when Lucila had him park the car.

On either side Sheridan was lined with handsome old apartment buildings of copper-colored brick, fronted by small, neatly clipped lawns. She nodded across the street to a three-story courtyard building.

"That's where Martin Bixby lives."

Rosen said, "It's Wednesday morning. Bixby must be in school."

"That's what I'm counting on. We're going to search his apartment—give you a chance to 'sift' through his belongings and maybe find something to connect him with Nina's death."

"Even assuming we could get in, that would be breaking and entering. I'm a lawyer, an officer of the court—I can't do that."

"We're not breaking in. A few weeks ago Kate and I visited Bixby to drop off an art catalogue. We got to talking. He's interested in putting on a theatrical production of *Carmen* and asked me to make some costume sketches. Told me to drop them off any time—even showed me where he kept the spare key." She lifted her sketchbook. "So I made a few drawings, and I'm dropping them off."

Before Rosen could reply, she left the car and hurried across the street. There was nothing to do but follow her.

He walked between two concrete statuettes into a narrow court-yard and joined Lucila in the entranceway at the far end. Martin Bixby's name was on the mailbox marked "1A." An inner doorway with a buzzer secured the residents from uninvited guests.

Through the door's window, they watched an old woman drag a two-wheeled shopping cart down the stairs. As the woman opened the door, Lucila peered into her purse, pretending to fumble for her keys.

"Thanks," Lucila said, holding the door.

She led Rosen up a stairway to the first door on the left —1A. She knocked loudly, "Just to make sure," and receiving no reply, untaped the key from behind a faded landscape on the hallway wall. After unlocking the door, she returned the key to the picture, and they walked inside.

Having seen Bixby's disorganized office at school, Rosen expect-ed the apartment to be as cluttered. However, it was tidy and bright, the polished hardwood floors reflecting the sunlight slant-ing through the windows. A set of Scandinavian furniture was arranged on a swirling blue and orange rug; built-in book cases, including a sound system, encased the entire far wall, and a com-puter and printer rested on a desk against the wall to his right, just past the kitchen entrance. On the near wall, beside the doorway, hung a dozen framed photographs of Bixby over the years directing students in a variety of productions.

Studying the photos, Rosen saw that most of the students were girls. The last showed Bixby standing beside Nina, with Sarah sit-ting at the piano. His hand rested lightly on Sarah's shoulder. Rosen's skin prickled.

"Nate, did you hear me?"

Lucila stood in the kitchen entrance.

"No, I was looking these over."

"I said he's a tea drinker like you. The guy eats well. His freez-er's filled with steak and chops and those cute little packages of gourmet vegetables. Quite a wine rack too—something you'd expect of a guy like him. And a cupboardful of cookies and chips."

She stood beside Rosen and looked at the photographs. "What do you think—Bixby brought the girls here, gave them cookies and got them drunk? Maybe that's what he wanted to do to Nina. Maybe she said no, and he killed her."

He didn't know what to say, so he walked across the room to the computer. Lucila followed him. Putting down her sketchbook and purse, she rummaged through the desk drawers, then two flip boxes filled with disks.

A gold plaque hung on the wall above the desk. Rosen read the words aloud: "Arbor Shore High School, Teacher of the Year, Martin Bixby, 1991."

"More lies," she said, continuing her search.

Next Rosen scanned the bookshelves on the far wall. One shelf was filled with photo albums. The first album, dated 1971–74, contained photos, theatrical programs, and local reviews of Bixby as a Northwestern University student. Bixby had acted in dozens of plays, always as a supporting player rather than the lead. Courtier, villain, pirate, businessman, clown, monster, child, even a woman. Never the same character more than once—always behind a new mask.

The last album, only half filled, went back two years—with photographs and program copies of high school productions, as well as notes of appreciation from parents and students. Bess sat primly in the photo of a cast party; Bixby stood behind her, each arm around a female student. Everyone was smiling.

The last item in the album was a thank-you note from all the students who'd participated in the frosh-soph "Arts in Life Festival" the previous week. "To more than just a great teacher, to a great friend." Among the signatures were Chip Ellsworth's, Nina's, and Sarah's.

Flipping back through the pages, Rosen again wondered what kind of man Bixby was. All the wonderful photographs and congratulatory letters said one thing, but to Lucila and Esther Melendez the teacher was someone quite different. As if Bixby were walking through a hall of mirrors that kept changing his shape.

"Find anything?" Lucila asked, sitting on the edge of the computer desk.

"No."

"Me neither. At least, that's the way it looks. All the disks are labeled for school—grade books, lesson plans, rehearsal schedules. It'd take too long to run through every file. Maybe after, I'll boot up a few and do a spot check."

"After?"

"One more place to look."

Bixby's bedroom was more what Rosen had expected. The furniture was Early American, and not merely factory reproductions. Sturdily crafted of dark, polished wood, the furniture didn't quite match, as if Bixby had inherited it piece by piece. From left to right—a round table on a faded blue oval rug, the bed, and a tall dressing cabinet. Opposite the foot of the bed, a low chest of drawers supported the television and VCR.

A half-finished glass of wine and bag of chips lay on the table, and the morning paper had been strewn across the floor between bed and closet. This was obviously the "real" Bixby.

Lucila said, "Kind of funny, Bixby not having a TV in the living room. Maybe he didn't want his guests to think he was a lowbrow. Or . . ." She touched the VCR. "Why don't you check the closet."

Rosen stood against the closet doors, not bothering to look inside. He'd intruded enough into another man's privacy. Besides, he kept seeing Denae Tyler's sobbing mother after the girl's murderers had been acquitted—acquitted because an illegal search had tainted all the evidence. Yet as Lucila rummaged through each drawer, he did nothing to stop her. He wanted to be fair, but he'd seen Bixby's hand on Sarah.

She knelt to open a bottom drawer, then gasped as her hands jerked back. Moving beside her, Rosen saw the rows of video tapes, in black plastic cases, completely filling the drawer. Titles like "Leather Lovers" and "Chained Lust"—all sadomasochistic.

Lucila stared at her hands, balled into fists with whitened knuckles, and willed them to open. Walking to the dressing cabinet, she searched the drawers, then tossed a whip onto the bed.

"I won't bother showing you the kind of magazines he has in there. Or the handcuffs."

Rosen's stomach tightened, and sweat began to slide under his collar. He almost sat on the bed, but drew back at the sight of the whip.

Lucila asked, "Now do you believe me?"

He leaned against the doorjamb. "I don't know."

"What do you mean—you don't know?"

"Maybe he just fantasizes."

"Oh sure—he's got a drawer full of fantasies on videotape, and the whip and the handcuffs. And that's supposed to be okay? Tell me, Nate, is that normal? Is that what you fantasize about?"

She was breathing heavily. He watched her breasts rise and fall, and his face grew warm. Even looking away, toward the floor, he traced the curving lines that defined her thigh and calf. Did she know what he fantasized?

"Well?" she demanded.

Rosen swallowed hard. "It doesn't mean Bixby was involved with Nina."

"No, he wasn't involved with Nina. She'd never be involved with scum like him"—she motioned toward the whip—"in that way. He went after her though, and when he went too far, she resisted. Then he killed her."

"But there's no proof."

"Damn you, you're just another lawyer, with your talk of 'proof.' Why don't you offer to represent him? Maybe you'd get him off, just like you did those other two murderers. Doesn't it bother you that he might've been after your own daughter?"

"Of course it bothers me! I . . . !"

He stopped suddenly and rubbed his eyes. Hadn't Bess said just the opposite—that he, as a lawyer, was too aggressive in going after Bixby? When he'd started working for the CDC, his boss, Nahagian, had said with a grin, "If both sides criticize you, you're doing a good job."

Maybe he was doing a good job, but he didn't think so. With Sarah involved, he didn't feel free to act, as if she were being held hostage. And then there was Lucila. She bothered him too, but in a different way.

"Well," she asked, "what are you going to do?"

He took a deep breath. "First, we're going to put everything back in place."

She clicked her tongue. "All right. Then?"

Rosen checked his inside coat pocket. The tickets were still there, where he'd put them a few days before.

"Then," he said, "we're going to see Martin Bixby."

"At school?"

"Do you like baseball?"

"What?"

"Do you like baseball?"

"What a question to ask a Dominican."

"Good, because we're going to the ballgame."

Chapter 13

Rosen's favorite place in the whole world was Wrigley Field. Everything else from his boyhood had either changed or disappeared. So too had all other major league ballparks; they'd put in artificial turf, or domes, or gigantic exploding scoreboards. Only Wrigley Field had stayed the same.

Glancing at the ticket numbers, he led Lucila into the ballpark. They walked between the cool gray pillars, past the souvenir stands, and up a concrete incline into the sudden sunlight of the grandstands. They stood at the top row, deep in left field, near the yellow foul pole. Above the stadium, team pennants twisted in the wind. He pointed across the stands to the left field bleachers.

"That's where I saw my first Cubs game. September 7, 1969, against the Pirates. The Cubs were in first place but on a three-game losing streak. The Mets . . . well, you know what happened in 1969."

Lucila said, "In 1969 I was in first grade in Santo Domingo, making little dolls from mango seeds."

"The ivy on the walls was thick and green, not brown like today, and Billy Williams was playing left field. He was there with Santo and Kessinger and Beckert and Hundley. And Ernie Banks. It was a game we should've won." He smiled. "Guess I sound pretty nostalgic."

"You sound like a guy talking about the first time he ever had sex." She rubbed her arms. "It's cold up here in the wind. Let's find our seats, then you can tell me the rest of the story."

They walked down to a middle row and found their two seats on the aisle. Their section was filled with Arbor Shore students and a few chaperones. Margarita Reyes huddled with a group of girl-friends two rows down. Bixby sat beside Chip Ellsworth and joked with the students, as if he were one of them. Noticing Rosen and Lucila, he waved.

"Glad you could make it! Should be a great game, though I'm not much of a baseball fan! Can't tell one end of the stick from the other!"

"Bat, not stick!" one of the boys shouted, and the kids all laughed.

Rosen glanced at the clock on the scoreboard. "Game should be starting in a few minutes. Hungry?"

When she nodded, he bought two hot dogs, watching a cloud of steam rise from the vendor's metal box.

Settling back, he chewed slowly through the frankfurter's tough skin.

Other vendors walked up and down the aisle. "Hot dogs! Get your hot dogs!" They threw mustard packets, like confetti, into the stands.

"Beer! Cold Beer! Here, buddy, pass that down."

"Peanuts! Here you go—catch!"

He watched Lucila wipe the mustard from her mouth and asked, "Want another?"

"God, no. My stomach can't take more than one of these."

"Really? There's no place hot dogs taste better than at the ball-park."

"That must be a guy thing—part of the romance of baseball. Well, aren't you going to finish the story about your first game at Wrigley Field?"

"You really want to hear it?"

"As long as it's more interesting than your sponge story."

Again he looked into the left field bleachers. "I was fourteen. I'd never seen the Cubs play."

"You mean live. You must've watched them on TV."

"We didn't have a television. It only distracted you from study-ing Talmud. My father was away that weekend. It was about six o'clock Sunday morning when my uncle woke me up. My mother's younger brother, a contractor who lived in the suburbs. Very modern, and for that reason unwelcome in our home—at least when my father was around. He and his two boys had come to take me to the ballgame."

"At six in the morning?"

"It was September, and the Cubs were still in first place. They hadn't won the pennant since World War II. Everyone wanted a ticket, and to be in the bleachers—to be a 'bleacher bum'—that was something special."

"It was nice of your uncle to come for you."

"He took me in, after . . ." Rosen shook his head.

"He took you in, after what?"

"Nothing. Just another story. Anyway, he did it for good luck. You see, the Cubs were on a losing streak, and he thought having a real yeshiva boy along might turn things around."

"Like a rabbit's foot?"

"Exactly. I knew my father would've never let me go, but my mother didn't say a word. After all, I already had my bar mitzvah; I could make my own decision."

"What about your brothers?"

"Aaron had escaped—he was away in college, and David . . . well, to question our father like that would've never entered his mind."

"But you went."

Rosen nodded. "I said my morning prayers and went. It was really something, that first time I went into Wrigley Field. I'd never been inside something that big. The huge concrete pillars, the mass of people shouting and cheering—at first, a little frightened, all I could think of was Samson in the Philistine temple. But then I saw Banks, Williams, and Santo trotting onto the field—names I'd only seen in the paper or heard occasionally on the radio. They were my first heroes less than two thousand years old."

Lucila asked, "The Bible was all you knew?"

"That and the stories of the Old Country my grandfather used to tell. But that day I learned something else—a different kind of faith. It was a great game, a battle on a biblical scale. First the

Pirates led, then the Cubs came back, then the Pirates, then the Cubs, then once again the Pirates. In the bottom of the eighth, Jim Hickman put us ahead 5-4 with a two-run homer. It went right over my head. Days after, my ears were still ringing from the cheers."

"So the Cubs won."

He shook his head. "You don't know the Cubs. Two outs in the top of the ninth—Willie Stargell the last Pirate hitter. He had a 2-2 count; one more strike was all we needed, and the wind was blowing hard against him."

"I take it this is not a happy ending."

"He cracked the ball through the wind into the right field bleachers. That tied the game, and the Pirates went on to win it in the eleventh. The Cubs lost three more in a row, while the Mets kept winning. Kept winning and won the pennant and the World Series."

"And the Cubs?"

"You know what the Jewish people used to say for centuries? 'Next year in Jerusalem.' It's sort of like that for Cub fans—'Wait'll next year.'"

Lucila asked, "Why did you stay a fan?"

Looking onto the field, Rosen could almost see Billy Williams spitting into his mitt, waiting for a fly ball. "I learned something that day. Not just about forgiveness—Cub fans are always forgiving the team. I learned that love wasn't predicated by success; one could fail, not meet someone's expectations, and still be loved."

"But surely your family—"

"My mother—yes, and my grandparents. But my father ran the house, and his word was law, as if the words were engraved in stone tablets. No, all those people trudging from the ballpark after the game, talking about how we'd win the next day—how *we'd* win, as if members of the same family. Seeing my uncle hugging his two boys, then taking their hands, and wishing my hand was in my father's."

At that moment Rosen felt the warmth of a hand closing over his. He turned to see Lucila, her smile as gentle as his mother's used to be.

She said, "So, you can talk about yourself, after all."

"I shouldn't have rambled on."

"It was a lot better than the sponge story."

He laughed, and she joined in his laughter, squeezing his hand before letting it go. They chatted more about baseball, and she told of how her countrymen played the game in the alleys back home—fielding rag balls and stones that took every bad hop imaginable—until they became the best infielders in professional baseball.

"Their ticket out of the bohios, the shacks."

They stood for the national anthem and cheered as the Cubs took the field. The breeze slackened, and under the warm sun he was no longer interested in the game's progress. At that moment, he didn't even care about Bixby. Just sitting beside Lucila was enough, and for the first time in a long time, he was happy.

Everyone else in the grandstand seemed to be happy as well. Five or six rows down, near the warning track, three big Latinos, wearing jackets with a tree service's logo, kept buying each other rounds of beer.

The man in the middle waved his hands and shouted, "Hey Ump! Hey, Fat Boy!"

Some of the Arbor Shore students egged him on, insulting the umpires and paying the beer vendor to take free drinks to the trio. One of the chaperones finally stopped the students, but Bixby laughed along with them, mimicking perfectly the drunk's accent.

"Hey Ump! Fat Boy!"

Directly in front of Rosen, a teenage girl, ignoring the ballgame, explained about her "stupid father" to her friend.

"And so he says I have to be in by eleven, but like Brian had already bought tickets to the late show that started at 9:30. And he says we better not go, 'cause last time I got home late he got in *so* much trouble. And his dad like plays golf with mine, so they're always talking, and it's so rude for him to be spying on me."

The way the girl confused her antecedents—who was "he"?—reminded Rosen of his daughter and Nina and why, after all, he was at the game. He watched Bixby continue to clown with the students. How to get him alone?

147

A few minutes later Chip Ellsworth left his seat and walked up the aisle, probably going to the bathroom. Rosen was tempted to sit beside the teacher, who was still surrounded by students. Instead, he followed Chip into the lower level.

Compared to the sunlit ball field, the area inside the stadium was cast in cool gray shadows, people flicking through the darkness, hurrying back to the game. He leaned against a pillar. Leaving the men's room, Chip walked toward the incline leading back to the grandstand. Seeing Rosen, he stopped dead in his tracks.

"Hello, Chip."

"I got to get back to the game."

"We didn't get a chance to talk yesterday morning in the school auditorium. By the way, that was a fine impression you gave of Dr. Winslow. You're quite an actor."

The boy looked around nervously.

Rosen asked, "Are you looking for Masaryk—Soldier?"

"Wh . . . what?"

"Are you looking for Soldier? He does keep close tabs on you, like at the funeral."

"What're you talking about?"

Rosen didn't want to frighten the boy into running. "Let's talk about the night Nina died. You remember that night."

"Yeah, I guess so." His hand trembled as it brushed back his hair.

"What were you doing that night?"

"I already told the police."

"Tell me."

"There's nothing to say. I was home that night—all night."

"Any friends over?"

"No. You can ask my dad—he already talked to the police. I was just kinda tired, so I stayed home. No big deal."

Rosen shook his head. "I don't believe that a popular guy like you would've stayed home alone on a Friday night. I'm going to ask around—check with your friends, the local liquor stores and bars. Maybe you were with Margarita Reyes."

"No."

"Or maybe Nina."

148

"What?"

"She lived in your house. You must've seen her every day. A pretty girl—it'd be easy for the two of you to make plans to slip out that night to the park. You got into an argument and maybe you pushed her a little too hard."

"No! I never had anything to do with Nina."

"Then where were you?"

The words came softer. "I told you. Nowhere."

"You're lying."

Chip reddened, and his jaw trembled.

"I was wrong," Rosen said. "You're not a very good actor. Now tell me the truth."

The boy took a deep breath, exhaling slowly. "It's no big deal . . . I mean, nothing to do with Nina. After it got dark—about eight-thirty—me and a couple friends—two guys—went into the ravines with a couple six-packs."

"Just a little beer bash?"

"That's right. Well, one guy had a bottle of vodka from his dad's liquor cabinet, but I wasn't drinking any. I don't like to mix beer and the hard stuff."

Chip was talking too much, adding too many details. Lying again.

Rosen asked, "Who were these friends?"

"Just some guys at school. Look, I don't want to get them involved."

"Involved with what? According to your story, you weren't involved with anything."

"That's right. I mean . . ." He shrugged. "You know."

Rosen stared at Chip, who looked away. Part of the boy's story was probably true—about him not being with Nina. But there was something more.

"What time did you get home?"

"I'm not sure—I was buzzed. I remember checking my watch around eleven. Guess I went home a little after that."

"Nina was probably already dead by then. Did you see or hear anything in the park or on the beach?"

Chip shook his head emphatically. "We were in the ravines, on the other side of my house. I didn't pass the park or beach."

"You didn't happen to see your landscaper, um . . . what's his name? Henry?"

"Hector. Hector Alvarez. No. Why would he be in the neighborhood so late at night?"

Why, Rosen wondered, did Chip know the name of the family landscaper? Maybe it wasn't beer the boy had partied with.

Chip said, "I told you where I was. Like I said, it has nothing to do with whatever happened to Nina. I'd better get back to the game."

Rosen put a hand on the boy's shoulder, which tensed as if struck. "Why did your father say you were in all evening?"

"Do you really have to ask that question? He didn't want our name involved. Bad publicity for his precious company."

"Did you see your parents that evening, either before leaving or when you came home?"

"No. I came in through the back gate and kinda sneaked upstairs into my bedroom."

"Were they home?"

Chip shrugged. "I don't know—the house was dark. Wait, they musta' been. At least one of them, because the TV was on in their bedroom. I remember, because at first I thought it was them arguing. But it was only the TV."

"Do they argue a lot?"

"Isn't that what marriage is all about?"

For a moment their eyes locked, and in that instant Chip became a little boy, frightened and filled with a child's hate.

Rosen said, "I understand that Soldier lives on the premises. Was he at home?"

"How the hell would I know?"

"You didn't see him?"

"No. On my way into the house, I passed his room—he's got these patio doors. The curtains were drawn, and the light was out."

"It seems that Soldier and your mother—"

"Shut up!"

With a muffled sob, Chip ran up the incline into the grandstand. Leaning against a pillar, Rosen tried to imagine what had happened in the park the night Nina died, but instead couldn't stop thinking about Chip sneaking up the darkened stairs of his family's mansion. No hug or greeting; only the television muttering like an argument in the cold silence. What was going on in that house?

"About time," Lucila said, as he sat beside her. "You missed the seventh inning stretch." She rubbed her arms gingerly.

"Cold?"

"I'm okay." Leaning closer, she half whispered, "Did he tell you anything?"

Rosen recounted his conversation with Chip. While he spoke, the students around him grew quiet. For a moment he thought they were eavesdropping.

Then someone shouted from a few rows down, "You think it's funny, man!"

The drunken Latino who'd been mocking the umpires stood and pointed at Bixby. "You been makin' fun of me and my friends!"

Bixby sat very still, a Cheshire grin frozen on his face. The chaperones and students were as quiet, each looking away.

"Hey, man, I'm talkin' to you!" the drunk shouted. "Son of a bitch!"

Lowering his head like a bull, he stumbled up the aisle toward Bixby. His two friends, mumbling to each other, trailed behind.

When Rosen stood, Lucila grabbed his arm. "Let them hurt him. It's the least he deserves."

"I'm thinking about the kids."

She followed him down the aisle to intercept the three men.

He reached the end of Bixby's row first and raised his hands in front of his chest, like a catcher. He'd only have to stall them until security came; of course, he could have a few broken ribs by then.

The drunk cocked his head. "Get outta the way!" He pushed up his sleeves. "Unless you wanna lose a few teeth!"

"Take it easy," Rosen said. "Why don't you go back and enjoy the game."

"Why don't you mind your own fuckin' business!"

151

He shoved Rosen, who took one step back and let the man stumble to his knees.

"Mierda," he muttered, struggling to his feet.

The other two men tried to calm their friend, who pushed them away and let fly a string of curses. Turning to Rosen, he raised his fist.

Lucila stepped between them. The drunk blinked hard, as if she were an apparition. Eyes blazing, she spoke rapidly in Spanish, not letting him reply. The drunk's fist was now a finger pointing at Bixby. She glanced back at the teacher, then said something to the three men, who began laughing.

She whispered to Rosen, "It's all right, but you'd better get Bixby out of here."

"I'm not leaving you alone with—"

"I said it's all right. I told them you're taking him away, among other things. Besides, you said you wanted to see him alone."

Taking the teacher by the arm, Rosen led him past a pair of security guards up toward the exit. Bixby's brown suede jacket was zipped to his throat, like a little boy's, and that's the way he walked—in short, wobbly steps. He wiped his forehead several times, and Rosen smelled the other man's sweat.

"Wh . . . Where are we going?"

The top row, near the exit, was half empty. Rosen pulled Bixby into a seat beside him. He looked up at the scoreboard. It was already the eighth inning. The Cubs were down 2-1.

"You'd better stay here until the game's over, although security will probably throw those men out."

Bixby swallowed hard. "Yes, of course. You don't suppose they might wait outside the stadium?"

"I don't think the man after you can even see the ballpark anymore, and his friends didn't seem interested in causing trouble. Besides, Lucila won't let them get at you."

"Yes, Miss Melendez. Remarkable woman." Unzipping his jacket halfway, he took a deep breath and smiled sheepishly. "I'm still a little on edge. I'm not used to real violence."

"Real violence?"

"I've acted and directed many scenes involving fighting, even murder. But the real thing's something else, isn't it?" When Rosen didn't reply, the teacher continued, "I'm afraid I acted like a real ass."

"Well, you are an actor."

Bixby spurted bits of laughter. "I didn't set a very good example for my students."

"It must be difficult to be a teacher. You're held to higher moral standards than most other professions. Don't you find that so?"

"Oh yes. When I first started, a teacher was expected to be some sort of ascetic monk. Holier than thou."

"Not anymore?"

Bixby giggled, lacing his fingers over his stomach. "I think the media has pointed out the foibles of those we once considered heroes, from athletes to presidents. Made it easier for teachers to show their human side as well."

"Like what?"

"Hmm?"

Rosen leaned closer. "What's your human side?"

"Oh, I don't know. I suppose being a bit irreverent with authority."

"Like with your principal?"

He mimicked Dr. Winslow's voice. "*Uh*, yes."

"Dressing very casual?"

"Yes."

"Clowning around with the kids?"

"Yes."

"And watching sadomasochistic movies on your VCR?"

Bixby's eyes popped wide, and his face turned fish-belly white. He slowly zipped the jacket up to his throat.

Rosen said, "The handcuffs—were they for more than just watching?"

"How . . . ?" The words came in a hoarse whisper. "How did you find out?" He turned his head away, as if not wanting to know.

"Tell me about your relationship with Nina Melendez."

But Bixby wasn't listening. He leaned forward, moaning softly, and gripped Rosen's arm. "I don't mean any harm. I don't hurt

153

them—not really. They can't make me give up everything—twenty years of teaching, because of . . . a hobby."

He spoke with a kind of barroom intimacy. And his hand was on Rosen's arm, the way one friend might touch another.

"I don't mean anything by it. I mean, the girls I pick up . . ." Blinking hard, he stared at Rosen. "You're a lawyer. If I get into trouble, will you represent me?"

Rosen grimaced, a cold clamminess shivering through his body. He didn't know whether to pity Bixby or hit him in the face. Pulling his arm away, he repeated, "Tell me about Nina."

"Nina?" Rubbing his face, the teacher muttered, "I don't want to talk to you anymore. I want to go. I want . . ." The words guttered in his throat, and he began crying.

Rosen shouted Bixby's name, but the crowd suddenly erupted into a roar of cheering, as a home run shot into the left field bleachers. Rosen watched as everyone jumped to his feet. Everyone except Martin Bixby, who couldn't find forgiveness even in Wrigley Field.

Chapter 14

The next twenty-four hours was what his boss, Nahagian, called a "throw-away day." It came whenever an especially tough case was concluded, and a lawyer needed time to get away and just relax. Only this time the case was far from over. In fact, Rosen still wasn't certain a crime had been committed.

He'd spent an hour after the ballgame at Lucila's apartment, arguing over that very point. She'd wanted to corner Bixby and force a confession from him. Rosen had refused, worried that her temper could jeopardize any case against the teacher—if, indeed, there was a case. All that resulted from their argument was that his headache roared back; the long rush-hour drive to the Nahagian condo only made it worse. At six-thirty he lay down for a few minutes' nap. He woke up at nine-fifteen the following morning.

Feeling better, Rosen had a big breakfast at the local deli—thick potato pancakes made with plenty of onion, fried crisp and served with sour cream. Returning to the condo, he called Sarah, only to learn from Shelly that she'd gone to school.

Shelly had added, "Come over for supper around six. It's Thursday—I'm getting Chinese."

Rosen dialed the high school and was told that Bixby had called in sick. There was no answer at his apartment. Lucila wasn't home either. Uneasy at failing to contact either her or the teacher, Rosen took the long walk south through downtown Evanston to Bixby's apartment.

It was like so many of the spring days he remembered as a child—cool even in the warm sun because of the lake breeze.

155

Almost noon; streets were filled with the lunch crowd and mothers strollering their babies before nap time. The fresh air cleared his head, or maybe it was just watching the young mothers with their children that made him feel clean.

The feeling faded quickly as he stood in the courtyard of Bixby's apartment. The window shades were drawn. Was the teacher really ill, or had he crawled into his room to hide? Maybe he'd driven somewhere to dump the videotapes and handcuffs, promising to put such thoughts from his mind forever. But what about the girls he'd mentioned?

Could one of those girls have been Nina? Rosen had asked himself that question over and over. Any other time, he wouldn't have needed Lucila's prodding. Bixby was vulnerable. Just a little more pushing to learn the truth—whatever it was. Yet again Rosen hesitated. Standing within Bixby's courtyard, he finally understood why.

The old people peeking through their curtained windows, and a short, thin woman limping past him, hands clutching her purse, once again reminded Rosen that he was a stranger, an outsider. So too was Bixby. The harder the teacher tried to be one of the kids, the more pathetic he became—as he had at the ballpark yesterday. Nor could he fit in with Kate Ellsworth and her wealthy friends who patronized the arts. He was merely an amusing hanger-on. As for friends or a romantic relationship . . . ? There were those videotapes hidden in his drawer. As much as Rosen wanted to despise Bixby, he pitied him even more. What if, after all, the teacher were a murderer?

The breeze must have stiffened, because Rosen shivered. Turning, he looked up and down Sheridan Road at the line of parked cars; Lucila's beat-up old station wagon wasn't among them. He hoped she'd stayed away. With her temper, seeing Bixby would only make matters worse.

Leaving the courtyard, he kept a steady pace while walking home. By the time he reached the condo, his undershirt was soaked with sweat, but the headache was finally gone. He took a long, hot shower and flipped through the art book that featured some of Lucila's work. At four o'clock, figuring Sarah would be home from school, Rosen drove up to Arbor Shore.

Eva, the Polish housekeeper, answered the door. "Hello, Mr. Rosen. Nobody here."

"Sarah's not home from school?"

"Yes, she come home but go out maybe ten minutes ago."

"Where?"

The woman hesitated.

"Where, Eva?"

"She go over to Ellsworth house. See Nina's mother."

"What?"

"Each day this week she go see Nina's mother. Sarah good girl."

Rosen rubbed his eyes. "I'm going over there to get her. We'll be back in time for supper. Dr. Gold invited me."

Eva said, "I know. Thursday night—Chinese food. What Mrs. Gold calls 'whole megillah.' See you six o'clock sharp."

Again Rosen decided to walk. The Ellsworths lived just a few blocks south, across Sheridan Road. Entering the park, he approached the wooden fence that overlooked the beach where Nina had fallen to her death. The yellow police tape had long ago been removed, as had the gold chain and scattered rose petals. The land had healed, but after all there'd only been a few scuff marks in the grass—hardly a scratch. Even Rosen wasn't quite sure where the girl had fallen.

Some would want to forget—neighbors and the mothers who brought their children to play. But Nina's classmates would remember. They'd keep her death alive, because it gave a spirituality to their carefully crafted, safe suburban neighborhood, just as Native Americans believed the ghosts of their ancestors inhabited the land. Teenagers would whisper about seeing Nina's ghost; the braver ones would make out here at night, nicknaming the cliff something like "Lover's Leap." Years from now, none of them would remember exactly what had happened or who the girl was. None except Sarah.

The gate in the Ellsworths' fence was ajar. Rosen pushed it open and walked inside the estate. He was too close to the house to comprehend its true size, only that it was a two-story Tudor that seemed as high as the Tower of Babel. There was a railed wooden deck attached to an Olympic-size swimming pool, and behind that a gazebo bowered by giant oaks, with one or perhaps two tennis courts in the distance.

In the nearest corner of the house, Rosen saw a set of sliding glass doors. Chip had referred to that as Masaryk's room. The floor-length curtains were drawn. On the same side of the mansion stood an attached one-story coach house.

Knocking on the coach house door, he had to knock louder a second time before it opened.

"Daddy, what're you doing here?"

He kissed Sarah's cheek. "Shelly invited me for supper."

"Oh yeah, it's Thursday—Chinese night."

"Eva told me you were here. I haven't seen much of you lately. You look much better."

She did look better, or maybe Rosen just liked seeing her without any makeup or earrings, wearing the faded Georgetown Bulldog sweatshirt he'd given her last year. For a moment, she seemed once again his little girl. But she stepped back from his embrace, and they both knew after what had occurred over the past few days she would never again be that little girl.

"We have about an hour before dinner," he said. "Let's go back home."

"Okay. I need to say goodbye to Mrs. Melendez."

"Of course. I'd like to pay my respects."

"You won't upset her?"

"What do you mean?"

"You won't ask her any questions. She's still . . . just promise me you won't ask her any questions."

"All right."

On the kitchen wall were an intercom and a telephone. The phone Nina answered the night of her death.

He asked, "Is this phone on a separate line from the main house?"

"Uh huh. I think everybody has their own number, including Chip and Mr. Masaryk. If the Ellsworths need Esther for anything, they use the intercom."

Rosen followed his daughter through a narrow hallway into the first room on the left. This had been Nina's bedroom, from the kitten posters on the wall and the chairful of stuffed animals in the far corner. The white muslin curtains were drawn, and a single candle burning on the dresser under the darkened windows gathered light like a magnet. The light illuminated a photograph of Nina, and a gold cross hung over the frame. Rosen recognized the workmanship of the chain. It was like the one found where the girl had died.

"She was beautiful, my Nina. Como una angelita."

In the dimness he saw Esther Melendez sitting on the bed. She wore an old robe tied loosely at the waist. Her hair was down, splashing over her round shoulders and onto her heavy breasts. No makeup or jewelry, she sat very still with the heart-breaking beauty of the peasant women her sister-in-law painted. Only her eyes, which somehow caught the candlelight, glimmered with their own fire.

Esther sang a lullaby in Spanish. Kneeling beside the bed, Sarah rested her head on the woman's lap. Rosen watched them for a long time and felt the same vague uneasiness as when he'd watched Bixby at the ballgame. Pity and disgust tangling around his throat, making it even harder for him to breathe. He coughed hard, then coughed again until Esther stopped singing.

He said, "We need to be going."

Esther stroked Sarah's hair. "She a good girl, your daughter. Another angel. When Nina was little girl, I brush her hair like this. So soft, so pretty." Again the woman lapsed into a lullaby.

After watching them for a long time, he repeated, "We need to be going."

Esther looked up. "Lucila called me last night. She told me—"

"Let me send Sarah home first. Then we can talk."

As if waking from a dream, his daughter slowly stood. "I'll come by tomorrow after school."

"Vaya con Dios," the woman replied—Go with God.

Rosen walked Sarah to the kitchen door.

"Go on home. I'll be along in a few minutes." When she hesitated, he said, "I promise not to ask any questions."

Sarah nodded, then blurted, "What happened to Nina?"

"I don't know, Shayna."

"There're all sorts of rumors at school, but nobody really knows, do they?"

"Not yet."

"Last year when one of the seniors died from a drug overdose, there were all these counselors coming into our classes. They were so worried how the guy's death would affect the other kids. But nobody's saying anything about Nina—not Dr. Winslow, the teachers, or even the counselors. Only the kids whispering in the halls."

"Whispering what?"

"That's just it. They don't know either. They only say 'maybe'— maybe she got drunk and fell, maybe she was doing drugs and freaked, or maybe she committed suicide. All that talk's crazy, Daddy. Nina wouldn't have done any of those things."

"What does your mother say about this?"

"She doesn't tell me anything. She says the police are calling it an accident, but that's not saying anything. I mean, why was Nina in the park that night? And who called her? I keep wondering—I can't get it out of my head—what happened to her?" When he reached for her, she stepped back, shaking her head hard. "Since Nina died, I haven't seen much of you."

"I didn't think you wanted to see me, and your mother said—"

"I know. I didn't mind really, because Mrs. Melendez said you were investigating Nina's death. I'm glad. I told her you'd find out what happened. I think that's what keeps her going. If it weren't for you . . ." Stopping suddenly, she bit her lower lip.

"What?" Rosen asked.

"Sometimes I'm afraid of the way she can get."

"Because of Nina's death?"

"No . . . yes. I mean even before, she could get kind of angry. If Nina didn't do exactly what she said, she'd . . ." Again Sarah shook her head.

"She'd what?"

"Nothing. Just remember what I said about not getting Mrs. Melendez upset. I'll see you back home."

She let Rosen hug her for a long time, then walked toward the gate, while he turned, carrying the warmth of her embrace back into the dead girl's bedroom. He stood beside the dresser, where the candle burned brightly.

Esther had remained sitting on the bed, but on her lap lay the spiral notebook—Nina's diary. Opening the notebook, she read slowly. In the darkness she could barely see the words; still she read them slowly in her thick accent.

"'After rehearsal, he picked me up on his way home. We went to the park overlooking the beach. His eyes, so stern with everybody else, looked so gentle tonight. We kissed.'" She handed Rosen the open diary. "You finish."

He read silently the rest of the passage. "'He says I'm not a girl to him but a woman. A woman! I think we might make love. Should I tell Sarah?'"

"Why don't you say the words?" Esther asked.

"I know the words. I heard them last week in the principal's office." He handed back the notebook.

Her voice was soft, as if blanketed by the darkness. "It good you remember. I remember too. It hard for me to read English, but I practice. Every day I read over and over and now I know the words without reading them. Like the prayers they teach us in church when I was a little girl. No puedo olvidar—I can't forget. 'He says I'm not a girl to him but a woman. A woman. I think we might make love.'" She laid the diary on the bed. "Lucila said you saw the teacher yesterday. You know he a bad man."

"That doesn't mean he killed your daughter."

"Lucila told me what you found in his apartment—what kind of man he is. Dirty things, and he a teacher. In my country, you know what they do to a man who . . ." She searched for the right words. "Molestador—a man who hurts children. You know what they do to such a man? Cut off his balls, then cut the rest of him into little pieces. That what they should do to this teacher. Don't you think so?" When Rosen didn't reply, she continued, "Look at that face. Una angelita."

He stared at the photograph, but what interested him at that

161

moment was the gold cross hanging over the picture. A small velvet case lay open near the candle. The name inside read "Brissard Jewelers" with a North Michigan Avenue address.

"That's a beautiful necklace," he said. "Was it Nina's?"

She hesitated before answering. "No. A Christmas present last year. For me from the Ellsworths."

"Very expensive. Doesn't Kate Ellsworth have a necklace with the same kind of chain?"

"Yes."

"And isn't the chain like the one found in your daughter's hand?"

"Nina always like my necklace. Sometimes I let her wear it. When the police show me the chain, I thought it was my necklace, but no. Mine was in my room."

"How do you think she got the chain?"

Esther said, "Ask the teacher. Maybe he got it for her."

She leaned forward. Candlelight softened her round face, except where the shadows deepened under her eyes. Her eyes were alive, glowing like embers, and something about them seemed familiar.

He asked, "What about the rose petals found by the cliff? Who do you think gave your daughter roses?"

"The teacher."

"Could she have taken them from the house?"

"I told you—the teacher. I told, I told you. The teacher!"

Her eyes widened, as if some hateful secret stoked the fire behind them. Rosen should've stopped; he'd promised Sarah no questions. But he'd promised something more important—to discover the truth.

"Did Nina have many friends?"

"Sarah was her friend."

"Besides Sarah. Did she have any boyfriends?"

"She was a young girl, too young to think about boys. I don't let her date."

"But the diary . . ." Her eyes made him pause. "I mean, it's natural for any high school girl to think about boys. Chip Ellsworth, for example. He seems like a nice boy, and with you and Nina living on the estate—"

"What are you saying?" She rose to her feet. "What are you saying about my Nina?"

"The necklace and the flowers had to come from somewhere. Then there's the telephone call that night. Who made that call?"

Nostrils flaring, she said, "So you think my daughter was bad? You think she run around chasing men?"

"I didn't mean—"

"I told you what happened. The teacher, he trick her with his lies. The teacher! Lucila tell me you a good lawyer. Why he not in jail?"

"I told you, there's not enough evidence—"

"Maldito!"

Trembling, Esther continued to curse him in Spanish, then stopped abruptly in midsentence. From deep inside a whimper grew steadily into a moan so primal, as if the earth itself were wrenching apart. She sank back onto the bed, but her eyes never left his. Eyes big and dark and burning. Rosen suddenly realized where he'd seen those eyes before—in the painting at Kate Ellsworth's gallery, Lucila's *Flowers of Madness*.

He took a step back into the dark corner, still not able to look away. Then a shadow passed between him and Esther, breaking her spell. He blinked and saw Byron Ellsworth sitting on the bed, his arm around the woman.

"No llores," he whispered to her, gently brushing the hair from her face. "No, no, don't cry."

He held her in a tight embrace, and they rocked together. He kissed her and kept whispering, "No llores. Don't cry."

Gradually Esther quieted. When Ellsworth's hand moved inside the woman's robe to caress her breast, she stiffened and nodded toward the corner. Rosen stepped from the shadows. Ellsworth froze. He started to speak, then checked himself.

Leaving the bedroom, Rosen heard footsteps hurrying after and, as he reached the door, felt a hand on his arm.

Ellsworth was no longer the confident financier sipping a drink and spinning big deals in his office. He seemed older, tired, and his eyes shifted from Rosen's stare.

"I . . . uh. I don't want you to get the wrong idea." When Rosen didn't reply, the other man sighed. "You know how it is. Sometimes things just happen. Kate and I never seemed to be at home together. Esther was always here. She's a beautiful woman."

"Sure. Not like the ones at the country club."

"No, not at all. I know what you're thinking. She's the housekeeper and I'm the boss, and so I took advantage of her. But it's not like that."

"You really care about her."

"Yes, I do."

"And you plan on divorcing your wife, marrying Esther in the Episcopal Church downtown, and living happily ever after, sipping martinis and eating sancocho by the fireplace."

Ellsworth reddened. "You don't understand. Look, all I'm asking is that you don't make things worse. There's no need for anybody else knowing."

"You think no one else knows about your affair?"

"I suppose Kate has her suspicions."

"Suppose?"

"We've never discussed it, but the way she's acted these past few months—I think she suspects something."

"Did Nina know?"

"I'm sure she didn't. We were very discreet. If the girl had found out, Esther would have . . ." Ellsworth shuddered. "No, Nina couldn't have known."

"What about your son?"

For a moment Ellsworth's jaw tightened. "Leave Chip out of this."

"If your wife suspects, then certainly your son—"

"I said, leave him out of this! It's none of your business anyway. You're looking into Nina's death. That has no bearing on my private life."

Rosen stared hard at the other man. "I don't know if your housekeeper would agree."

"Of course. I didn't mean the girl's death was unimportant."

"Why are you so worried about your son? Did he know about

your affair with Esther? Did he think, like father like son? Was he the one who called Nina that night. Met her with flowers and—"

Ellsworth pushed him against the door.

"Shut up," he hissed, his hands balled into fists.

Rosen kept his hands at his sides. He said very slowly, "Go ahead—hit me. Then I'll hit you back, and Esther will walk in on us fighting, and you can explain the reason for the fight."

The color drained from his face. "No, she's suffered enough. She couldn't stand anything else. It's just, why involve the boy? I give you my word he had nothing to do with it. I thought you were looking into that teacher, Martin Bixby. Esther's certain he's the man responsible."

"I thought you believed Nina's death was an accident."

"An accident? Yes, possibly." Ellsworth ran a hand through his hair. "Girl wandering out at night. It's possible."

"Sure," Rosen said, looking past the other man into the darkened house. "Sometimes things just happen."

Chapter 15

Rosen sat with Sarah around the large beige "island" in the middle of the kitchen. Bess took her place between them, setting the brewing teapot on a ceramic hot plate. He followed her gaze to the digital clock on the wall—5:58. When the last number changed to a nine, she poured the tea. Exactly one minute later a car entered the garage, and a door closed loudly.

Shelly walked into the kitchen, juggling four carryout orders, which Bess helped to place on the table.

"Four?" she said.

"We do have a guest. Hi, Nate."

"Hi. I didn't want you going to any trouble."

"No trouble at all."

"Quite a feast. Where'd it come from?"

Staring at each other, Bess and Sarah burst out laughing.

"Well," Shelly said, placing his tea cup at the center of the table, "here's our house in Arbor Shore." He distributed the carryout bags geographically around the cup. "First, on my way home, I stopped at Mah Din—it's a Thai place—for their pad thai. Then Bob Po's, on Green Bay Road, for wonton soup, egg rolls, and sweet sauce. You know, it's a common failure of takeout restaurants not to pay attention to their sweet sauce. Bob Po's is excellent."

"Enough with the dissertation," Bess said, "we're starving."

"Then up to Chin Ho's in Highland Park for shrimp egg foo yung, lo mein noodle combo and combination fried rice. In Nate's honor, I stopped in downtown Arbor Shore at the Lotus Palace. Its

167

only really excellent dish is moo shu, although the plum sauce is a little on the sweet side."

As he finished, Bess and Sarah opened the cartons with assembly-line precision.

"First the soup," Bess said, ladling it into four bowls.

"Then the egg rolls and pad thai," Sarah added, placing them onto four plates.

The next ten minutes were spent enjoying the appetizers; Rosen murmured his approval between bites. Then Shelly carefully served the main courses. Not a noodle fell onto the table.

After sampling each dish, Rosen leaned back in his chair and sipped his tea. "This is really some meal."

Shelly concentrated on rolling his moo shu into a perfect dumpling. Only after folding both ends with his chopsticks did he acknowledge Rosen's compliment.

"Thanks. Guess I've always liked Chinese food."

Bess put a hand on Shelly's arm and smiled. "Next to feet, it's his great passion."

"Don't laugh. You could say it caused my divorce. For me, Thursday's always been Chinese night. Eileen and the boys knew that. So one night, I come home with the goodies, and she says we're going to some 'farchadat' bridge game with her friends. 'No time for Chinese food,' she says, 'we're having finger sandwiches there.' What kind of food is that for a man to eat?"

Rosen said, "I take it you didn't go."

"I told her where she could put her finger sandwiches. She didn't like that. I guess things hadn't been going so good for a long time."

"Sort of the chopstick that broke the camel's back."

Shelly laughed, and so did Sarah. It was the first time since Nina's death that Rosen had seen his daughter happy. Once again he was grateful to Shelly.

"Yeah," Shelly said, "we got a divorce. It's kinda strange at first—you know what I mean. Being on your own."

Rosen nodded.

"At first I threw myself into my work. That's when my podiatric clinics really took off. Within a year I had eight going."

"Nine," Bess said.

"Huh? Oh yeah, the one in Buffalo Grove. Was it like that for you?"

Again Rosen nodded. It was the sort of question he'd always tried to avoid, but coming from Shelly, it didn't sound threatening or even unpleasant. It was the kind of question one friend might ask another. How long had it been since he just kibitzed with a friend?

"Yeah, but . . ." Shelly paused to take a bite of moo shu. "But after awhile a guy gets lonely, so he starts to date."

"Did you go out with many women?"

"Not at first. There was always something wrong with whomever I'd meet. Like this one woman whose car had a bumper sticker, 'I love Baby Shamu.' For Chrissakes, how can you take a person like that seriously?"

Bess wiped his chin with a napkin. "Some playboy."

"Eventually I got the hang of it, once I learned the strategy. You know—never date a widow, because you'll always look bad in comparison to her dead husband. Now, a divorcee's different. You *always* look better than her ex-husband. Jeez, Nate, I didn't mean—"

Rosen smiled. "That's all right."

"I really didn't mean anything."

"It's all right. So, how did you and Bess meet?"

"It was a professional visit—at my office in Highland Park. She came in one day after school with a student—some dancer in a show."

Bess said, "The girl was in tears complaining about her foot. I called her mother, who met us at Shelly's office. The girl had quite a bunion."

"Yeah. Besides the fact that she had a congenital predisposition for bunions, she didn't have enough ligamentous stability. That's a common problem for women athletes. But the girl eventually healed, though not in time for the show."

"No. That caused us quite a time, trying to find a replacement. Eventually Bix convinced one of the senior—"

Bess stopped suddenly, her face reddening as if she'd told a dirty joke. Sarah's face grew as flushed as her mother's, and she looked down at her plate. Shelly made small talk, which Rosen didn't bother to follow. He kept glancing at Sarah, who sat so still she might've been at prayer. Bess got up, returning a minute later with a tray of cookies, which no one touched. No one wanted to stay, yet no one left the table, not even when the doorbell rang. Only when it rang again did Shelly get up.

It was a long time before he returned, and then he said with a sheepish grin, "Look who's here."

"Hello, Nate."

It was his brother.

"Sit down," Shelly said, offering his own chair.

"No, no, I didn't mean to interrupt your supper. Looks like quite a celebration."

"Not at all. Just Chinese night. Here, let me take your coat."

Aaron removed his topcoat with great deliberation. The same way he did everything, as if the most mundane task were a ritual. He wore a gray suit with a red splash of a tie. No matter how expensively tailored, suits never seemed to fit Aaron. Unlike Rosen and their brother David, Aaron had taken after their mother. He had the same stocky build and strong hands—hands that seemed made for laying bricks rather than performing heart surgery. His face was broad like their mother's, eyes set wide apart like an owl's. He had her owlish patience too. What had Shelly once said about him? ". . . like Moses coming down from Sinai."

Sarah walked to him. "Hello, Uncle Aaron."

He smiled and hugged her. "My little Sarah, how quickly you're growing. Just like my Debbie. It's a shame, two cousins about the same age who never see each other. And what, do we live at each end of the world?" He gazed into her face. "How beautiful you've grown. You have your grandmother's eyes. Doesn't she, Nate?"

It was a trick—coming at Rosen through his daughter. Still what could he do but nod?

Still holding Sarah's hand, Aaron sat across from Rosen. "I called here about an hour ago. The housekeeper said you were coming over for supper. I hope you don't mind. It's just that you've been here a week, and I haven't heard from you."

"I've been very busy."

"Yes, that case involving those two boys. I saw it on the news. They say you won an important victory for civil liberties. Something to make the family proud."

"I suppose."

Aaron waited for something more, but Rosen didn't care. His brother could wait until they both wasted away to skeletons, as brittle and fragile as their mother's remains. Let him wait.

Pulling a chair beside Aaron, Shelly said, "And what about you? Head of cardiology, and how old are you—forty-four, forty-five?"

Aaron measured out a small smile. "I feel humble beside you, Shelly. My name's not a household word, or my face a celebrity's. Those commercials of yours are really something. No wonder you have a big house in Arbor Shore."

"Don't tell me you couldn't move up here, if you wanted to."

"I suppose so. I just wouldn't feel comfortable."

"I know what you mean. Once I saw this nature show about lions and hyenas. Hyenas are always hanging around, never daring to attack the strong lions but waiting to get at the weak ones. That's the way I feel about these goyim—some of them. They're nice and polite, but you know what they're saying about you at their little cocktail parties."

"You knew that would happen when you moved here."

Shelly drank his tea, then grimaced as if it had been a shot of bourbon. "Yeah, I knew what to expect, but the hell with them. What did Bogart say to Peter Lorre in *The Maltese Falcon*—'You'll get slapped and like it'? Well, that's what I say to my blue-eyed neighbors."

There was a long moment of silence, then Shelly giggled nervously. "I guess that sounds hard-nosed, but it wasn't easy for a little Jewish guy from the city to make it."

"I understand," Aaron said.

"Do you, Dr. Rosen? I wonder. Podiatry isn't exactly the same as cardiology. People weren't exactly beating down my door to—"

Bess took her husband's arm. "I think it's time for Sarah to do her homework, and I have a few things we need to discuss. It was nice seeing you, Aaron."

"Yes, we really should get together more often, especially with Debbie and Sarah so close in age. I'll have Eileen call you."

Rosen and his brother waited for the others to leave the kitchen. Then Aaron sighed.

"Such a coarse little man. I wonder why Bess . . ." He shrugged.

Rosen's cup was empty. He filled the teapot with cold water, then put it on the stove to boil.

Keeping his back to his brother, he said, "I like Shelly."

"Of course. You always liked that kind."

"What kind?"

"Oh, you know. I guess they could be called 'colorful,' like Uncle Jack always smoking that big black cigar when he came to visit Mama. And he'd dress up in those ridiculous outfits whenever he'd go to the ballgame."

"How do you know? You never went with him."

"You told me. Remember?"

"Sure."

After a few minutes the hot water whistled, and Rosen filled two cups. He dunked a fresh tea bag into Aaron's cup, hesitated a moment for the cup that wasn't there, then did his own. Once again he sat across from his brother, handing him his tea.

"Thanks. You split the tea bag between us. I remember when David and I were studying at the kitchen table, how Mama would pour three cups of hot water, then let you dip the tea bag. What was it—five times for each of us? I remember how serious you looked bringing David and me our tea. So slow you walked, and so serious. Papa walks just as slow now. Yes, you looked just like Papa. Umm, this is good."

Rosen wondered why his brother was here. Not just a social visit; that wasn't like Aaron. Maybe something was wrong with their father. Still, Rosen couldn't bring himself to ask.

"Ever think of the old days?" Aaron asked. "I mean, back when we were growing up?"

"No. Have you heard from David?"

"Poor David. He's still living with that group of militants in the West Bank, or Judea and Samaria, as he calls it. I always send him a check during Hanukkah. He wrote back that real Jews don't give presents at Hanukkah; only ones pretending it's really Christmas."

"Does he return the checks?"

"No, he cashes them. That's what worries me. I suppose he has to eat like everyone else, though sometimes I wonder. I write asking him to come home, but he won't. I should show you his letter. What did he say—'I want nothing more than to spend my days with the Righteous.' Strange. Of course, Papa thinks he's wonderful, a pioneer in the Holy Land. Between you and me, I question David's sanity."

Rosen asked, "Did you ever think that the money you send him might not be for living expenses?"

"What do you mean?"

"That this group of his might be buying more weapons, more bombs?"

"Bombs, no I—"

"Forget what I said. It was a stupid question to ask."

"That's all right."

"Of course you knew."

Aaron's eyes widened, and he slowly rubbed them, rubbed them like an eraser across an ugly mistake. Then, gazing with the soft eyes of their mother, he put a hand over Rosen's.

"We don't have much family. We need to hold onto what little we have."

Rosen felt his hand was a little bird, that he was that little bird slowly being stifled by his his brother's palm.

"Nate?"

"So how are Eileen and the kids?"

"Come to dinner and see for yourself." He paused, his grip tightening. "Why don't you ask about *him*?"

"You'd let me know if anything was wrong."

"You're talking like a lawyer, not a son."

Rosen pulled his hand away. "I'm not his son—remember."

"That was all a long time ago. He's an old man. Each day he gets older."

"I'm not his son."

"I see him once a week, usually Sunday. We visit Mama's grave. He's still in the old neighborhood. You should see how it's changed."

"I was in the old neighborhood last Monday."

Aaron smiled. "Then you saw——"

"No. I was there on business. I ran into old Hyman, the tailor who used to work with . . . Papa." The last word tasted like Passover's bitter herbs. "Hyman didn't recognize me. I asked him about Papa's sons, and he couldn't even remember my name."

"He's an old man—older than Papa." Aaron bent closer and tapped his head. "Papa's not all there. It started a few months ago. We'd be talking, and he'd drift off in midsentence, reminiscing about . . . no, actually speaking about the old days as if they were the present and I was still a boy."

"Like you said, he's an old man."

"He'd have me read biblical passages aloud—his eyes aren't very good anymore. You know what he keeps asking me to read? Genesis 37."

Rosen thought for a moment. "How Joseph's brothers betrayed him?"

"He keeps repeating what Jacob said when he thought his son had been slain by a savage beast: 'I will go down mourning to my son in Sheol.'" Aaron paused; his eyes locked on Rosen's. "He's talking about you, Nate. He won't . . . can't admit he was wrong, but he's talking about you. You were always his favorite. He loved you the most."

"No."

"He still does."

Rosen felt his face grow warm and the blood pulsing in his ears. "Why are you doing this?"

"Because Mama's dead, David's a basket case, and who knows when you'll be back in town? I want to salvage what family I have. For God's sake, don't you think, after all these years, it's a time for healing?"

Aaron reached out, but Rosen batted his hand away.

"Healing? Healing what—your guilt? Papa didn't love me the most—I was his last chance."

"His last chance? For what?"

"For respect. For that godlike respect that comes to a zaddik, a saint. Someone he could never be, because it took more than learning. It took compassion. Who would go with their troubles to a man sharp as flint? So he turned to his sons. Such students of the Torah would make perfect rabbis! And what did you do? Never said yes but never said no, until you moved away and entered medical school. I remember you telling Papa, 'Don't worry—David is so much more serious. He eats the word of God like it was food.' And they say that lawyers have oily tongues."

"It was true. You saw how devout David became. Why he even went to live in the most dangerous area of the Promised Land."

Rosen grimaced. "That was his escape, a bit more literal than yours. He'd rather face the PLO than Papa. He never felt comfortable among people, let alone being their shepherd. So who did that leave?"

"Of us three, you were the best. You had the compassion, as well as the learning. David and I knew it, the same as Papa. Even Mama—"

"Leave her out of this!"

Now Aaron was blushing. He lifted his teacup, then put it down. "You know I never did anything deliberately to hurt you."

"You never did anything. Remember when I showed up at your dorm because I couldn't take him anymore? You got me to leave by promising to talk to Papa, but you never talked to him."

"What could I have said that would've made any difference?"

"And when he threw me out to live with Uncle Jack, how many times did you come to see me?"

"He'd forbidden it."

"Well, hasn't he still forbidden it? And aren't you here now?"

"Don't, Nate. For God's sake, I'm your brother."

"You didn't even tell me Mama was sick. It was Uncle Jack who told me she'd died—not you, brother. When Papa wouldn't let me come to the funeral, what did you do, brother? Oh I know—what could you do?"

Whatever Aaron was about to say died in his throat. Rosen stared into his teacup and saw the three of them as little boys sit-

175

ting at the kitchen table. His father walking behind each boy in turn. Rosen felt his father's hands like talons on his shoulders. He rubbed his eyes, trying to erase an image that wouldn't go away. Maybe Aaron had been right all along—what could he have done?

His brother's chair scraped the floor. "Maybe I'd better go."

Rosen blurted, "How I feel about the family. It's not you—"

"Come over for dinner Saturday night. Bring Sarah. It would mean a lot to me."

"I'll have to let you know. I'm involved in something right now—something having to do with Sarah."

"This little investigation of yours, about that Mexican girl's death?"

"Dominican." Rosen tensed, the way he did before interrogating a hostile witness. "How did you know I was looking into Nina Melendez's death?"

"I've known the Ellsworths for years. Kate's a remarkable woman. She's helped organize dozens of fund-raisers for the hospital. And Byron's a highly respected member of the community."

"I suppose he's made generous contributions to the hospital."

"As a matter of fact, he has. We have one of the best cardiology units in the Midwest, in part because of his corporate donations."

Rosen shook his head. "How did you know I was looking into Nina Melendez's death?"

"I really don't remember. Perhaps Bess mentioned it."

"When did you talk to Bess?"

"As I said, I really don't remember."

"Maybe you heard it from Byron Ellsworth while he was writing out a check to the hospital. That's the real reason why you're here, isn't it?"

"Don't be ridiculous."

"What's it like, trying to run with the hyenas?"

Aaron's lips trembled. He stood and put on his coat.

"Nate, in your own way you're as twisted as David. Won't you come with me to see Papa?"

Rosen gripped the table edge, watching his knuckles whiten. Otherwise, he would've struck his brother in the face.

"Nate?"

"Go back to the hospital, to the hearts you're able to mend."

Aaron's big shoulders gave a slight shrug, the same gesture their mother made to end an argument, and Rosen felt a deep yearning cascade over his anger. He almost spoke his brother's name but held back until Aaron closed the door behind him.

Only then did he whisper, "Aaron."

As if in response, the doorbell rang. Rousing himself, he walked to the door. What would he say to his brother now?

But it wasn't Aaron.

Police Chief Keller stood in the doorway. The porch light glinted off his gray hair as if it were iron. His leather jacket smelled of tobacco, and he nervously fingered the pipe bowl in his right hand.

"Good evening, Mr. Rosen. Glad I caught you here."

"Is it something about Nina Melendez's death?"

"I'm afraid I'm going to have to ask you to come along with me."

"Why?"

The policeman ran his thumb rapidly over the pipe bowl. "I'm afraid there's been another death. I'd rather not talk about it here. We'd better get going." He started down the walk.

"Another death—who?"

Keller turned, and the light seemed to draw all the blood from his face. "Do you know Lucila Melendez?"

Chapter 16

Rosen sat in the passenger seat and, as the squad car pulled away, saw Bess framed in the doorway. He'd barely said good-bye. Arms crossed, she raised her right hand slightly, the way she used to when he'd leave on an out-of-town case, as if half a farewell gesture would make him return sooner. Only now he remembered something else—the way another woman had crossed her arms the first time they'd met.

"Lucila," he whispered.

Craning his neck, Chief Keller watched the Golds' house disappear around a corner. "Lucila Melendez isn't the one who's dead."

"But you said—"

"She's involved, but she isn't the one who died." He paused, shaking his head. "It's Martin Bixby. Sorry for the confusion, but I didn't want to mention Bixby's name in that house. I know he was Mrs. Gold's colleague and your daughter's teacher. I also know how you felt about him. The people in that house have gone through enough. Besides, the last thing we need is more rumors to start flying."

Rosen asked, "What happened?"

"I don't know. Lt. McCarthy of the Evanston Police called about a half hour ago. He asked if I could have you picked up and brought to him for questioning. When I filled him in about Nina Melendez's death, we both thought it best if I drove down too."

"He wanted me 'picked up for questioning'?"

Fumbling in his shirt pocket for his pipe, Keller nervously blew through the pipe stem. "I'm sure it's only a routine part of McCarthy's investigation. He's a very thorough man."

"So are you. How'd you find me so fast?"

"The Evanston police checked the condo where you're staying and found you weren't home. McCarthy gave me your rental's license-plate number. He figured you might be visiting your daughter."

"But how—" Rosen caught himself, but not before Keller gave the answer he expected.

"I guess they know you pretty well from the Denae Tyler case."

The last thing Rosen wanted to do was become involved with the Evanston police—not after he'd embarrassed the department and caused two of its officers to be suspended. Maybe that's why Keller had picked him up, to make sure he'd come.

Rosen asked, "Is this a murder investigation?"

"McCarthy didn't say. I'm sure everything will be explained when we get there."

"Can you at least tell me where we're going?"

"Bixby's apartment. It's down in south Evanston on Sheridan Road. That's where it happened."

"You said Lucila Melendez is involved?"

Keller shrugged. "I'm sure Lt. McCarthy will explain everything."

The policeman concentrated on the drive down Sheridan Road. It was beautiful, the streetlights hanging like a pearl necklace on the black velvet throat of the night. For a moment Rosen thought of Lucila and how a necklace might look against her throat. But then the pearl necklace became one of gold, the one found where Nina had fallen to her death.

Squeezing his eyes shut, Rosen leaned against the armrest, trying to get comfortable. He'd ridden in a few squad cars before, handcuffed and thrown in the back seat for participating in some demonstration or pushing the police too far in an investigation.

In comparison, he rode beside Keller in comfort. Instead of a shotgun, a portable computer rested between them. Still, anyone glimpsing him at that moment might wonder why he was arrested. Might call Bess, might embarrass his daughter. What a fool—to have agreed to ride in the squad car. He hadn't been arrested. Why in the world . . . ?

Of course. He'd heard Lucila's name and followed like a sheep. Was that the real reason why Keller had mentioned her, to get Rosen to follow like a sheep? He glanced at the policeman, who stared straight ahead while chewing thoughtfully on his pipe stem. Sighing softly, Rosen looked past the streetlights deep into the stars. What were his problems compared to the immensity of the universe?

As his rabbi had always said, "If you can't show understanding, at least show patience until you learn."

Now he would be patient, not only until he learned what had happened to Nina, but to Bixby as well.

Twenty minutes later they arrived at Bixby's apartment building. Keller parked a half block down, behind a squad car. Walking past two others with flashing red lights, they made their way through a small group of passersby before turning into the courtyard.

Lights blinked from the apartments on either side as people peeked through their curtains, then drew away before being seen.

"Innocent bystanders," Keller said, shaking his head. "Don't want to get involved. They might as well be stars up in the sky for all they care about their neighbors. Guess maybe that's why I like fishing up in Wisconsin. Stars seem a lot closer. A lot friendlier too."

"Some people say that about God," Rosen replied.

"Huh?"

"That He's as indifferent to us as stars in the sky."

"You sound like a cop talking. Seeing the kind of things I've seen, even in Arbor Shore, kind of tests a man's faith."

"Are you religious?"

Keller stopped to light his pipe and took several puffs. "Me and the Mrs. go to church every Sunday morning. Of course, that's expected of us. Can't say that I feel anything but tired in church. But it's different up in the woods by the lake. I feel God there, in the smell of pine and the silver flash of fish. You know what I'm saying?"

"I wish I did."

Rosen looked up at the apartments, lights blinking like stars as people peeked through their curtains. That afternoon, standing inside the courtyard, he thought he'd seen Bixby's curtains flutter. Had the teacher seen him? Had he been afraid and . . . ?

They reached the entranceway. Keller said a few words to the policewoman on duty, who stepped aside to let them walk up the short flight of stairs. A second police officer guarded the door to Bixby's apartment. Near his head a rectangular patch of wallpaper appeared brighter than the rest. A picture had been removed, the landscape that had hid Bixby's key.

"I'm Chief Keller from Arbor Shore. Here to see Lt. McCarthy."

"Yes, sir, go right in. He's expecting you."

"Is the body still here?"

The policeman yawned. "Oh, no. They carted it away about an hour ago. Not too messy. We're just cleaning up. Be outta here pretty soon." He narrowed his eyes at Rosen. "You look real familiar. Haven't we met?"

Rosen looked away.

Bixby's living room, which had been so tidy only a few hours before, was filled with the haze of cigarette smoke. Styrofoam cups fought the Dunkin' Donut boxes for space on the coffee table, and the polished wooden floors were streaked with dirt and scuff marks. Uniformed police and plainclothesmen mingled in small groups, as if at a faculty party instead of a murder scene. After eyeing the newcomers, they resumed their conversations. Rosen heard his name mentioned a few times.

A yellow strip of tape had been drawn chest-high across the kitchen entrance. No doubt the place where Bixby had died. Following Keller to the tape, Rosen looked into the kitchen. The chair nearest the entrance had been drawn from the table; blood stained the floor beside it. On the table, in front of the chair, lay a plaque—Bixby's Teacher of the Year Award, which had hung on the living room wall. Beside it was an eight by ten framed photograph. It showed a group shot, but from where he stood, Rosen couldn't discern the images. A coffee cup and a plate with burnt bread crust had been pushed to the center of the table. Dark spots speckled all the objects. More blood. A uniformed officer built like a redwood pushed into Rosen, almost making him break the tape.

Instead of apologizing, the policeman looked Rosen up and down. "Watch it. Smart lawyer like you should be careful about evidence. No telling what might go into a court of law. Or who."

"That's worth remembering," Rosen replied. "Why don't you spread the word to your buddies. Some of them need the advice a lot more than I."

Clenching his fists, the policeman whispered hoarsely, "The two cops you suspended were friends of mine. Friends of a lot a' guys here. We're all gonna take real pleasure, if it turns out that you—"

"That's enough, Bruner."

A short, balding man in a corduroy sports coat approached them. His wide mouth and bulging eyes resembled a frog's, eyes that glanced from the policeman to Rosen, as if deciding which were the more appetizing fly. The big cop walked away.

Slowly blinking, the other man shook hands with Keller.

"Hello, Otto. Been awhile."

"Too long. Jim, this is Mr. Rosen."

"Jim McCarthy," the policeman said, extending his hand. "We've never formally met, but I saw you at the Tyler trial. Thanks for coming. Maybe you can clear up a few questions we have. Shall we?"

Like a maitre d', the policeman removed one end of the tape and led the two men into the kitchen.

Keller said, "I assume that everything's already been photographed and dusted for prints."

McCarthy nodded. "This is where the body was discovered. Bixby called in sick this morning but asked a colleague to drop off some papers after school. The teacher came by around four-thirty. Bixby didn't answer the buzzer, but a neighbor let the guy into the building. He knocked on the door but again got no answer. Know how he got in?"

Staring at Rosen, the policeman waited for a reply. When none came, he continued, "Bixby kept a key behind a picture in the hallway outside the front door. Guess all his friends knew about it. Well, the teacher let himself in and found Bixby slumped over in this chair. Dead. One bullet in the right temple."

"Murder?" Rosen asked.

"An old revolver was lying on the floor near Bixby's right hand. One bullet had been fired. Bixby's prints on the handle. We've already received some preliminary information from the medical examiner. Powder burns around the head wound, and traces of powder burns on Bixby's hand."

"So you're saying it was suicide?"

"He died around noon, give or take an hour."

"Was it suicide?"

For a long time, McCarthy's big eyes stared at Rosen without blinking. "We didn't exactly find a suicide note, but maybe a psychiatrist would say these'd do."

He pointed to the table. Bixby's Teacher of the Year plaque and the photograph were dotted with blood, larger droplets than those scattered across the table. The photo contained another red mark, more methodical. Rosen had seen the picture yesterday morning on Bixby's wall: the teacher stood beside Nina; Sarah sat at the piano, with Bixby's hand on her shoulder. A circle had been drawn in red ink around Nina's head.

McCarthy said, "We found a red pen beside the photo. Lifted a partial print belonging to Bixby. When I learned that he taught in Arbor Shore, I called Chief Keller, who filled me in on the death of this girl, Nina Melendez. Chief Keller also told me about the suspicion, held by the dead girl's family, that Bixby murdered her. You're asking me if Bixby committed suicide? What do you think?"

Rosen stared, not at Nina, but at Bixby's hand on Sarah. The man was dead, yet still he didn't know.

Keller said, "It looks like Bixby did murder Nina Melendez—otherwise, why circle her face on the picture? Maybe he was brooding over what he'd done and finally couldn't take it anymore. Either he thought the girl's family would keep after an investigation, or his conscience got too strong. So he took his revolver . . . Do you know if that was his gun?"

McCarthy shook his head. "No record of Bixby owning any handgun, but he could've picked it up on street for a few bucks. Weapon was a piece of crap—could've just as easily blown off his hand. Would've been better for him if it had."

"So he went out and bought the gun, or maybe he already had it. He brooded all morning over his coffee."

"Tea."

"His tea. He takes down his award from the wall, thinks about how he's not only taken a human life, but betrayed a trust and destroyed his reputation. I guess a teacher's like a cop—nothing's more important than your reputation. He can't bring himself to write a confession, so he takes down the photograph with the girl's picture, circles it, then kills himself. That how you figure it, Jim?"

McCarthy rubbed his jaw. "Could've happened that way. The way you lay it out makes sense. One thing, though."

"What?"

"On the phone, you told me you had no evidence linking Bixby to the crime."

"No, that's true."

"Then why would he commit suicide?"

Keller took a deep draw on his pipe. "Like I said—maybe his conscience was getting to him?"

"Maybe, but it takes a pretty powerful conscience to make a man blow his brains out." McCarthy returned his gaze to Rosen. "Do you have any ideas?"

Rosen shook his head, a lawyer's reflex, but again remembered earlier that afternoon when he thought Bixby's curtains had fluttered. The conversation they'd had at the ballpark yesterday. Rosen had discovered the other man's pornographic fantasies and had guessed there was even more. Seeing Rosen walking up the courtyard—had that been enough to frighten the teacher into taking his own life? Was Rosen responsible for Bixby's death?

"Sure you have no ideas?" the policeman repeated.

"Why are you asking me?"

"According to Chief Keller, you've been pushing him to investigate Nina Melendez's death as much as her own family has. Besides . . ." Again he pointed to the photograph. "Your daughter was the dead girl's best friend. Isn't that her at the piano? The one Bixby has his hand on?"

Rosen nodded.

"And you still can't think of—"

"No."

The policeman nodded, more a twitch of the head. "This way, please."

They followed him back into the living room, through the hallway and into Bixby's bedroom. Lucila stood near the closet. Her jacket unbuttoned, she wore a baggy white sweatshirt and faded jeans, both stained with paint blotches of a dozen colors. So too was the scarf under which her hair had been tucked. Her arms were folded, but not in defiance. She held herself to keep from shivering, and her eyes were those of a frightened animal, shifting from one man to another.

"Of course you both know Ms. Melendez," McCarthy said. "I called her apartment, and she was kind enough to come right over. Very civic-minded."

McCarthy stared at Lucila, who looked away while rubbing her arms. What kind of game was the cop playing? Rosen kept quiet, waiting for the policeman to continue.

"You haven't noticed?" McCarthy asked, still watching Lucila. "On the bed?"

It was all there, neatly arranged on the bedspread. The whip and handcuffs, the two dozen videotapes.

He said to Rosen, "The deceased had some strange habits. Well, maybe in this day and age, not so strange. We've run through a few of the videotapes on his machine here. Pretty strong stuff—leather and bondage. Some of the women aren't much more than girls, probably the age of the dead girl. And your daughter." He shook his head sadly. "I asked you and Miss Melendez here to help figure out what happened to Bixby."

"You've already determined it was suicide," Rosen said.

"Does seem that way. Tell me, did either of you know about Bixby's interest in this kind of sleaze?"

"I'd rather not say."

"Well, at least you didn't lie. Do you know that both of your fingerprints are on file back East? What was it . . . uh, Mr. Rosen arrested for an abortion rights demonstration and Miss Melendez for some civil rights marches down South? No, I believe it was the other way around. Anyway, we found both your fingerprints all over this apartment and, I mean, all over. Living room, kitchen . . . well, just Miss Melendez's there, and in here. Closet, dresser drawers. It looks to me like you both were searching the place. What for—proof that Bixby was a pervert and maybe a murderer? Well, Miss Melendez?"

Trembling, Lucila was about to reply. Rosen shook his head to silence her.

McCarthy sighed, then nodded to a policeman standing in the doorway. The policeman left the room and, a few minutes later, returned with a short woman about sixty. A green turtleneck sweater hung loosely on her thin frame. Something about the woman seemed familiar. It was only when she stepped forward with a slight limp that Rosen recognized her. That same instant he knew the real reason why McCarthy had him picked up, the thought gripping him like a cold hand on his shoulder.

McCarthy said, "This is Mrs. Tonelli from upstairs. She went shopping today a little before noon. Bumped into a man standing in the courtyard. Mrs. Tonelli, do you recognize that man?"

The woman looked back at the policeman who'd brought her as if she needed his protection. Then she nodded and pointed at Rosen.

"He's the one."

"You're sure?"

"Yes, sir. He was just standing there, looking at the door I'd just come out of."

"The door that leads up to this apartment."

"Yes, sir."

"Thank you. We appreciate your cooperation. Officer Berens will take you back to your apartment."

The woman left the bedroom, while McCarthy stared at Rosen and waited. Rosen had to give some explanation, but what? How ridiculous the truth would sound—he'd just gone for a walk and stood in the courtyard for a few minutes before returning home. He had no alibi during the time Bixby had died. Quite the contrary; an eyewitness had just placed him a few steps from the dead man's apartment. Then add his fingerprints all over the apartment. If Bixby's death wasn't suicide, Rosen was the prime suspect.

Tired of waiting, the policeman turned his attention to Lucila.

"What goes for Mr. Rosen may also go for you, Miss Melendez. You've admitted having no alibi for the time of Bixby's death."

She looked down at the floor. "I told you. I was working in my studio all day."

"And you were alone."

"Of course I was alone. I was working."

Rosen remembered calling her just before taking his walk to Bixby's condo. If she'd been home, why hadn't she answered the phone?

The policeman asked, "Can you explain your fingerprints being all over the apartment?"

Again Rosen cut her off. "I thought you'd come to the conclusion that Bixby's death was suicide."

"Loose ends, Rosen. They're bugging the hell outta me. You two don't want to talk. Fine. Let's go down to the station. We like nothing better than having a lawyer call his lawyer."

"No," Lucila blurted. "We did search Bixby's apartment, but not today. We came yesterday morning."

The policeman asked, "How'd you get in?"

"The key behind the picture."

"You knew about the key?"

"I was here before with Kate Ellsworth. Bixby and I talked about a theatrical project he was working on. He asked me to drop off some costume sketches. So we weren't really breaking in."

"Weren't you? Did Bixby also ask you to go through all his personal belongings?"

"No. It was like you said. We were looking for something to prove Bixby killed my niece. It was all my idea. Nate . . . Mr. Rosen just came along. But this happened yesterday, I swear."

"Did you find a revolver?"

She shook her head.

McCarthy's wide mouth broke into a self-satisfied smile, as if she and Rosen were flies and the policeman had swallowed them both.

"All that's very interesting. You know, Rosen, if the police had done the same as you, entering and searching this apartment without a warrant, a lawyer like you'd be all over us. Isn't that what happened in the Denae Tyler case?"

Feeling his cheeks burning, Rosen swallowed hard. "You heard what Ms. Melendez said. Bixby had given her permission to—"

"Of course. After all, we have her word for that."

"You can check with Kate Ellsworth."

"Oh, we will. Of course, even if Mrs. Ellsworth substantiates what Miss Melendez has said, you two still can't prove you entered the apartment yesterday and not today."

Rosen almost replied that it was the police's job to prove the opposite, but didn't want to goad McCarthy into arresting them.

Instead he asked, "Do you intend to charge either Ms. Melendez or me with a crime?"

Still smiling, the policeman replied, "I like the way you say that, like you've had lots of practice. No, you're both free to go for now. I only gather the evidence. We'll see what the medical examiner's final report says. Who knows, maybe more evidence will turn up. Did Martin Bixby kill himself, or was he murdered? Interesting, huh? Don't worry—I'll keep in touch with both of you."

Keller thumbed his pipe bowl. "Uh, come on, Mr. Rosen. I'll drive you back to your car."

Rosen's eyes locked on Lucila's. She said, "That's all right. I'll take him."

"Very neighborly," McCarthy said. "Gives you both a chance to get your stories straight."

Taking Lucila's arm, Rosen led her from the bedroom and through the gauntlet of policemen's stares. He walked quickly into the courtyard, kept walking even when Lucila struggled against him.

She twisted away and rubbed her arm. "You hurt me."

Hands balled into fists, he looked up at the apartments, at the people hiding behind their curtains, inscrutable as stars in the heavens. He was angry at Lucila for breaking down before McCarthy, angry at McCarthy for his veiled accusations, angry at Bixby for dying without revealing the truth about Nina.

Most of all, Rosen was angry with himself. Had the curtain fluttered this afternoon? Had Bixby, seeing Rosen coming like an avenging angel toward him, panicked and committed suicide? If so, then Rosen wasn't merely Bixby's prosecutor, but his executioner as well. A man's blood was on his hands. A man he'd tried to hate but who was, after all, like him, made in God's image.

Chapter 17

"Where are you going? Nate!"

Rosen stopped at the end of the courtyard and waited for Lucila to catch up.

She stopped a few feet from him. "I told you I'd drive you home."

"Maybe I'd better walk. It's not much more than a mile, and I think we'd be better off if—"

"Please."

Her eyes shimmered behind a well of tears—dark eyes growing darker. He wanted to put his arms around her to stop the trembling, but was afraid that would only make things worse. He waited for her to take a deep breath, the air shuddering in her lungs.

"All right," he said.

Passing a knot of hangers-on and the police cars with their flashing lights, they continued a half block up Sheridan, crossing the street to Lucila's old brown station wagon.

As Rosen opened the passenger door, he noticed that the edge of the right front bumper had buckled.

"Did you have an accident?"

"What?"

"Over here."

She walked around the car and looked at the dented bumper.

"You didn't know?" he asked.

Not saying a word, she continued to stare at the bumper. Then the tears rolled down her flushed cheeks. Shaking uncontrollably, Lucila kicked the tire.

"Damn! That's all I need! Damn, damn, damn!"

This time Rosen did hold her, letting her sob into his shoulder, feeling her hot forehead against his cheek. She cried like little girls do, bridling against him, her hands sometimes clutching, sometimes beating on his chest. A few strands of hair, loosened from under her scarf, brushed across his cheek. Smoothing them back, inhaling the fragrance of her shampoo, he felt his heartbeat quicken and her sobs echo in his ears. His hands tightened on her back.

After a few minutes, Lucila's crying settled into a soft seesawing against his chest. Hesitating, she stepped away from him, then took another minute to regain her composure. He handed her his handkerchief.

Drying her eyes, she said, "I'm sorry. That was real stupid of me."

"Forget it." Taking the car keys from her hand, he opened the passenger door. "This time you'd better let me drive."

Traffic crept up Sheridan Road and continued to move slowly when he cut over to Chicago Avenue.

"What time is it?" he asked.

Lucila checked her watch. "Almost eight-thirty."

"Feels more like midnight, doesn't it?"

She closed her eyes. "God, yes."

She almost looked asleep, her breasts softly rising and falling, and her lips parted as if they'd just been kissed. Passing the Nahagians' condo, Rosen turned right and pulled into a space along the perimeter of the park.

"Lucila?"

Her eyes fluttered open.

"Like to come upstairs for a cup of coffee?"

Nodding, she let him take her arm, and they walked through the park, not unlike the other couples strolling by. A pair of teenagers sat together on the swings; leaning toward one another, they kissed. The sky was as clear as it had been earlier that evening.

Watching the stars wink back at him, Rosen remembered what Keller had called them—"innocent bystanders," indifferent to the actions of those on whom they shone. Too cold a thought for such a beautiful night, with him walking beside such a beautiful woman.

When Lucila also looked up at the stars, he remembered something else.

"What was that poem you recited for your niece in church? Something about the stars."

She stopped, and her eyes slowly widened.

"'Sleep, my little one,
sleep and smile,
for the night-watch of stars
rocks you awhile.

Sleep, my little one,
sleep and smile,
For God in the shade
rocks you awhile.'"

Lucila spoke the last words very softly and, for a moment, seemed about to cry again. But she cleared her throat and tossed back her head.

"Yes. Now, my little one, you can sleep. You can finally sleep."

Inside the condo, Rosen took Lucila's jacket and noticed a small rip on the left shoulder seam of her sweatshirt. As she moved, a bit of her soft brown skin played peek-a-boo through the hole, as if daring him to touch it. She walked past him into the living room and suddenly stopped.

"I've been here before. Who owns this place?"

"The Nahagians. He's my boss's brother."

"Of course—Ana Nahagian. She's on the board of the Art Institute and a good friend of Kate's. She's a real enthusiast for Latin American art . . . well, that's pretty obvious." Lucila studied the paintings on the wall.

"I'm afraid I lied to you," Rosen said.

"Hmm?"

"I asked you up for coffee, but there's only instant. None of that espresso you brew in a sock."

"You mean colador. That's all right. Tonight I'm your guest, so I'll have some tea."

Rosen walked through the hallway into the kitchen and put on the kettle. While the water heated, he stepped out and called, "What kind of tea would you like! I've got regular and some herbal that's decaf!"

"I'll split a bag of whatever you're having!"

After filling the cups, he took out a Lipton tea bag and started to dunk it, just as a little boy he'd done for his brothers. He let it steep, watching the dark tea ooze from the bag through the water. Aaron was like that—smooth and patient and inexorable. Again he heard his brother's voice, "What could I have said?" Aaron the doctor, the good husband and doting father, the eldest son, who'd gained his father's blessing. As the Patriarch Isaac had said to his son, "Be master over your brothers. . . . Cursed be they who curse you, Blessed they who bless you."

Taking out the bag to brew the second cup, Rosen wondered again why his brother had visited him earlier that evening. Was it to be the elder brother, loving and forgiving as Esau had been after Jacob's years of wandering? Or was he just another lackey for Ellsworth-Leary? Rosen remembered what Jacob had said to his brother after having been away for so many years: " . . . to see your face is like seeing the face of God. . . . "

"Oh, Aaron," he whispered, then, blinking hard, carried the teacups into the living room.

Lucila stood by the bookshelves, admiring the statuettes and other pieces of art. "It's like being in a museum. I'd forgotten how beautiful they are."

Handing her a cup of tea, he took a book from the shelf. "Let's sit on the couch."

He laid the book on the coffee table and turned the pages. "*Daughters of Frida Kahlo: Art of the Latin American Woman*. A very interesting book."

"She was quite a woman." Lucila turned to examples of Kahlo's paintings. "Her art showed the same simplicity, the same strength as that of her husband, Diego Rivera. But she was much stronger than him. I guess she had to be, to survive as an artist. You can sense that strength in her paintings. Do you see?"

Rosen turned to the double-page spread of Lucila's work. "Kahlo isn't the only woman with that kind of strength. Personally, I like these Melendezes."

Lucila tried to stifle a smile. "Some of my earlier work, first ever featured in an art book. Do you really like them?"

"Yes."

She clicked her tongue. "What could you say besides yes?"

"They're very moving, especially this one." He pointed to the painting of a pregnant woman being crucified. "The woman looks just like your sister-in-law, Esther."

"Uh huh. I've become a little less dogmatic, but back then I was so angry at how motherhood became a prison for Latin American women. Esther had been so good to my brother, but he was cheating on her even while she carried his child."

"Nina?"

Nodding, Lucila tried to speak, but her voice broke. She rubbed her eyes hard.

"Pobrecitas"—poor little ones.

Rosen handed her the teacup. It trembled in her hands as she sipped.

She said, "Sorry for the way I've been acting. I know you didn't want me to say anything to the police about our having been in Bixby's apartment. Guess I kind of fell apart."

"That's all right—our fingerprints were all over the place. Besides, you were trying to cover for me."

"I wish I was that noble. You don't know how afraid I am of police."

"I find that pretty hard to believe. McCarthy said you'd been arrested for some pro-choice marches."

"That was out in the open, with hundreds of other demonstrators and the TV cameras rolling. The arrest was just procedure. We were released almost as soon as we walked into the station. But tonight." She shivered.

"Did they threaten you?"

She shook her head. "You don't understand. You couldn't, growing up in America. As a little girl in my country, I heard so many stories about the dictator Trujillo—the anonymous phone calls at night, then the knock on the door and the people who disappeared, fed to the sharks in Santo Domingo harbor."

"That was a long time ago."

"When you lose two uncles like that, you never forget. When Lt. McCarthy called and said he'd send a car for me, I panicked. It took me several minutes just to agree to drive over by myself. Guess I was kind of a basket case."

Rosen drank his tea. Over the rim of his cup, he saw Lucila's glance dart away as she chewed on her lower lip.

He said, "That's not the only reason you acted the way you did."

"No, it's not. Guess I just couldn't believe it was finally over. Didn't want to believe. Crazy, isn't it?"

"Didn't want to believe what was over?"

"Our going after Bixby. I loved Nina so much, it seemed that as long as we were hunting Bixby, she was still with me. I don't have much family, and Nina was like my child. It gets so lonely. I don't know what I'm going to do."

She put her teacup down and stared into Rosen's eyes. "We're taught that hating is wrong, yet hating Bixby kept Nina alive for me a little bit longer. Was it bad for me to hate him so much?"

"I don't know. There's a story in Genesis about a man named Shechem raping Jacob's only daughter. Even though the man loved and wanted to marry her, Jacob's sons slew not only Shechem but all the men of his tribe. By comparison, your hate is very small."

Lucila's dark eyes, so deep he could drown in them. Again he smelled the simple fragrance of her hair and saw the softness of her shoulder through the torn sweatshirt. He felt a little drunk and, though she said something, couldn't hear it. All he wanted to do was touch that bare spot of shoulder. He moved toward her.

"Careful."

He blinked hard.

"You're spilling your tea."

Setting his cup down beside hers, he rubbed his eyes. "You were saying something?"

"Just strange, your bringing up a story about rape and murder.

Never mind. Esther and I owe you a lot. You said you'd help us, and you did. Now I guess it's time we start putting all this behind us."

Lucila touched his arm, almost brushing the bare spot of her shoulder against him. Her lips parted, about to smile—about to kiss him? Rosen wanted to kiss her. He was as lonely as she. Easy to put an arm around her, to draw her close. Why not forget about everything else? It all could end so easily. It already had.

He shook his head. Something wasn't right. Besides, he owed more to Sarah and to the girl who'd been her best friend.

"Are you sure Bixby killed Nina?"

She cocked her head. "What?"

"Are you sure—"

Of course I'm sure. A pervert like him. And look at the way he died. How can you ask such a thing?"

"When we searched his apartment yesterday, we didn't find a gun."

"McCarthy said he might've bought it last night."

"It's not so easy for someone like a teacher to go into the streets and just buy a gun."

"Maybe he had it in his car all along."

Rosen shrugged. "Maybe. The real question is, why would Bixby kill himself? There was no evidence connecting him to Nina's murder."

"But we were pressuring him."

"There were only a couple months left in the school year. He could've resigned and gone away. That's a lot less drastic than committing suicide."

Lucila pulled at her hands. "His conscience. He just couldn't live with what he did."

"Pretty inconsistent. On the one hand you think he's a sick pervert, and on the other so very sensitive."

"You're just confusing things with . . . just your lawyer talk."

"Am I? Why wasn't there a suicide note?"

"You saw the photograph—the red circle around Nina."

"Anyone can draw a circle around a photograph."

Her eyes narrowed. "What are you saying?"

"Besides, there're some things that bother me about the physical evidence."

"What are you saying?"

He moved close enough to kiss her but instead asked, "Have you seen your sister-in-law today?"

"No—why?"

"I saw Esther late this afternoon, at her place. We had a long conversation. She strikes me as being unstable."

Lucila raised her eyebrows in mock surprise. "Unstable—God, what a revelation. After her daughter's been murdered, you find Esther unstable. How would you have felt, if it'd been Sarah?"

"You know it's more than that." He nodded toward the art book. "Esther's been the subject of more paintings than this."

"What're you talking about?"

"The painting in Kate Ellsworth's gallery—*The Flowers of Madness*."

"Stop it!"

"It wasn't chance that made her your subject for a madwoman. There's something wrong with her, isn't there?"

Lucila's eyes flashed as she grabbed his arm. "Now you're the one who's inconsistent. How can my sister-in-law be so crazy and yet so coolly plan a murder to look like suicide?"

He looked away for a moment. They both knew Lucila was right, just as they both knew what his next question would be.

"Where were you today?"

"You heard me tell McCarthy I was working in my studio all day."

"No answer this morning, when I called you."

"I never answer the phone when I'm working. It breaks my concentration."

"You answered McCarthy's call."

Her nails dug into his arm. "The phone kept ringing every five minutes."

"So that particular call—"

"What're you saying? That Esther and I drove over to Bixby's apartment today? That we brought a gun, forced him to put the barrel against his head and pull the trigger? That we circled Nina's picture and did everything else to make it look like suicide?" Lucila's voice softened, and her breath felt warm against his cheek. "Is that what you really think?"

He shook his head hard, not in answer to her question, but to stop the blood pounding in his ears. "I think your sister-in-law's capable of killing Bixby. You once said if it weren't for me looking into Nina's death, Esther might—"

"I'm not talking about Esther. I'm talking about me." She pointed her right index finger like a gun against his temple. "Do you think I could've killed Bixby?"

"I think you loved your niece very much."

She pressed harder against his throbbing forehead. "Do you think I'm a killer? Do you!"

Twisting her wrist, Rosen pulled her close. His other hand gripped her shoulder, the bare spot where her sweatshirt was torn. The more Lucila struggled to free herself, the tighter he held her, and when she turned toward him, he kissed her hard, as he'd wanted to do for so long. He wouldn't let her go, wouldn't give himself a chance to think, just kissed her and then forgot everything else when her hands went around the back of his neck.

She drew him onto the couch and, arching her back as his hands crept under the sweatshirt, fell to the wooden floor while dragging him with her. She let him pull off her sweatshirt and held him tightly while he kissed her neck and heavy breasts.

Her hands running through his hair, she murmured something in Spanish, something that sounded like kisses. He tried to lift her back onto the couch, but she wouldn't let him, nor did she let him push away the coffee table that restricted their movements. She pulled off her scarf, and the fragrance of her hair overpowered him. And so they struggled with each other's clothing in a space no bigger than a coffin, and when he finally entered her, they sweated and moaned and gasped for breath as if sharing a coffin. One he'd never want to leave.

Sometime later, she led him by the hand into the bedroom and, throwing off the blanket, made love to him again. She was slow and deliberate, as if every touch, every kiss intended to erase any thought that dared wander from her. Afterward, she curled against him and fell asleep.

The bedroom was dimly lit by the hallway, its light feathering over the soft curves of her hips and shoulders and over her long legs stretched against his. Her scent was on him; with each breath he inhaled it and grew excited again, more excited than he'd ever been with Bess. He wanted to wake her, to once again . . .

Shaking his head, Rosen drew the blanket over their bodies, naked as Adam and Eve. No, not quite. When Adam had tasted the forbidden fruit, at least he'd gained knowledge. "Then the eyes of both of them were opened."

With Lucila it had been the opposite. She'd made love so that Rosen would forget. But her body, perfect as it was, wasn't enough. He hadn't forgotten, and he still had to know.

Chapter 18

The clock on the night table read "8:32," and light spilled like sugar between the vertical blinds. Rosen began to smile, thinking of a dream he'd had that night. Turning, he realized he hadn't been dreaming, for Lucila lay beside him, dark strands of her hair tangled like a silken web across the pillow. How beautiful she looked asleep.

Since his divorce, he'd made love a few times but never spent the whole night with a woman. Somehow falling asleep together made them closer than having sex; the unspoken trust more intimate because it needn't be spoken. He imagined her body under the covers, but even more was captivated by her soft breathing, which made the silken hair on her pillow tremble. At that moment he'd do anything to protect her. Would he have felt that way about any woman lying beside him, or was he falling in love with her? God, he hoped not; that would only make things worse.

Slipping from bed, Rosen gathered a clean set of clothes and walked through the hallway into the bathroom. He hesitated before turning on the shower, letting her scent linger on him a few more moments.

"Idiot," he whispered, then turned on the water full blast.

Twenty minutes later he sat at the kitchen table, drinking tea, eating a bagel, and listening to the all-news radio station. It was the lead story under local news:

"We have more information concerning the death of Martin Bixby in his south Evanston apartment. Police are now saying that the popular thirty-nine-year-old drama teacher, from Arbor Shore High School, may have committed suicide. However, Lt. James McCarthy of the Evanston Police cautions that his investigation is continuing. Otto Keller, Police Chief of Arbor Shore, who visited the victim's apartment last night, refused to comment on whether Bixby's death might in some way be connected with the death last week of Arbor Shore student Nina Melendez."

Rosen wondered how Sarah was taking the news of Bixby's death. If she knew anything about his relationship with Nina, if he'd made advances toward Sarah, maybe she'd finally open up.

He called Shelly's house, but there was no answer. It was 9:15; Sarah and Bess were probably in school. He'd stop by later in the afternoon to see his daughter and pick up his car. There was something he could do in the meantime. He dialed the number.

"Hermes Communications." The voice, deeper and slower, wasn't that of Elgin Hermes' daughter-in-law Sherry.

"Good morning. I'd like to speak to Mr. Hermes."

"Who shall I say is calling?"

"Nate Rosen."

After a long moment, the secretary said, "Sorry to keep you waiting, Mr. Rosen. It seems that Mr. Hermes is out of the building. He'll be gone all day."

"Can you tell me where I might reach him? This is very important."

"I'm afraid not. He didn't leave his schedule with me. However, I will leave a message that you called."

"Sure. Where's Sherry?"

The woman hesitated. "She . . . uh . . . she's home sick today."

"Is Mr. Hermes' son Jason in?"

"He's with his father. I'll tell Mr. Hermes you called. Good-bye."

Rosen squeezed the receiver in his hand, as if that might force the truth from it. It was obvious that the publisher, who'd been so friendly, who'd even offered Rosen a job, not only wanted to avoid him, but wanted Rosen to know he was avoiding him. Could that also have something to do with Bixby's death?

"Morning."

Lucila walked into the kitchen. She had showered and dressed and was toweling her wet hair.

She asked, "You don't have a blow dryer?"

"I don't think so. I'll look in the hall closet."

"That's all right, I'm almost done. I never sleep so late. What's for breakfast?"

"There's tea."

"Of course."

"And cereal. I have bread for toast, or bagels."

"Bagels—that would be good. Cream cheese?"

"In the refrigerator. Here, let me."

"I can help myself."

Polite chatting, more like the conversation between acquaintances than lovers. Were they lovers? Coming into the kitchen, she hadn't kissed him or even smiled shyly to acknowledge what had happened between them last night. Maybe for her a moment of weakness, an embarrassment she was trying to forget. Or worse, something she did so often, it wasn't worth a second thought.

Tucking the towel like a turban around her head, Lucila made herself breakfast, then joined Rosen at the table. Her face was beautiful; freshly scrubbed and without makeup, she looked like a teenager. She looked like Nina.

She nodded toward the radio. "Any news about Bixby?"

"The police are leaning toward suicide, but the investigation's not closed."

"Suicide. So that's that."

"The report also indicated there may be a connection between Bixby's death and that of your niece."

She chewed the bagel thoughtfully. "Did the radio mention you or me?"

"No."

"Good. Why don't we drive up to Arbor Shore? You need to pick up your car, and I'd better see Esther. Besides, she'll want to thank you for all your help. With Bixby dead, she can begin to put Nina's death behind her."

Lucila spoke casually, as if their disagreement over Bixby's death hadn't taken place last night, or that it had been resolved in bed. Rosen didn't want another argument, but he also wanted her to know that, for him at least, it wasn't over.

He said, "I need to go downtown. You can drop me at the "L" station on your way to see Esther."

"Your business—it can't wait? I'm sure Esther would like to hear from you what happened to Bixby."

Lucila was giving him one last chance. What would they do after seeing her sister-in-law? Go out to dinner, then back to her place to make love? Or would that too be over?

He shook his head. "It really can't wait."

They finished their breakfast in silence. Afterward, as he was washing the dishes, she stood beside him and dried them. How often he and Bess had done the dishes just like this. No need to speak, just being together had been enough. He almost sighed, feeling a greater longing than he'd had last night.

Lucila left the kitchen, and a few minutes later returned with her long hair, brushed to a luster, once again gathered by the red scarf. They put on their jackets, and he followed her out the door.

Five minutes later she stopped her car across from the Davis Street "L." Rosen might have been any commuter being dropped off by his wife. Bess used to drop him off like this, a quick kiss before hurrying to catch the train. Should he kiss Lucila, or at least say something about seeing her later?

"Thanks," he said and walked across the street.

He rode the "L" to Grand Avenue, the last exit before the Loop, and walked three blocks east to Michigan Avenue. It was another clear day, in the upper fifties. Leaning into the wind that sliced off Lake Michigan, Rosen zipped the jacket to his throat and wished he'd also worn a sweater.

He turned north to walk briskly up Michigan Avenue. The stores and upscale boutiques were filled with shoppers, whose bags thumped against their bodies like battered flags in the wind. Just across Ontario he pushed open the door to Brissard Jewelers. An electric chime tinkled "Diamonds Are a Girl's Best Friend."

The store was shaped like a box, with cream-colored walls and plush carpeting the color of pewter. One long glass-enclosed counter, shaped like a boomerang, occupied three of the corners. A variety of jewelry was displayed in the cases, as well as on the ear-lobes and swanlike necks of black velvet busts. Several chains were crafted with the same twisted strands of gold as the one found in Nina's hand and the one he'd seen in Esther's room.

Two salesladies, one old and one young, were dressed identical-ly—a white-embroidered blouse and long black skirt. Each wore earrings, a necklace, and a ring like those in the display case. The younger woman was helping a businessman in a crisp blue suit select an engagement ring.

"Such simple elegance will always be fashionable," she said, while the man smiled in agreement.

The older woman waddled along the opposite side of the counter to where Rosen was standing. Her back curved slightly, making her lean forward like a goose.

"May I help you, sir?"

"I hope so. I'm thinking of getting my daughter a necklace for her birthday."

"Very wise. So many parents these days settle for Nintendo games. How long do *they* last? But jewelry—not only a gift but also an investment." She swept her hand over the glass. "Do you have any particular necklace in mind? I'd be happy to make several sug-gestions that would please a young lady."

"Actually, I wanted something like the necklace worn by a friend of mine. Esther Melendez."

"Melendez . . . no, I don't believe I know that name. We've done business with a Mr. Martinez from the Spanish consulate."

"The necklace was purchased for her by Mr. and Mrs. Byron Ellsworth."

Her eyes widened. "Oh, Mr. Ellsworth. He and his corporation are one of our most important clients."

"His corporation?"

"Why yes. Ellsworth-Leary often purchases gifts for its cus-tomers. Individuals in the corporation buy presents as well."

"Which are charged to the corporation's account?"

"I'm sure it's just for billing purposes."

The color rose in her pale cheeks like claret filling crystal. They both knew what was really going on—executives buying presents for their mistresses through the corporation, so that their private charge cards wouldn't show evidence of the purchase.

She cleared her throat. "I really shouldn't be—"

"Of course. Just idle curiosity on my part. If you could look up the type of necklace Mr. Ellsworth purchased for Mrs. Melendez."

Again the color rushed to her cheeks.

"It was a Christmas present from Mr. *and* Mrs. Ellsworth."

"Oh, I see. Of course. One moment please."

She waddled to the middle of the counter and returned with a leather-bound ledger. She turned the pages slowly.

"The order would probably have been placed in late November. Here we are. Oh yes, a beautiful piece from our DeLiani line. Tuscan craftsmen, really superb artists. Like these."

She placed a tray from the display case on the counter. "Exquisite, aren't they. All handmade in eighteen-carat gold. Here, this is the one the Ellsworths purchased—a yellow-gold rope with a white-gold box link twisted in. Let it run through your hands. It feels just like silk, doesn't it?"

"Yes, it's beautiful."

"This one came with a gold cross. Would your daughter like a cross as well?"

Rosen suppressed a smile, which felt sticky against his lips, as he thought about his next question. It was a question he'd been formulating ever since seeing Ellsworth in Esther's room.

"Didn't Mr. Ellsworth order two such necklaces?"

"No, I only see one here."

"Perhaps the second was ordered more recently."

"Let me see." She flipped through the ledger. "Why, yes. Now I remember. A second necklace was delivered last month."

"With a cross?"

"Yes—identical."

"Delivered to . . . ?"

"The Leary Building, as usual."

"But Mr. Ellsworth placed the order personally."

"No. We haven't seen him in a few years. Once a bond of trust is established . . . you understand. Besides, our jewelry speaks for itself."

"So he just calls in the order."

The saleswoman cocked her head slightly. "I really think it would be better to concentrate on your purchase. Now that we've settled on the chain, we can turn our attention to an appropriate charm. If you'd step over to this counter."

Rosen said, "It's a beautiful necklace, but I'd like to think it over. Thanks for your time."

Standing very still, she said in the same pleasant tone, "You weren't intending to make a purchase. This was just a ruse to gather some information about one of our clients."

He shrugged.

"I should have known. You have the look of a cheap detective. Your jacket—Sears, no doubt."

Rosen nodded. "Such simple elegance will always be fashionable."

Leaving the jewelry store, he walked down Michigan Avenue. He trembled—not from the wind, but from the ultimate conclusion drawn from the last question he'd asked the saleswoman. Martin Bixby was as much a victim as Nina.

He crossed the street, hailed a cab, and ten minutes later was in the heart of the Loop, in front of a small gray building. Climbing the stairs, he walked into Elgin Hermes' office.

A heavy black woman, her hair set in poodle ringlets, smiled from behind the desk. "Hello. How may I help you?"

"I'd like to see Mr. Hermes."

"Do you have an appointment?"

"No, but he'll want to see me."

"Indeed. Your name, please?"

Her hand reached for the intercom button.

"Nate Rosen." When the woman's hand froze in midair, he continued, "Go ahead. I think you'll find he's changed his mind."

She pressed the button gently, as if tapping her boss's shoulder.

"It's Mr. Rosen."

"I told you to say I'm not in!"

"But he's here. He'd like to see you."

The intercom went dead.

"Mr. Hermes?"

"All right. Send him in."

Hermes sat behind his desk, the fingers of his right hand drumming on a yellow legal pad. He motioned to the chair opposite him. Rosen noticed that the pad's top sheet was blank. It was there as a prop, to make Hermes appear busy. But his red eyes, the stubble on his face, and the wrinkled suit told another story.

Rosen said, "I thought you were anxious to see me."

"Hmm?"

"About the job offer."

"Oh that. Could we take it up another time? I'm pretty busy."

"Writing another scathing editorial?"

Hermes stared at the blank pad. "Yeah."

"Maybe I can help you."

"No, you can't help me."

"What's it about? Some sort of corruption, I'll bet. Threats, intimidation."

The publisher fixed his gaze like a knife on Rosen. "What is it you know?"

"It's what I don't know. What you promised to get for me—remember? Information on Byron Ellsworth and his family."

"Like I said, I've been busy." His fingers returned to drumming on the legal pad. "Besides, I thought you wouldn't need any information."

"Why not?"

"Well, because of Bixby."

"What about Bixby?"

"Goddamnit, because he's dead. Because he must've killed that friend of your daughter's, then committed suicide."

"How do you know that?"

Hermes rubbed his raw eyes and winced. "It's been on the radio all day. And the newspapers."

"They're all guessing, just like the police are guessing. No one knows for sure. That's why I need your help."

The other man shook his head wearily.

"I need your help to get to Ellsworth. At least to get him somewhere alone, away from Masaryk and his army of well-dressed goons. I think Ellsworth's the key to the deaths of Nina Melendez and Bixby."

"Now *you're* guessing."

"Maybe. Let's deal with what we both know. They got to you."

"Who?"

"Ellsworth or, more likely, Masaryk acting for Ellsworth. Somehow they got to you. Not with money. They've got something on you or threatened you. Either way, I'm disappointed."

"What the hell do you know?"

Rosen nodded up toward the portrait on the wall. "Your grandfather would've been disappointed. What do you think he'd have said?"

Hermes glared at Rosen. "He would have quoted Shakespeare. I'm sure you know the passage: 'If you prick us, do we not bleed? If you tickle us, do we not laugh? If you poison us, do we not die?' This investigation of yours—you're doing all this for your daughter, right?"

"Yes."

His jaw trembled. "Well?"

"Well?" Rosen suddenly caught the glint of fear in the other man's eyes. "Your daughter-in-law. Where is she?"

"She's home safe. There was an accident last night. Nothing much. Sherry and my son Jason took the train to the station where their car was parked. From there it's only a five-minute drive home. At a stop sign one block from their house, one of those big four by fours—some kind of jeep, hit their car from behind, then took off."

"Were they hurt?"

"Shaken up a little. Jason banged his knee. You know, Sherry's pregnant. It'll be my first grandchild."

"I'm glad they're all right, but I don't understand. If it was an accident—"

"Last night, fifteen minutes after coming home from the hospital, I received a call from Masaryk. He offered his condolences over the accident. He said the kids needed to be careful—that there were crazy drivers all over the streets and something like that could happen anytime, anywhere. That we'd better have a good lawyer, but not some out-of-town Jewish lawyer. He was warning me to stay away from you."

"How did he know you were helping me?"

The publisher shrugged. "I'd begun making some inquiries about Ellsworth. Masaryk must've backtracked them to me. He also said we should be especially careful, since Sherry's expecting."

"How did he know that?"

Hermes banged his fist on the table. "The son-of-a-bitch knows everything!" Breathing heavily, he leaned over the table. "Sometimes I think he's the devil himself. Know what else he said?"

Rosen shook his head, afraid to ask.

"Had some good news for me, he said. Ellsworth-Leary had decided to present the city college system with a performing arts scholarship in my grandfather's name. Something I'd been planning to do for a long time. The Oliver Jones Scholarship. Know why they did it?" He looked away. "It's a little lesson, so that I won't ever forget their intimidation."

Ashamed for Hermes, Rosen also looked away. Neither man spoke, but as Rosen got up to leave, he saw Jason Hermes standing in the doorway. The young man leaned on a cane, his right leg bent at the knee.

He grimaced. "Dad, tell him what he wants."

"You're hurting. Why don't you go home."

"Damn right I'm hurting, but not from the knee. It's the same thing that's hurting you. I want you to help Mr. Rosen."

"You don't know what this Masaryk is like. If you don't want to think about yourself, think about Sherry. Think about your baby."

"I'll protect her. I'll get a gun if I have to, but I won't live like this."

"You don't know what the hell you're saying."

Shutting the door behind him, Jason hobbled into the room. "Don't I? Mr. Rosen, what can I do to help you?"

Rosen glanced from father to son. "Maybe I'd better go."

"What is it you want to know?"

"How to get at Ellsworth."

Jason shook his head. "I don't know. I wish I could help." He narrowed his eyes. "About a year ago, we were looking into the relationship between Ellsworth-Leary and a Chicago alderman. It had to do with a zoning variance downtown EL was seeking. We had a tail on Ellsworth—"

"Jason!" Hermes shouted.

The words came quicker. "One Friday night, our man followed Ellsworth to the Palmer House. We knew EL kept a suite there for out-of-town clients, but that time Ellsworth was the client. He spent the night with a call girl. Green eyes, long blond hair—very nice."

Rosen shook his head. "I don't see how that helps me."

"Last month—it was a Saturday night, Sherry and I attended a small dinner party at the Palmer House. As I was walking to the men's room, who do I see but Ellsworth in the lobby. He met a woman near the elevator door, and they went up together to the company suite."

"Another blond?"

"No, she was dark—Latino. Nice looking but not the type you'd expect to be hooking. Dressed real plain."

"So you think Ellsworth has these trysts every weekend."

Jason shrugged. "I don't know, but it might be worth a try. At least Masaryk wouldn't likely be around."

Rosen walked to the door, then turned. Bent over his desk, Hermes seemed even older. In contrast, Jason stood ramrod straight, as if the father's energy had flowed into the son.

Rosen said to Hermes, "I guess this means you're retracting the job offer."

"Uh . . . yes. I don't think it's wise for us to continue any sort of relationship."

"I understand. I don't really know if I would've taken it. Thanks anyway."

Hermes asked, "You know James Williams—Denae Tyler's

uncle—the one who was in court? The one who threatened your daughter?"

A chill ran down his back. "What about him?"

"Last night one of the boys who murdered his niece made the mistake of walking down Williams's street. Williams came out of his house with a gun, ran after the boy and put three bullets in his back. Killed him dead, then turned himself in."

Rosen gripped the door handle so hard his knuckles whitened.

"You're a lucky man," Hermes continued. "The man who threatened your child is in jail. Bixby, the man who killed her friend, can't hurt anybody else either. Yeah, you can fly back to Washington tomorrow without a worry in the world."

Rosen nodded slowly. "Sure, and now there's a scholarship named in honor of your grandfather. That makes us both lucky, doesn't it."

Staring into the empty legal pad, Hermes ground his fist against the desktop.

Chapter 19

After leaving Hermes' office, Rosen walked back to Michigan
Avenue to spend the afternoon at the Art Institute. It had been one
of the places he'd enjoyed with Bess and Sarah. They'd especially
liked the turn-of-the-century French painters—Seurat's *Sunday
Afternoon*, cliffs and beaches transformed under the sun strokes of
Matisse's brush, Degas' dancers about to step onto the stage. And
their favorite, Renoir's *Two Sisters*. Each time he'd take a few steps
back to admire Bess and Sarah as they admired the beautiful girls
sharing a hushed moment on the terrace.

It had never been the same since the divorce. In Renoir's world
even the simplest acts, like bathing and combing one's hair, were
done with the hands of angels. As long as Rosen had his family, he
could forget for a moment the real world's deceit and cruelty. He'd
come home each night to Sarah's eyes, innocent as the painting's little red-haired girl. One stroke of vermilion on a coal-black canvas.

But that afternoon he'd stayed away from the Impressionists.
Wandering through the museum's exhibits, he stared into the
stained glass world of Chagall until he saw his grandparents walking alongside a creaking wooden cart to escape the Tsar's pogrom.
Stared into Edward Hopper's *Nighthawks* until he stood at the
counter with the other customers, drinking black coffee in the midnight silence. Wandered through the museum but never found
what he was looking for. Never found the eyes that stared back at
him the same way as the woman in Lucila's painting, *The Flowers of
Madness*.

It was nearly five o'clock when Rosen walked downstairs to call Sarah. Bess answered. "I've been trying to get you all day."

"I had some things to do."

"What happened with Chief Keller yesterday? It was about Bix's death, wasn't it? God, how awful."

Rosen hesitated. What should he say; what did she expect him to say?

"Nate, what in God's name happened?"

"Keller drove me to Bixby's apartment."

"Why?"

"Just routine."

"What do you mean?"

"I think Keller wanted to close the book on Nina's death. He believes that Bixby killed her, then, out of remorse, committed suicide. How's Sarah?"

"Shaken up, like everybody else at school. Linda Agee—you remember, Sarah's counselor."

"Sure."

"Linda spent about a half hour with Sarah this morning. As terrible as Bix's death is, I guess because it makes some sense—"

A soft click, as someone picked up another receiver.

"Daddy?"

"Hello, Shayna. How're you doing?"

"Daddy, is it really true? Did Mr. Bixby kill himself because of what he did to Nina?"

"It's possible. Look, I don't want Bixby's death to hurt you the way Nina's did."

"It's not. I mean, Nina was my best friend. If Mr. Bixby really did kill her—"

"We don't know that yet, not for sure." He heard her breathing heavily. "Shayna?"

"Mrs. Agee and I talked for a long time. We talked a lot about Nina. You know, we didn't really like Mr. Bixby all that much. I once said he was kind of twerpy—the way he always tried to act like one of the kids, and she laughed—"

"Wait a minute. I'm a little confused. Who laughed—Mrs. Agee or Nina?"

214

"Sorry. It was Nina who laughed. She called him a 'mojón.' That's a Dominican expression. It means . . . well, it means a turd."

Rosen shook his head. "But the way Nina described Bixby in her diary. She seemed quite taken with him."

"I know. I don't understand. That's why I didn't say anything about it before."

"Maybe Nina was pretending to agree with you and hiding her real feelings. I guess having a crush on a teacher could be embarrassing."

"I've thought about that. Maybe, but Nina . . . I don't know. I just don't know."

Bess said on her extension, "Don't start cross-examining her."

"Daddy, can you come over? It'd be nice if you were here tonight."

All the times Rosen had wanted her to say just that. To really need him. All the times, and yet he said, "I can't. I have something to do that just won't wait. But I'll be over tomorrow morning. We'll spend the whole day together. All right?"

"All right."

Bess interrupted again. "Sarah, would you hang up, please. I'd like to talk to your father." After a receiver clicked, she continued. "There's something more, isn't there? Something not right about Bixby's death."

"I don't know."

"For a lawyer, you never were a very good liar."

"I've got to go. See you tomorrow."

And so, instead of taking the train to his daughter, Rosen turned up his collar and walked through the Loop for another hour. He stopped at some pancake house where, according to the menu, breakfast was served all day "with a sunny-side-up smile."

The booths were pink, the walls alternating pink and black tiles, with little art deco lamps hanging on chains from the ceiling. The waiter, a thin East Indian whose complexion resembled a meerschaum pipe bowl, took Rosen's order. Only a few tables were occupied, each by a single customer—an old woman with a coat too heavy for April, a man in a threadbare suit reading the *New York Times Book Review,* and a teenaged boy with dirty hair and bright eyes who kept spooning sugar into his coffee, as if that would make him forget about the fix he needed. It could have been another *Nighthawks*.

The potato pancakes were surprisingly good, coarsely grated and cooked to a golden brown. He swirled each piece in sour cream and felt its weight on his fork before biting into it. The tea was hot, the lemon fresh, and the meal made him full and almost happy. After all, tomorrow was Saturday, and no matter what happened, he'd spend it with his daughter.

After dinner Rosen walked for another half hour, then entered the Palmer House. He'd often visited the hotel but was always amazed by the lobby's nineteenth-century opulence. With the same brashness a young Chicago had used to link the nation with railroads and stuff its mouth with slaughtered meat, the city's first great hotel had condensed centuries of European art into one room.

The lobby was two stories high. Chandeliers, their branches outstretched nymphs holding candles, hung on golden columns, which rose past heavily draped dark balconies. They supported golden vaulted arches, covered with carved flowers and vines, and a ceiling filled with more nymphs and angels than God Himself could create.

In the center of the lobby, a large circle had been formed of high-back chairs, round end tables, sofas, and tall ferns. The furniture was green with a pattern of white moths. Sitting in one of the chairs, Rosen spent the next two hours reading *Time* and *Newsweek*. Every few minutes he glanced toward the elevators.

Yawning, he thumbed through the *Chicago Reader*, pausing at the personal columns.

"DWF seeking same to share bed and plan revenge against ex-husbands."

"SWM seeking tennis partner. Must be willing to play in the nude."

Rosen tossed the paper onto an end table with the magazines. Stretching, he walked slowly across the lobby. Only then did he notice the red carpet's floral pattern. The flowers were roses, like the petals scattered where Nina had died. He followed them up an incline that led to the men's room.

216

After urinating, he washed his hands and face with cold water. Someone handed him several paper towels.

"Thanks."

Looking into the mirror above the sink, he saw the reflection of a short, powerfully built man wearing a dark suit. The man was about thirty, his sandy hair receding prematurely and making his green eyes even more prominent. Eyes that glinted like jade as he grinned. He was a stranger, yet something about him was familiar.

Rosen continued to watch in the mirror, as if the other man weren't really there, but rather some projected image. Even as the stranger pulled out a gun and laid his other hand on Rosen's shoulder, so that each man faced the other.

Without breaking his stare, the man quickly patted Rosen down.

"My wallet's in my inside jacket pocket."

Rosen started to reach for it when the other man slapped his hand away. "Take it easy." He unbuttoned Rosen's shirt, running a hand over his undershirt. "I'm not after your money. Just checking to see if you're wired. Okay, you can button up now."

Putting the gun under his suit coat, the man turned once again to face the mirror. He combed his hair, then nonchalantly adjusted the knot in his tie. In doing so, his cuff slipped down to reveal his watch, which looked just like Rosen's. The man removed the watch and tossed it onto the sink between them.

"Cheap piece of shit. Not worth even spare change."

Spare change—what the panhandler had wanted before mugging Rosen and taking his watch. The thickset panhandler with eyes the color of jade.

"You're the one who—"

"Shut up. You lawyers always talk too much. Just pick up your watch and go back to the lobby."

The man waited patiently for his instructions to be obeyed. Finally, Rosen put the watch on his wrist and left the men's room.

A second man, wearing a light brown suit, stood against the wall just outside the door. Taller and thinner, with short blond hair, nevertheless he resembled the gunman. Arms folded over his chest, eyes fixed on some point on the other side of the room, he showed the same arrogance.

The hotel was crowded. What was to stop Rosen from simply walking out the door? What could the two men do—shoot him in the back? He took a few steps toward the exit, then stopped. Why had he been frisked and told to "go back to the lobby"? Why had he come to the hotel in the first place, if not to get at Ellsworth?

Walking through the lobby, Rosen returned to his chair. He straightened suddenly, gripping the armrests, then settled back, trying not to look too concerned that Edward Masaryk sat across from him.

Masaryk wore a cocoa-colored turtleneck under a camel hair jacket. The blue sunglasses were tucked into a breast pocket, and his gray eyes were almost lost behind his dark brows. His clothes fit perfectly, the jacket sleeves smooth and tight over his arms like cylinders over two pistons.

From an inside pocket, Masaryk opened a silver case. He removed a dark cigarillo, which he lighted and puffed contentedly for several minutes. The smoke trailed off into filaments delicate as a spider's web. Rosen leaned back even farther in his chair.

Finally Masaryk said, "I wonder what kind of animal you'd make. A beaver digging in the dirt trying to stem the tide. Or maybe a jackal—the way you're always hovering around dead bodies."

"Like Martin Bixby?"

"Like Bixby."

"We both know there's a good reason for my interest. I wonder what kind of an animal you'd make."

Masaryk flicked his cigarillo over an ashtray. "I am an animal. I always act on instinct. Ever since we met at Nina Melendez's funeral, I knew you'd have to be followed."

"You did more than that. What about the man—your man—who mugged me and took my watch?"

"That was just to see what you were made of."

"Those Mexicans in Highwood, near Hector Alvarez's house. The ones who tried to rape Lucila Melendez. Were they your men too?"

Masaryk shrugged. "Aren't you getting a little paranoid?"

"That's good coming from you—having me followed the past week. Aren't you the one who's paranoid, surrounding yourself with all these . . . what do you call them—'security experts'?"

"They're not for me."

"I know."

After taking a few more leisurely puffs, Masaryk asked, "What're you doing here?"

"Why don't you tell me?"

"A good lawyer trick, answering a question with a question. Well, let's see—you've had quite a busy day. After going to Brissard Jewelers this morning, you dropped by Elgin Hermes' office for a chat. You spent the afternoon at the Art Institute. Better than a bar, I guess. By the way, what fascinates you so much about that *Nighthawks* painting?"

Rosen remembered what Hermes had said about Masaryk, "That son-of-a-bitch knows everything!"

"You had dinner in a two-bit pancake house, then settled here for a couple hours with your magazines. My first guess is that the public library is closed. No? Well then, maybe you're waiting for somebody. Is that it?"

Rosen nodded.

"I don't think he's going to show. Will I do?"

"Can you tell me what happened to Martin Bixby?"

"I understand it was suicide. Why don't you ask Police Chief Keller?"

"I thought I'd cut out the middleman. We both know Bixby didn't kill himself."

Masaryk leaned forward. "How about this? Your girlfriend Lucila Melendez and her sister-in-law murdered Bixby because he killed Nina."

Rosen shook his head.

"Don't tell me it hasn't crossed your mind. Lucila has quite the Latin temper. And Esther . . . we both know she's got a few screws loose. You've seen what she's like. You've looked into her eyes. Don't you think she'd have killed Bixby if given half a chance?"

"Maybe, but she didn't kill him."

"Who did?"

"You."

Masaryk slowly crushed his cigarillo in the ashtray. Leaning back, he placed both hands on the armrests. "You're right. I killed Bixby."

They sat in the lobby of the Palmer House, dozens of people passing within an arm's length of their chairs, yet Masaryk spoke as casually as if discussing a baseball game.

"I knew Bixby was home yesterday morning, so I went up his back stairs and let myself in with a skeleton key. I sat at the kitchen table with his dirty breakfast dishes until he came in. I used one of my old throwaways, a .38 revolver, to make him sit down across from me. Then I put the gun on the table, and we had a little chat. We'd met before at Kate Ellsworth's art gallery."

Forcing himself not to shiver, Rosen asked, "What did you talk about?"

"Mostly about the Melendezes. About how they thought he killed Nina, and about how I was going to have to kill him."

"How did you—"

"When I moved toward him, Bixby picked up the gun and fired. Unfortunately for him, I'd emptied the first chamber. By the time he tried again, I'd grabbed his wrist and forced the revolver against his temple, then pulled the trigger."

For a moment Rosen closed his eyes, seeing Bixby's head jerk back from the gunshot. He swallowed hard. "That's why there were more powder burns on his face than his hand. Your hand covered his when the gun was fired."

"You're a smart lawyer."

"What if Bixby had been able to fire that second shot?"

"I'd be dead. But he hesitated, like I knew he would. No animal instinct for survival. Remember that. Don't wait to fire the second shot."

Rosen stared hard at the other man. "You took a big chance killing Bixby. Shooting him in the middle of the day. Not even using a silencer."

"How do you know I didn't use a silencer?"

"You can't put one on a revolver."

Masaryk almost laughed. "So what? Rigging Bixby's death to look like suicide—the gun by his hand, the photograph with Nina's face circled—that was easy. I had some practice in that sort of thing years ago in Latin America. Know why I killed Bixby?" Opening his silver case, he lit another cigarillo. "Because of you."

"Me?"

"Because you wouldn't accept Nina's death as an accident. Her aunt and mother—who cares what a couple of spics think? But you kept after Bixby. Maybe you believed he killed Nina, or maybe you just went through the motions to get into Lucila Melendez's pants, but you kept after him. So I gave you all what you wanted—a conscience-stricken Bixby blowing his brains out."

Could Masaryk have known that too—that Rosen had already blamed himself for the teacher's death? He wanted to get up. His throat was dry. He wanted to get up and walk away. Just walk away and keep walking.

"It was a happy ending for all concerned," Masaryk said.

"Except Bixby."

"Like I said, your fault."

"That's right. You had to kill him . . ."

The other man nodded.

". . . to protect your boss, Byron Ellsworth."

Masaryk smoked his cigarillo, his eyes locked on Rosen's. "See what I mean? You don't give up."

"What happened? Did Ellsworth like sleeping with Esther Melendez so much, he wanted to try Nina too?"

"Careful."

"He ordered a necklace for her, just like the one he bought Esther. He met her in the park that Friday night, brought her the necklace and flowers. Then what—he got too rough, they struggled, and she fell over? Or did she threaten to tell her mother, and he killed her? You're right, I have seen Esther's eyes. The thought of her finding out must've terrified Ellsworth. So after killing the girl, he went to you, and you took care of everything. You've made a living out of taking care of Ellsworth and his family, haven't you?"

"We all have our weaknesses. Byron happens to like women. That's hardly a vice."

"My God, Nina was just a girl."

Masaryk cocked his head slightly. "What?"

"I said—"

"You know, in some cultures there's no such thing as girls. They're babies, then women. I've seen it in Vietnam, El Salvador, Guatemala. Running after you in the street, like little birds with broken wings. They hop and shake and flutter, and once you get them upstairs, they fuck your brains out for the change in your pocket. So if a man like Byron Ellsworth wants to have a little fun—"

"No," Rosen said, his jaw tightening, "he's not getting away with it. Neither are you."

As if watching a willful child, Masaryk shook his head sadly. "What're you going to do? Tell the police that, in the lobby of the Palmer House, I admitted murdering Martin Bixby? Where's the evidence?"

"I'll work on it."

"See what I mean—the patience of a jackal."

"Suppose I tell Esther that Ellsworth killed her daughter?"

"You won't. You know about the accident?"

Rosen nodded. "The rear-end collision involving Hermes' kids. So now you're threatening me with—"

"Not that accident. The one involving your girlfriend. Her dented bumper—you know about that?"

Again Rosen nodded, but more slowly.

"Did she tell you how she got it?"

"She didn't know."

Masaryk puffed contentedly; he seemed to enjoy making Rosen wait. Finally he said, "Yesterday morning about noon, a house painter reported to the Chicago police that an old brown station wagon, while speeding south down Sheridan Road, hit his parked car. Suppose somebody suggested that the Chicago cops ask Lt. McCarthy to match the chipped paint from both the painter's and Lucila's cars?"

Rosen leaned back in his chair, trying to appear casual. "So you paid someone to lie. Even if his testimony stands, it's circumstantial."

"You know it's more than that. Suppose an eyewitness, a realtor working the neighborhood, happened to see Lucila coming down the back stairs of Bixby's apartment ten minutes to noon?"

"A realtor who has dealings with Ellsworth-Leary?"

"Suppose the police find a gang banger in Logan Square who admits selling your girlfriend the murder weapon? Suppose . . . well, I could go on, but you get the idea. Nina Melendez was killed by Bixby, and Bixby committed suicide in remorse. If you don't like that, then your girlfriend's arrested for murder. Stay away from Byron Ellsworth."

Rosen's arms felt heavy, as if pinned to his sides. The same feeling as in Highwood, when one man had held him down while two others attacked Lucila. But then Rosen could struggle against somebody—could strike his fist against flesh and bone.

Now he could only swing at the shadows Masaryk threw across his eyes. One, two, three . . . how many were there? As many as it would take to keep him silent.

"You know," Masaryk said, stubbing out his second cigarillo, "Joseph Stalin once wanted to take over a certain city on the Baltic coast. When he couldn't, he simply included it on all Soviet maps as Russian. Two generations of his people grew up believing that city was theirs. You're a lawyer—I shouldn't have to tell you that a lie's as easy to believe as the truth. Sometimes easier."

Picking up the copy of *Newsweek*, Masaryk began flipping through the pages as if Rosen weren't there. And, of course, he wasn't.

Chapter 20

"Cab, sir?"

Rosen stood outside the hotel. Couples in their evening clothes strolled past him, their laughter sounding strangled in his ears. Above the glare of streetlights stretched the deep black night, where stars flickered like the yahrtzeit candles he lit each year to remember his mother and grandparents. As a little boy, he'd imagined the stars as candles lit by God to commemorate each new death. Scanning the sky, he wondered which two stars flickered for Nina and Bixby.

"Cab, sir?" the doorman repeated.

"What time . . ." No, he didn't have to ask anymore. He stared at his watch as if it were a scar, a scar of a fight he'd not only lost but in which he'd been humiliated. Was Masaryk's man standing behind the doorway, still grinning as he had in the bathroom mirror?

"Yes," Rosen said a little too loudly. "A cab."

He blurted Lucila's address to the driver and settled back while the cab angled its way northwest toward Logan Square. Why Lucila? To warn her about the frame? Or was it because Masaryk, who knew everything else, knew that too? How much Rosen wanted her and, being able to do nothing else, would take her to bed.

Like Masaryk had said, ". . . a happy ending for all concerned."

Rosen rubbed the skin under his watch. It felt raw.

It was only when the cab arrived at Mercado Jimenez that he wondered whether Lucila would be home. A light shone from her second-story studio, and her car was parked in the small lot beside the staircase. Climbing up the wooden stairs, he knocked loudly several times. He was about to give up when the door opened.

Lucila's eyes grew wide. "Nate?"

Her sweatshirt and jeans were splattered with paint, as was the plastic shower cap under which her hair was bunched.

"I should've called."

"No, I finished working a few hours ago. Actually I nodded off. Come in."

He followed her through the narrow hallway into her studio.

She turned to face him. "I'm glad you came by." Noticing him staring at the shower cap, she blushed. "You don't know how hard it is to get paint out of your hair."

Pulling off the cap, she shook her head, and her hair splashed around her shoulders. For a moment, the room filled with the heady fragrance of her shampoo. She'd blushed because, despite their having made love, they weren't much more than strangers. His heartbeat quickened.

"Working on a new painting?"

"Uh huh. With things finally cleared up about Nina's death, I feel like working again. I painted most of the day. Quit when it started getting dark. I don't like mixing natural and artificial light. Colors aren't the same."

"May I see it?"

"Over there in the corner."

But he never made it to the corner. Directly across from the couch, *Flowers of Madness* leaned against the wall. He stared into the mad eyes of the woman holding the blood-red roses.

"I brought it home from the gallery," she said.

He couldn't tear himself away from those eyes. "Why?"

"I don't know, I just . . ." He felt her hand on his shoulder. "Come on, Nate. Come sit with me on the couch."

She was pulling him, and when he did follow her, Rosen saw she was blushing again. On the old captain's chest lay Nina's diary. He picked it up and thumbed through the pages.

He kept rereading one of the passages: "After rehearsal he picked me up on his way home. We went to the park overlooking the beach." There was something wrong, something he couldn't quite understand.

". . . don't think Esther wants the diary," Lucila was saying, "but I couldn't just throw it away. All so sad, so horrible—Bixby killing Nina and then himself."

Rosen returned the diary to the captain's chest. "Why did you bring the painting home?"

"I . . . uh . . . I'm working on something with a similar color scheme, so I brought it home as a point of reference."

"Is *Flowers of Madness* going to be in your show?"

"There's only so much space and so many canvases allowed. I'm not sure yet."

"Why didn't you tell me the truth?"

Hands tightening into fists, she stared into the eyes of the painting.

Rosen asked, "Why didn't you tell me about Esther? She's killed before, hasn't she? She killed her husband—that's what you'd start-ed to tell me once."

"Yes." The word crackled through the air like lightning. "But it was so long ago."

"It was her temper."

Lucila continued staring into those eyes. "Back in the Dominican Republic. My brother was cheating on her—he was always cheating on her. She found out, they got into an argument, and he started beating her up. She grabbed a knife. I don't even think she knew what she was doing."

Rosen shook her arm until she turned away from the painting. He said, "That's not the only time she's acted like that."

"What do you mean?"

"You must've seen it before, to have painted the eyes on that canvas. That's why you brought the painting home. You were afraid other people would see the madness in her eyes. Don't look at it; look at me! I've seen it too, when she talked about Bixby."

"No, she didn't kill him!"

For a moment, Lucila's eyes flashed hot as Esther's, then they shimmered in the welling tears.

"I know."

At first she didn't seem to understand. Narrowing her eyes, she said, "What?"

"I just came from Masaryk. He admitted murdering Bixby."

"What do you mean? He just came out and said it?"

"Yes," and Rosen repeated what Masaryk had told him about killing the teacher.

"But why?"

"I think he killed Bixby to protect his boss, Byron Ellsworth. I think Ellsworth's the one who killed Nina."

"Ellsworth. Why would . . . oh, my God!"

"Yeah, because the mother wasn't enough for him."

The hot tears rolled down Lucila's cheeks, as her fists pounded against the captain's chest. "The bastard! The Goddamn fucking bastard!"

Rosen grabbed her, letting her fists flail against him. She kept screaming obscenities against Ellsworth until her voice grew hoarse and the breath shuddered in her lungs. She turned away from him, staring out the window into the darkness.

"You knew about Ellsworth and your sister-in-law?"

Lucila nodded. "Do you know what she'll do to him?"

"You can't tell her. Masaryk's fixed it, so that—"

"I won't try to stop her. No, I won't try to stop her. I'll help."

"You can't." He shook her until she looked at him. "Listen to me. Masaryk's fixed it so that if we try getting close to Ellsworth, you'll be framed for Bixby's murder."

He repeated what Masaryk had said about Lucila's car and the so-called witnesses. After he'd finished, they sat quietly for several minutes.

Finally she said, "It's the same everywhere. Masaryk might as well be back home, wearing a general's uniform. That's what the dictator Trujillo used to do—play with people as if they were toys. Wind them up and watch them do anything, even walk over cliffs. Oh, Nina." Again tears ran down her face.

"No," Rosen said, "not here, not in this country. There are laws, laws that even Ellsworth and Masaryk have to obey."

"You make beautiful speeches like all lawyers do. Lawyers—

they're good at making excuses for men like Ellsworth. He must have an army of lawyers. They're all whores; they just use their mouths instead of their cunts." Suddenly she rubbed her eyes hard. "He's not getting away with it."

Lucila walked to the corner beside the kitchen, which served as her bedroom. A drawer opened, then slammed shut. She returned holding a small automatic.

Rosen asked, "Where did you get that?"

"Julian, who owns the store downstairs, gave it to me. Said anyone living in this neighborhood should have one."

"And what're you planning to do?"

"What my father or brother would do if they were alive. I'm going to kill that bastard for what he did to my niece."

"You can't."

"What else would a lawyer say."

She grabbed her jacket from the kitchen counter, and when she turned, Rosen stood in front of her.

"Get out of my way."

"Listen to me. You can't go after Ellsworth. I'm not absolutely sure he did it."

"More lawyer talk."

When she tried pushing past him, he grabbed her arm.

"We've got to be sure. We've got to have evidence. And then we turn Ellsworth over to the police."

"The police! Men like Ellsworth own the police."

"The one loose end is the landscaper, Hector Alvarez. He was in the park the night Nina was murdered, and I think he knows something. He must feel pretty safe with Masaryk protecting him. I don't think he'd expect me to pay him another visit."

She bit her lower lip. "All right, we'll go see Alvarez."

Rosen looked at the gun in her hand. "I don't think you'd better come along this time."

"How are you going to make him say anything?"

"Then give me the gun."

"No. I'm coming with. Don't worry, I won't shoot him—unless I have to."

They stared at each other and, at last, she couldn't help smiling. And, as her lips opened, he couldn't help kissing them. His hands tangled in her hair, kissing her again, her arms around his shoulders and she kissing him back. Her breasts hard against his chest, and she murmuring something he couldn't quite hear because of the blood pounding in his ears.

"We'd better go," she whispered against his cheek. Yet she didn't pull away, as if waiting for him to make the decision.

Hesitating to inhale once more the fragrance of her hair, he nodded and stepped back.

"Here." He helped her on with her jacket. "It's a little chilly outside."

She put the gun in her purse while avoiding his eyes. He picked up Nina's diary from the captain's chest.

"There's still something bothering me about the diary. I'd like to look it over one more time."

As they reached the door, he stopped her. "What if Masaryk's having your place watched?"

"You don't think—"

"He knows everything we've been doing. Is there another car in the neighborhood you could borrow?"

She thought for a moment. "I've got a friend one street over."

"Good. If someone's watching your apartment, he's probably doing it from across the street."

"Okay. Just follow me."

They hugged the wall of the building as Lucila led him downstairs, through the small parking lot and into a back alley that led to a street one block west. He followed her along the dimly lit pavement until they reached an old frame house in the middle of the block. He waited outside the back door, while she talked to her friend in Spanish. Five minutes later, a key chain jingled in her hand.

"I'll drive," she said. "I know the neighborhood better."

It was an old green Chevette, its motor sounding like a marimba band as the car wove its way through the side streets of Logan Square. Every few minutes, Rosen glanced over his shoulder.

Lucila turned another corner. "I'll zigzag up to Irving Park, then catch the expressway. Don't worry. Anybody trying to follow us is already lost."

Settling back in the passenger seat, Rosen thumbed through the pages of Nina's diary, reading as best he could under the flickering street lights. Again he paused at the passage— "After rehearsal, he picked me up on his way home. We went to the park overlooking the beach."

He rubbed his eyes. Something was wrong.

"You shouldn't try reading without a light," Lucila said.

"My mother used to say the same thing when I was a little boy."

"Your mother was right." After pausing a moment, she added, "I wonder what kind of a little boy you were."

"I was a juvenile delinquent."

"No you weren't. You were probably the nicest little boy in the neighborhood. I bet you carried your mother's groceries for her, and gave up your seat on the bus to little old ladies, and ate all your spinach without having to be told to."

"What're you making me out to be?"

She glanced at him. "A nice guy. One nice guy in a world of Ellsworths, Masaryks, Bixbys, and Alvarezes."

Clearing his throat, he asked, "And what kind of little girl were you? Did you run around town kick-boxing all the boys?"

She laughed, her head thrown back, sending a ripple through her waves of hair. "I was a little tomboy, running barefoot in the cornfields."

"Cornfields? I thought you lived in the Dominican Republic."

"It wasn't all 'caña'—sugarcane. We lived up in the mountains. It was pretty there. The stars so close and bright, like you were living in God's house. I don't suppose you'd understand."

Looking up into the stars, so dim and far away, he said, "I lived in God's house too, but it wasn't like that."

"What do you—"

"Tell me more about your childhood."

Lucila did, painting a picture with words as skillfully as she did on canvas, so that he saw her climbing up the tall palm trees to shake the coconuts loose, then scampering down and, with one swing of the machete, whacking a coconut in half, drinking the milk as it dribbled down her chin. That and the sweet smell of mango and papaya filled the car as it sped up the expressway.

After another fifteen minutes, Lucila exited onto Route 22, which, in turn, led to Green Bay Road.

When she clicked on her left-turn signal, Rosen said, "Keep going to Sheridan Road."

"But Alvarez lives off Green Bay."

"Go up Sheridan and double back across the tracks north of Alvarez's street. That way we can see if he's being watched."

"Okay. You know, it's Friday night. He may not be home."

"Yeah, but his wife will. Without Alvarez around, she might tell us something."

They turned up Sheridan and drove north into Highwood, along the east side of the tracks that ran through the middle of town. The streets were crowded with all sorts of people. Workmen heading for a corner bar elbowed past couples in suits and furs walking into some of the finest restaurants in Chicagoland.

Lucila asked, "Where do you want me to cross the tracks?"

"Another two blocks. Hold on. Isn't that Alvarez's truck?"

"Where?"

"We just passed it. It was parked in front of that tavern, the one with the redwood trim. Pull over anywhere."

Andy's looked like a million other taverns, with its neon beer signs and lottery advertisements in the window. Its inside was just as common—cigarette smoke, rickety wooden tables, a corner dance floor that nobody used, and a jukebox warbling about somebody's broken heart. The joint was crowded, but no Alvarez.

A row of booths lined the wall to their left. Squinting through the fog of smoke, Rosen saw the Mexican sitting in the corner booth, near the kitchen door. He wasn't alone.

Rosen slid beside Alvarez. Across the table sat Margarita Reyes and Chip Ellsworth. Gripping her handbag, Lucila stood over the girl.

Alvarez fingered an empty shot glass, beside which stood a bottle of Corona. "Get the hell outta here."

232

Rosen said, "I'm glad you're here, Chip. I need to talk to you too." Before Alvarez's right hand could slip from the table, Rosen grabbed it. "What'd you have there?"

"None a' your Goddamn business!"

As the two men struggled, the small package in Alvarez's hand tore open, and something crumbled onto the table.

Releasing the other man's hand, Rosen asked, "Something you mowed today?"

Alvarez curled back in the booth. "Fuck you."

"Dealing drugs to minors. That's hard time."

"I said—"

"I know what you said."

Ita got up—not quickly, but as if she'd just finished chatting with a friend. "We're leaving. C'mon, Chip."

Rosen shook his head. "Chip stays. You can wait for him outside."

"Wait? I don't wait for men. I'll see you around."

Lucila bent toward the girl and spoke softly in Spanish. Rosen couldn't follow what she was saying, but he understood the word "puta"—whore. Ita replied curtly, then sauntered across the room. The men at the bar turned their heads when she passed, and a few whistled. Before stepping through the door she tossed back her head, as if laughing at them all.

Rosen said to Chip, "You could do a lot better in your choice of friends."

Chip looked down at his lap. Lucila sat beside him and reaching down, pulled up the boy's hands, which covered something thick and folded. It was a business envelope with the Ellsworth-Leary logo in the upper left-hand corner.

"How much?" Rosen asked.

Opening the envelope, Chip fanned out five twenty-dollar bills.

Alvarez laughed. "Don't say nothing, kid. They're the ones in trouble, not us."

"Really?" Rosen said. "We're talking about dealing drugs."

"So call the cops. Big fucking deal."

"Maybe I won't bother the police. Maybe I'll just call Soldier instead."

Chip's eyes grew wide as a frightened horse's. Alvarez, however, grew even cockier.

"Go ahead, call Masaryk. The kid knows the number. You want me to get you the phone?"

"No," Chip said.

"Go 'head, call. What you think I got, man—shit for brains? You, lawyer, you're the one who's got shit for brains."

Something was wrong. Alvarez should've been terrified of Masaryk finding out that he was supplying Chip with drugs.

Rosen asked, "You think Soldier will get you out of this?"

Alvarez lit a cigarette and took several deep drags. "What do you think, shit for brains?"

"Just like he got you out of trouble before—you and Chip. Is that why he arranged a high-priced attorney when Keller had you picked up?"

"Sure. We're old friends, me and Soldier. Ask him." He was chuckling, his eyes blinking away the cigarette smoke. "Now, get outta my way, cabrón. I got things to do."

Lucila said, "You're not going anywhere."

Grinning, he looked her up and down very slowly. "Ven conmigo. Me gustas, chica. Te deseo."

She pulled the gun from her purse. "You talk to me like that again, I'll do more than what I did to your friends in the alley. You think I've forgotten about that." She aimed at him from under the table. "How good would you be able to chase women 'sin los cojones'? Should we find out?"

The grin fell like broken glass from his face. "Crazy bitch. You wouldn't shoot me . . . uh . . . ."

"In public?"

"Yeah, in public."

"Why not? You know how hot-blooded we crazy Latin bitches are. But maybe if you start talking nice, I might calm down."

"You ain't—"

"Just answer Mr. Rosen's questions. That's all, 'mojón.'"

Reaching very carefully for his beer, Alvarez gulped down half the bottle.

Rosen asked, "What happened the night Nina Melendez died?"

Chip blinked hard. "What're you asking him about that? Bix killed her . . . that's what everybody says. He killed her, didn't he?"

"Why don't we start with you? What were you really doing that night?"

"Just what I told you. Me and a couple guys were down in the ravines."

"But you weren't drinking?"

"Yes, we . . ." He looked at Alvarez, who shifted away. "All right, so we were smoking some dope. Everything else I told you was true. We were down in the ravines and didn't see anything."

"You bought the marijuana that night from Alvarez."

"Yeah. Look, I told you what you wanted to know. Can I go now?"

Rosen turned to Alvarez. "That's what you were doing in the park that night."

The Mexican shrugged. "My crew and me, we worked late in the neighborhood—about 8:30. I took 'em to get a hamburger, we stopped for a beer, then I dropped 'em home and went to meet the kid and his friends in the park."

"Taking the truck; dumping the clippings in the corner of the park was a cover."

"Yeah. If anybody saw me there and called the cops, the kids take off, and I get hit with a littering fine. Big deal."

"I don't understand. You were almost in Ellsworth's backyard, selling drugs to his son. Weren't you afraid that Masaryk would find out?" Before Alvarez could answer, Rosen half whispered, "Masaryk had to know . . . he had to."

Alvarez gulped the rest of his beer, then leaned back contentedly. He sucked on his cigarette until the tip glowed. Dropped into the bottle, it hissed angrily like a trapped animal.

"Me afraid of Soldier, of anybody? Man, you crazy. He don't fuck with me, and I don't fuck with him."

"But if he'd found out—"

"We're men, not maricones. He goes his way, and I go mine."

Rosen shook his head.

Alvarez struck his fist on the table. "You think I'm afraid of

Soldier? Hell, a few minutes after I took care of the kid and his friends, I passed Soldier on Green Bay. Did I give a shit that he was on his way home—that I just missed him?"

"He was on his way back to the Ellsworth estate?"

"Yeah, that's what I'm saying."

"That must've been sometime between ten and ten-thirty, right?"

"Yeah, I guess it was around—" He stopped suddenly. "I'm through answering your questions."

Lucila brought the gun over the table edge. "You're through when we say so, 'mojón.'"

Rosen glanced from Lucila to Alvarez. What had the Mexican said to her—"Te deseo." "Te." Finally, it was starting to make sense. Reaching across the table, he stuffed the packet of marijuana into the beer bottle.

"Okay, you can both go." To Chip, "Don't forget your money. Just leave the envelope."

After Alvarez and the boy left, Lucila returned the gun to her purse. "Well, we got to talk to Alvarez, but I don't see what good it did."

Rosen picked up the empty envelope with the Ellsworth-Leary logo. He turned it slowly in his hands.

"What do we do next?" she asked.

"First we make sure the safety's on that gun. You weren't really going to shoot him."

She clicked her tongue impatiently. "What are we going to do?"

He smiled. "Get something to eat. I'm hungry."

"And then?"

"Then? Find a clean-cut young man in a white shirt."

Chapter 21

Shifting Nina's diary to his left hand, Rosen rang the Ellsworths' front-door bell. Almost twenty-four hours had passed since he and Lucila had driven from her Logan Square neighborhood to confront Alvarez in a Highwood bar. Yet tonight he felt no safer standing alone in the middle of the Ellsworth estate. The porch lights barely illuminated beyond the front steps, so that house and lawn appeared as some great ship lost in the spindrift of an empty sea.

When the door finally swung open, Masaryk stood before him, the telegram in his hand. He wore a forest green cashmere sweater and tan slacks, like any gentleman lounging on a Saturday night.

"Eight forty-one—you're late. Before coming in . . . well, you know the routine."

While the other man frisked him, unbuttoning his shirt to check for a microphone, Rosen asked, "Anybody else home?"

"Byron and Kate are out for the evening—together, for a change. Chip's gone too. All right, come on ahead."

The foyer was illuminated by a crystal chandelier; on the cream-colored walls hung idyllic landscapes of shepherds with lutes and sheep bleating under sun-blessed skies. Masaryk led him on thick Berber carpet under a winding staircase and down a long hall, past glimpses of what appeared to be the rooms of a museum. Everywhere he saw paintings—along the hallway, the staircase wall, the rooms—as if the house were overripe with them, waiting for harvest.

Masaryk opened the last door on the left, and Rosen walked into a small room stinking of cigarette smoke. The walls were bare, in startling contrast to the rest of the house. The hardwood floor was also bare. In the corner to his left a leather chair had been arranged with a small table and lamp. A wooden desk faced the far wall. To his right, the sliding glass doors led into the backyard. A tall lamp stood in the corner diagonal to the leather chair. The only light came from the two lamps, which spread the illumination unevenly through the room, like a piece of bread that hadn't been buttered properly.

Motioning Rosen to the leather chair, Masaryk sat at his desk. Lifting the telephone receiver, he pressed a button, then asked, "How does it look?" After listening for a minute, he hung up without saying good-bye. His face, barely distinguishable in the dimness, stared at the strip of paper in his hand.

"'Know truth. Must see you Ellsworth house tonight 8:30.—Rosen.' When I received your telegram this morning, I thought what a soldier always thinks—that somebody had died. I had to write lots of those during my career. Not the telegrams—they were sent by the Defense Department—but the follow-up letters to the family of the men in my unit who were killed. What do you say about men you hardly knew?"

Rosen shrugged.

"Really? I thought you'd be an expert. What did your telegram say—'Know truth'? Those words have a deep spiritual ring."

"I'm surprised you take them that way."

"Why, because I'm a soldier? Did you know that Stonewall Jackson was a deeply religious man; that he led prayer meetings for his troops and believed that his cause was God's?"

"God's cause—destroying the Union to perpetuate slavery?"

"Jackson believed—that was enough for him. It made him the most brilliant commander of the Civil War, greater than Lee. That belief, that moral certitude, makes all the difference. All the great military leaders had it. Alexander the Great, Caesar, Patton, . . ."

"Oliver North."

As Masaryk lit a cigarillo, his smile flashed, brief as the match's flame. "Yes, Oliver North. We had to free American hostages and fight the Communists in Nicaragua, and he did something about both. He was a good soldier."

"Not everyone agreed."

"What do you expect from civilians responsible for defining military operations? It just became too complicated to be a soldier—wars became 'police actions' or 'clandestine operations,' with more rules about what you couldn't do than what you could."

"That's why you left the army."

Masaryk nodded. "Heading security for an international corporation like Ellsworth-Leary was like the army the way it used to be. Hunting down terrorists who'd kidnapped our executives, dealing with industrial espionage, sabotaging campaigns of political opponents—"

"Like playing war with the whole corporate world as your battlefield."

"That's right."

Rosen shifted forward in his chair. "And when someone like me threatens your boss, a little bit of counterinsurgency. Like Guatemala."

"You should read up on Stonewall Jackson or Patton. Maybe then you'd understand."

Rosen opened the notebook. "I've been busy reading other things, like Nina Melendez's diary. I assume you know about it."

Masaryk smoked his cigarillo for almost a minute, then flicked the ash into a metal wastebasket beside the desk. "It shows that Bixby was after the girl. That he'd met her in the park at least once before. That he was the one who killed her. That everybody should be happy he's dead. Don't you think everybody should be happy?"

"You're right about people assuming Nina was infatuated with Bixby. Obviously, she was talking about her teacher when she wrote things like, 'Tonight at rehearsal he said Sarah and me we're good enough to be professionals.'"

"If this is the great 'truth' you've discovered, I'm afraid you've wasted both our time."

"Do you have children?"

"None that I know of."

"I have a teenage daughter . . . well, you know that. She's a bright kid but in many ways a typical adolescent."

Masaryk stubbed his cigarillo on the inside of the wastebasket. "Some people enjoy hearing about other people's children. I'm not one of those."

Rosen checked his watch. It was getting close to nine. He'd have to hurry.

"Teenage girls have their own way of talking. I was reminded of that several times the past two weeks, including listening to a conversation between my daughter and Nina. They kept mixing their subjects and confusing the antecedents."

"What the hell are you talking about?"

"Nina's diary. I think she wrote the same way she talked. It doesn't make sense any other way. Listen to this entry, which she wrote two days after the one I just read. 'After rehearsal, he picked me up on his way home. We went to the park overlooking the beach. His eyes, so stern with everybody else, looked so gentle tonight.'"

Rosen stared at the other man. "Bixby lives south of the high school, but Nina lives north—as, of course, do you. Picking her up would've been out of Bixby's way, but not yours. Besides, according to Sarah, Nina thought of the teacher as a 'twerp.' But 'His eyes, so stern . . .' and some of the other things she wrote in her diary fit you pretty well."

Masaryk lit another cigarillo. "What happened to your theory about Ellsworth and the girl? Everything you said about me could equally fit him."

Rosen checked his watch again. "At first I thought Ellsworth had bought the necklace for Nina, but the order was made by phone. You ordered it in Ellsworth's name and, as head of security, took the package when it arrived at the office. All the time I thought that you were protecting the Ellsworths—trying to hide Byron's affair with Esther Melendez and Chip's use of drugs, even comforting Kate Ellsworth. In reality, you were using the Ellsworths' wealth and power to protect yourself."

Masaryk's laugh came thin, vanishing almost before it began. "What're you saying—that I killed the girl?"

Just then, someone knocked on the sliding doors. Rosen checked his watch—nine o'clock. Cocking his head, Masaryk dropped the cigarillo into the wastebasket and crossed the room. The slider whispered open and closed.

Through the dimness, Rosen barely discerned the figure across the room. But the fragrance of her perfume hung heavily in the air. She took a few steps, her high heels clicking on the wooden floor, and flung off her long coat. She wore a filmy chemise, garters, and stockings. Everything white and, in the pale light, gleaming hard as ivory.

Throwing her arms around Masaryk, Margarita Reyes gave him a lingering kiss. She tilted back her head and grinned.

"I brought it, just like you said. Here."

Masaryk took something from her hand, then walked back to his desk. Starting after him, she saw Rosen and froze in her tracks.

"Porque esta aquí? Creía que—"

"Speak English," Masaryk said. "You're Mr. Rosen's guest, not mine."

"I don't understand. The man who brought your letter—"

"What man?"

"He looked just like one of your men. Short hair, white shirt and tie. He brought me this."

She bent to retrieve something from her coat, then hurried to Masaryk.

He stretched the envelope taut between his hands. "Company stationery—very clever." He took out the letter. "In Spanish—even better. 'Come to my study tonight at nine. We'll be alone. Bring the cross. I have the chain.' There's no signature."

Rosen said, "I didn't need a signature."

"No, I suppose you didn't. I underestimated you. That has serious consequences in my profession."

Ita stamped her foot and shouted at Masaryk, "You told him! He'll spoil everything!"

Rosen shook his head. "He didn't tell me. You did."

"Mentiroso! I never told you a thing!"

"Remember going to Lucila's apartment after the funeral? "You and Soldier spoke to one another in Spanish."

241

"Yeah, so?"

"You laughed at him and said, 'No te preocupes'—'Don't worry.'" Rosen paused, then repeated the phrase, "'No *te* preocupes.' You didn't use the formal 'se,' but 'te,' as if Masaryk were a close friend or a lover. Why else would he protect Hector Alvarez, a man dealing drugs to his boss's son? Under any other circumstance Alvarez would be in jail or worse. But he's your cousin."

Ita stared hard at Rosen, then suddenly grinned, arms akimbo. "That's right. We're lovers. So how do you know—"

Masaryk grabbed her arm to shut her up.

Rosen finished the sentence, almost sighing. "How do I know that you killed Nina Melendez?"

Masaryk and Ita exchanged glances, and she twisted her arm free.

"I didn't know for sure," Rosen said, "until you walked in with the cross, the one that came from around Nina's throat. That is what you brought?"

Opening his hand, palm upward, Masaryk revealed a small cross of gold. "It was my birthday present to her."

"You're the one who called Nina at ten o'clock the night she died."

"Yes. I told her to sneak out of the house and meet me in the park. She'd done it before. I wanted to give her the present."

Ita clicked her tongue. "I wasn't enough for you."

Masaryk closed his eyes for a moment. "We've gone over all this before."

"But she's right, isn't she?" Rosen asked. "Ita wasn't enough—too easy, like the young whores in Vietnam and Guatemala. What did you want—something more challenging? A virgin. What was that you told me—they're either babies or women?"

Glaring at Masaryk, Ita said to Rosen, "The bastard was in a hotel with me when he called her."

"The company suite in the Palmer House?"

"Yeah, that's right. Said he had a present for her—something real special. I was in the bathroom; he thought I didn't hear him on the phone."

Masaryk shook his head wearily. "I didn't give a damn if you heard me. He's right—you were too easy. Too common."

She moved closer to Masaryk, rubbing against him like a cat. "But you know better now, don't you, querido?"

"That's right," Rosen said. "Has any other woman ever killed over you?"

Again the other man shook his head. "How did you know?"

"It was the roses."

"Roses?"

"The morning after Nina's death, the police found rose petals scattered on the ground where she tripped and fell. Esther Melendez said her daughter didn't bring the flowers from the house. It seemed obvious that some man brought her a bouquet. At first, like everyone else, I assumed the man was Bixby. Later I thought he was Ellsworth, then you. But if one of you had brought her roses, they would've fallen down the cliff when she fell. They didn't."

"What?"

"There weren't any stems. That Friday night, you were with Ita in the company suite. Dinner for two, roses ordered from the florist downstairs. When she overheard you calling Nina and mentioning that special present, I can imagine how Ita felt. She's not exactly the most understanding of God's creatures."

Masaryk rubbed his forehead. "You've noticed that."

"You made some excuse to end the evening early and drove her home around ten-thirty, the bouquet of roses cradled in her arms. Her house is just around the corner from the park, but instead of going inside, she followed on foot, as you drove down the side street, across the bridge, and into the park."

"That's right," Ita said. "I stood behind a tree and listened to them goo-goo together. He kept saying how sweet she was, so soft and gentle. When they kissed, he kept his hands on her shoulders. Not like me, eh, querido? Not like when you can't wait to run your hands up my skirt and into my panties. I bet she smelled me on your hands, that little Snow White of yours."

Rosen asked, "And when he gave her the necklace?"

"Even from where I stood, I could tell it was expensive. What had he ever bought me—nada. Nada menos las flores."

"Then what?"

"They kissed, that's all." To Masaryk, "What would you've expected from me for something like that. On my knees, right?"

Masaryk grabbed her arm and pulled her down beside him. Ita tried twisting free, but his grip only tightened. She stifled a scream, biting her lower lip, then moved her hand slowly up his thigh. Masaryk released her hand. She rested her head on his lap while he stroked her hair.

Ita spoke very softly to Rosen, "After Soldier left, Nina stayed in the park. She was leaning against the fence railing, watching the moon and still trembling from his touch. She didn't hear me coming."

"Then what?" Rosen asked.

"Nina turned. She had a small smile on her face, like she thought he'd come back. I told her about Soldier and me, about how good I made him feel, and what a little bitch she was. No way was she getting that expensive piece of jewelry, so I ripped it from her throat. The chain fell onto the ground somewhere, but I held the cross in my hand."

"She went for it?"

Ita shook her head. "I expected her to fight for the cross, but instead, her hands moved down to her side. She couldn't stand to touch me. Like I was trash."

"So you pushed her over the cliff."

"Yeah, I pushed her. She grabbed at me but came up with a handful of petals before going over the cliff."

"You just watched her fall."

"Yeah."

"And walked home, still holding the bouquet of roses."

"He gave them to me, didn't he? Besides, I wanted him to see— to know what I'd done for us."

Rosen rubbed his eyes. The room seemed smaller, warmer— much too warm. His hands were sticky and his mouth dry.

Clearing his throat, he said, "That's why the police didn't find any stems. You took the bouquet home. I bet you put them in a vase. If the police had only bothered to look in your room."

"They were beautiful," Ita said. "I liked the damaged ones the best. I pressed one of them into a book so I'd always have it. I showed it to Soldier."

"You showed him the cross too?"

"No, I was afraid he'd take it away. I wanted a gold chain for the cross, but he wouldn't get me one—said it was too dangerous. Then I got his letter . . . your letter."

Rosen said to Masaryk, "So you covered for her—even killing Bixby."

Lifting her head, Ita grinned, the laughter rippling through her body. He looked into her widening eyes and realized it was more horrible than he'd imagined.

"My God, *you* killed Bixby. I should've known—risking murder in the middle of the day, the throwaway gun that might've blown up, no silencer. An act of impulse . . . of insanity."

She giggled. "Since Esther thought Bix killed her daughter, I figured his suicide would stop people from asking any more questions. So I cut school and went over to his apartment. I used the back stairs. He let me right in."

"You were one of the girls he . . ."

"Played his little games with. Yeah. Oh, how excited he got when he saw me. When we sat down in the kitchen, I told him I had a special surprise in my purse. Maybe he was expecting a new nightie, maybe a whip. When I took out a pair of white gloves, he started smiling, he was even licking his lips. Then I pulled out my cousin Hector's gun. Bix put up his hand, but it was too late. The look in his eyes, just before . . ."

She closed her eyes for a moment to linger over the memory. "Afterward, I pressed his hand on the gun handle and set up everything to look like suicide. Everybody thought it was suicide. Everybody but you!"

Rosen waited for his trembling to stop, then asked Masaryk, "Was it worth it?"

"He loves me," Ita said.

Rosen shook his head. "He's protecting himself. If the police found out about you, they'd find out about him and Nina. That would bring lots of publicity to the Ellsworths. Soldier couldn't have that. He wouldn't be doing his job."

Like a petulant child, she struck her fist on Masaryk's knee. "He loves me! Show him, Soldier. Show him how much you love me."

Opening the desk drawer, Masaryk took out a service revolver. Ita ran her hand lightly over the gun barrel.

"See, I told you he loves me. I killed for him; now he's going to kill for me."

"Not here," Rosen said. "Not in his own room in his employer's house."

Masaryk shrugged. "You'll be taking a trip with some of my men."

"I won't need to pack a toothbrush."

"I'm afraid you're going to have an accident, but the bravado's another nice touch. Am I to worry that you've been in contact with the police?"

"Haven't I?"

"That phone call I made, when you first arrived. One of my men checked the neighborhood for police cars—nothing but the usual patrol. And Chief Keller left yesterday for a long weekend in Wisconsin. Besides, I don't think you trust the police. I think you came here all by yourself."

Rosen shifted in his chair. He had to get Masaryk off balance. "Why would I do that?"

"Maybe you hoped to get Ita and me going at each other. Or that we'd admit everything, and in my megalomania, I'd let you walk out of here—to show I wasn't afraid of you. You do think I'm megalomaniacal."

"I think you're both crazy."

"The real reason you came is because you had to discover the truth, even if it cost your life. So which of us is crazy?"

"You're going to kill me and live happily ever after with Ita? You'll never be able to trust her."

"Trying to pit us against each other after all. I know my Ita very well. I'm willing to take the chance. I've seen a lot of this world—too much. Nothing really excited me anymore, even her. But when she murdered Nina, then Bixby . . . remember what Oscar Wilde said about fucking stable boys—it's like feasting with panthers; the delight's in the danger."

"You and your little whore."

"Kill him!" Ita yelled.

Masaryk reached for the phone. "Not here."

She grabbed for the gun. "If you won't shoot him, I will." The receiver clattered onto the desk as Masaryk moved his gun hand away from Ita. When she stretched across his body, he threw her onto the floor like a bothersome cat.

Rosen started from his chair.

"Hold it," Masaryk said. "The both of you—just hold it."

For a moment Ita's jaw set tight, then she grinned, running her tongue across her upper lip. Leaning forward, she whispered into his ear, her hand inside his shirt. Masaryk closed his eyes tight for a moment and nodded. She reached for his gun.

"No," he said. "No, I'll do it." To Rosen, "Plans have changed slightly. I'm sorry. I really wished you'd let well enough alone."

"Don't."

"Go on," Ita said. "Now, do it now!"

Grabbing the armrests, Rosen jerked as two shots cracked in the air. For a moment, everything held still as a painting. Then Masaryk slumped forward, sliding from the chair as his gun clattered along the floor.

Rosen turned to see Lucila leaning against the door frame. She'd been outside the door, as they'd planned. The gun quivered in her hand.

Rosen knelt beside Masaryk, where rivulets of blood formed a delta down the side of his chest. Swallowing hard, Rosen fought back the hot flash before his eyes as his left hand clawed at the desk.

"Take it easy. I'll call for an ambulance."

Grimacing, Masaryk gripped Rosen's right arm. "That girl of yours . . . didn't hesitate. Good soldier."

Another sound, soft whimpering like a frightened animal, but

Masaryk wasn't breathing anymore. It was Ita pushing past him, on her knees, toward the gun on the floor. Rosen couldn't stop her; Masaryk's hand still gripped him like an iron claw.

Then another figure swept past him, her long skirt brushing his cheek. Esther, holding a butcher knife, reached Ita just as she fumbled for the gun. One hand twisted in the girl's hair, Esther jerked back Ita's head to expose her throat. Jerked it back and let the body dangle, arms flailing like beating wings and strangled cries guttering as eyes grew wide.

But no wider than those of Esther, whose knife, slicing through the air, plunged into Ita's throat. Blood spurted over her chest, spraying her white chemise and spattering the wooden floor with droplets as finely shaped as rose petals.

It didn't matter that the girl hung lifeless under the woman's hand. With a sob, Esther made a second thrust through the first to complete the cross, Nina's cross, that Ita had so wanted to wear.

Chapter 22

The fog was damp enough for the wipers to sweep occasionally across the windshield, like a hand brushing away an irritating fly.

"Turn left here," Rosen said to Lucila. "Park anywhere on the street. Don't forget to turn off your lights."

Sunday morning it was easy to find a spot near the corner. Rosen and Lucila got out first, while Sarah moved carefully from the rear seat, trying not to damage the bouquet of flowers wrapped in green paper. Turning up his collar and zipping Sarah's jacket to her chin, he led them across the street into the little Jewish cemetery.

They were in his old neighborhood, a few blocks north of Gompers Park. The cemetery was small and almost forgotten, tucked between an auto-body shop and a Korean realtor. Its iron gates, mottled with rust, yawned open to an asphalt path bisecting the graveyard. In the fog everything looked gray or black—the path, monuments and headstones, benches, evergreen trees, and the catalpas, naked and tall, that stretched their limbs broadly as if just awakening.

They were alone; not even the sound of birds. Rosen wouldn't have come—too close to Friday night and the deaths of Masaryk and Margarita Reyes—but he was catching a plane for D.C. in two hours. Before leaving, he had to see his mother.

Sarah had wanted to come along. She'd spent the night with Rosen. They'd talked; rather, he'd talked while she listened to everything that had gone on among Bixby and Ita and Masaryk. She'd heard Rosen say, again and again, that her friend Nina had

249

done nothing wrong. An innocent victim who'd done nothing wrong.

All night Sarah had listened. She'd nod, ask an occasional question, look off, then change the subject. She didn't ask why, or clench her fists, or lash out, or cry—as if Nina were no more than a stranger mentioned in a thirty-second news spot. With Mrs. Agee's help, Bess was arranging private therapy for her. Rosen didn't want to leave, but the counselor said Sarah might take months to make any real progress.

"How far?" Lucila asked.

He nodded down the path. "To the left of that monument."

They passed a granite lion stretched over a family headstone.

He said to Sarah, "The first time I brought you here, you were maybe three or four. I thought the lion would scare you, but you said next time we needed to bring milk for the kitty."

Lucila laughed, but his daughter merely nodded.

Past the lion and a concrete bench, under a giant catalpa, rested a headstone that fronted a double plot. "ROSEN" had been carved across the top. Below, on the right half, were the words, "Rivka—Beloved Wife and Mother." Under that, the carver had inscribed, in Hebrew, words from Genesis 24:67, "and he took Rebekah as his wife. Isaac loved her."

There was also her picture, locket-shaped, set into the stone. She wore a dark, heavy dress, her head covered as it always had been. Her face, broad like Aaron's, but with a generous smile and soft, dark eyes that smiled too. Rosen could almost feel her arms around him while she sang him a lullaby.

The left side of the stone, blank, had waited patiently over twenty years for his father's remains to be interred beside her. He imagined the words forming inside his head, sent like lightning bolts through his eyes to burn into the stone: "Honor your father."

Sarah was saying something.

"What?"

"The flowers, Daddy. Here."

Kneeling beside the grave, he carefully unwrapped the roses. In the mist their redness took on a vibrant luminosity, as if, at that moment, all the color in the world had been concentrated into those flowers. As he laid them carefully across his mother's grave, Sarah spoke in a faraway voice.

"Grandma came over as a little girl from Russia. One day, not long after she got here, she was walking in the street, and a vendor gave her a red rose. She'd never seen anything so beautiful, so perfect. She said she saw God in that flower."

Lucila said, "You must've been very close to your grandmother."

"She died before I was born, but Daddy's told so many stories about her, she was with me all the time I was growing up."

"Sort of a guardian angel."

Rosen stood, spanking the dirt from his knee. "Let's sit down, like we used to do."

They walked to the concrete bench and sat down, Sarah in the middle. Rosen took her hand.

"I'm glad you remember what I've told you about my mother."

"So many stories," she said dreamily. "Like when her family was running from the Cossacks in Russia. It got so cold, she had to tie her father's books around her legs to keep warm. Or the time when the two of you were cooking latkes, the grease splattered and she burned her arm covering yours."

"There's another story," Rosen said. "One I've never told you. Would you like to hear it?"

Sarah nodded.

"I was five years old. My mother had taken me shopping, and we were on our way home, our arms filled with grocery bags. It was a spring day like this, damp and foggy—late in the afternoon. I had to walk fast to keep up with her, when she suddenly stopped. I remember bumping into her and almost spilling a bag of oranges.

"We were on the sidewalk where an alley snaked between two old buildings. I didn't notice him at first, but following my mother into the alley, I finally saw a rough-looking man—a bum, I guess. He was staring at the ground, wheezing, with a liquor bottle in his hand. I couldn't imagine why we were going toward him.

"My mother put down one of her bags, reached into her purse and took out some money. When she touched the man's shoulder, his arm jerked up and struck her in the face. I don't think he did it on purpose—when he looked at my mother, he was just as surprised as she was. I was scared and kept tugging on her sleeve, but she just stood there. I couldn't see her face, but I saw the look on his. It was a look I'd never seen before, and I started crying. Finally, my mother gave the man the money, picked up her bag, and led me back to the sidewalk. A block from our house she stopped and bent down beside me. I thought she'd wipe my tears away, but she only dabbed the blood from her mouth where the man had struck her.

"'Are you all right?' she asked me.

"Still crying, I nodded.

"'What did you see in that man's face?'

"I said, 'He's evil.' You see, I'd been taught by my father that evil was real—just as there were angels, so too were there demons. I thought the man was a demon.

"But taking my hand, my mother said, 'Evil is like a mask. You have to look behind it. I looked behind that man's mask, into his eyes, and you know what I found? He was hurt and afraid, more afraid than you were, little one. That's what makes evil—not demons, but pain and fear. Go ahead and cry, but cry for that poor man, for his pain and fear. For the pain and fear in all of us.'"

Leaning back in the bench, Rosen closed his eyes for a moment and saw his mother bend close to kiss him. His small hand trembled in hers. Then he realized it was the small hand he held that trembled. Sarah's hand trembling, and tears running down her cheeks. The crying came softly, as if very far away, and he thought again of himself as a little boy sobbing in his mother's arms. But now Sarah was sobbing, her shoulders heaving, and he held her tightly while his own eyes grew hot and wet.

Sarah cried for a long time, and when she finally stopped, Rosen gave her his handkerchief. She wiped her face and sat quietly, every other breath catching in her throat.

Finally she said, "Maybe w . . . we should be going."

"There's still time before my plane leaves. You know, I'll be back in a few weeks to see you."

252

"You don't have to. I'll be all right."

"I know you will, but I'd like to see you." He glanced at Lucila. "Besides, I still have some unfinished business here." Stifling a smile, Lucila stroked Sarah's hair. "It's cold just sitting here. Would you like to walk around?"

"Where?"

"Oh, you could show me who else in your family's buried here. If there's anybody else."

Sarah nodded and pointed to her right. "Great-Grandma and Grandpa over there. And I think there're some cousins and neighbors from where Daddy used to live."

"That's right," Rosen said and led them deeper into the cemetery.

"My grandparents." He pointed to another double plot, with the name KAPLAN engraved on the old granite headstone. The photos showed them as Rosen had always remembered—she shy and dignified, while he smiled as if the photographer were offering a glass of wine.

"Your mother's parents?" Lucila asked.

"Yes. My father's died in Russia."

Sarah touched the headstone. "Daddy says that Great-Grandpa was quite a character. He was a jeweler but not a very good one. He'd say, 'As a jeweler, I make a good challah.' But he could sing. Right?"

Rosen put his arm around her. "Yes, he could sing. He had a deep baritone voice that rattled the synagogue windows. People wouldn't let him sing near the cemetery for fear he'd wake the dead. He could dance too, singing his praises to God while kicking his big legs like a draft horse."

"What about Great-Grandma's friend Dvora?"

Pointing to the graves of relatives and family friends from the old neighborhood, he reminisced through the eyes of a boy. About Dvora, who lay "dying" in bed for over thirty years, outliving her eight children. And Mayer, who had the only kosher ice cream truck in the city. And Chana, who pestered Shmuel their entire married life, writing notes like "Close the ice box, Stupid!" but who died of grief a week after his death. And Yussel, Avrum, little Yudel, and all the others who peopled the few square blocks that were his world for sixteen years.

So long ago, yet Rosen saw them once again. Not as ghosts, rising stiffly through the gray morning mist, but as flesh and blood. He inhaled too the smells of the neighborhood—the warm sweetness of challah fresh from the oven, the strong iron smell of liver as it went through the grinder before the schmaltz was added, the odor of sewing-machine oil from his father's tailor shop. Smelling the oil, he even saw his father walking toward him. Yet something was wrong. How could his father be such an old man?

Rosen blinked, then his heart closed like a fist.

His father came down the cemetery path, accompanied by Aaron. Rosen hadn't seen him in almost twenty years, but he knew his father. The man was old, his beard gray, and the black hat and caftan engulfed him as if he were a little boy playing dress-up. Like a little boy, he gazed steadily at the ground. He walked very slowly, each step deliberate, while muttering to Aaron, who occasionally nodded a reply.

The wind whispered in Rosen's ear, "Honor your father and your mother."

Lucila asked, "Shouldn't we be going?" She didn't know who the men were, and Sarah hadn't noticed her uncle.

Rosen nodded. When Lucila turned toward the path, he said, "No, keep going this way. The old graves are in this area—very interesting."

Again the whispering, only harsher; the voice of a tyrant. "Honor your father!"

He followed Sarah a few steps, then his gaze locked upon his brother's. Eyes widening, Aaron smiled, about to tap his father's shoulder. Rosen shook his head once, then a second time. Aaron winced and looked away.

Rosen felt the wind cut through his coat. He held tightly to his daughter, as a drowning man clings to flotsam, and through the cold gray mist they drifted back to Lucila's car.